THE GOLDSEEKERS

Jim and Hoxie meet the Old Man in a Seattle bar. He's fought in the Civil War and the Mexican War. The Old Man has been around. He's even been to Alaska. Took out $35,000 in gold dust ten years back, and spent it on women and high living. Now it's time to go back and find the real cache he knows is still up there. All he needs are a couple more partners, fellow investors to help pay for the food and equipment they'll need for a tough winter near the Arctic Circle.

Once Jim agrees, Hoxie is in. After all, they're two Ohio boys looking for adventure. Why not? And soon young Lloyd—son of the rooming-house family they're living with—decides to join them, bound and determined to find his own independence. But none of them figure on the struggles it will take them just to get to the Yukon—nor the grit it will take to stay.

The Goldseekers

W. R. Burnett

STARK HOUSE

Stark House Press • Eureka California

THE GOLDSEEKERS

Published by Stark House Press
1315 H Street
Eureka, CA 95501, USA
griffinskye3@sbcglobal.net
www.starkhousepress.com

ISBN-13: 978-1-944520-29-8

Book design by Mark Shepard, SHEPGRAPHICS.COM

First Stark House Press Edition: June 2017

FIRST EDITION

TO THE MEMORY
OF
HOMER MEAD,
SOURDOUGH

The story of the big Alaska strike was not
so much the gold as getting there.
—HOMER MEAD

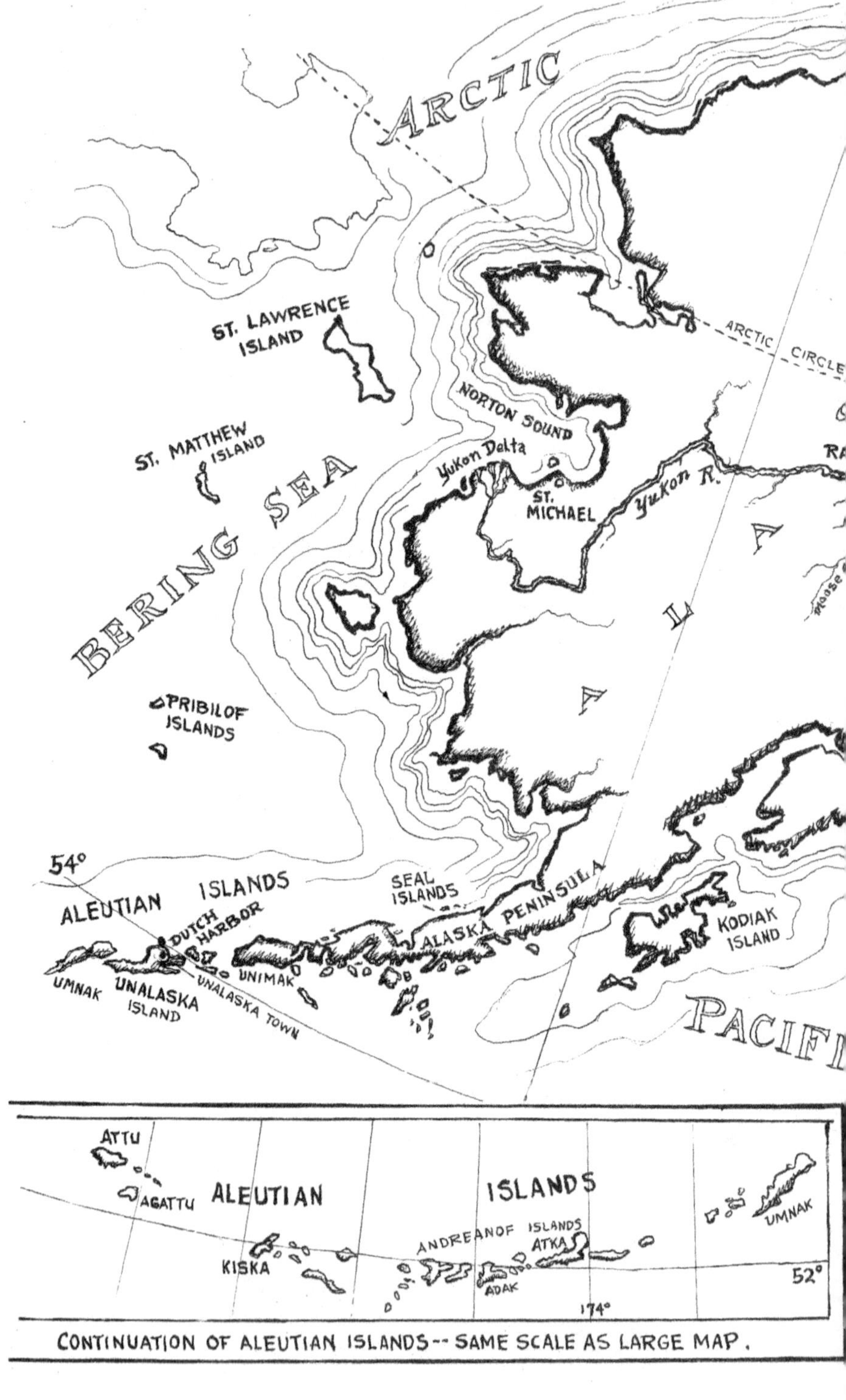

CONTINUATION OF ALEUTIAN ISLANDS -- SAME SCALE AS LARGE MAP.

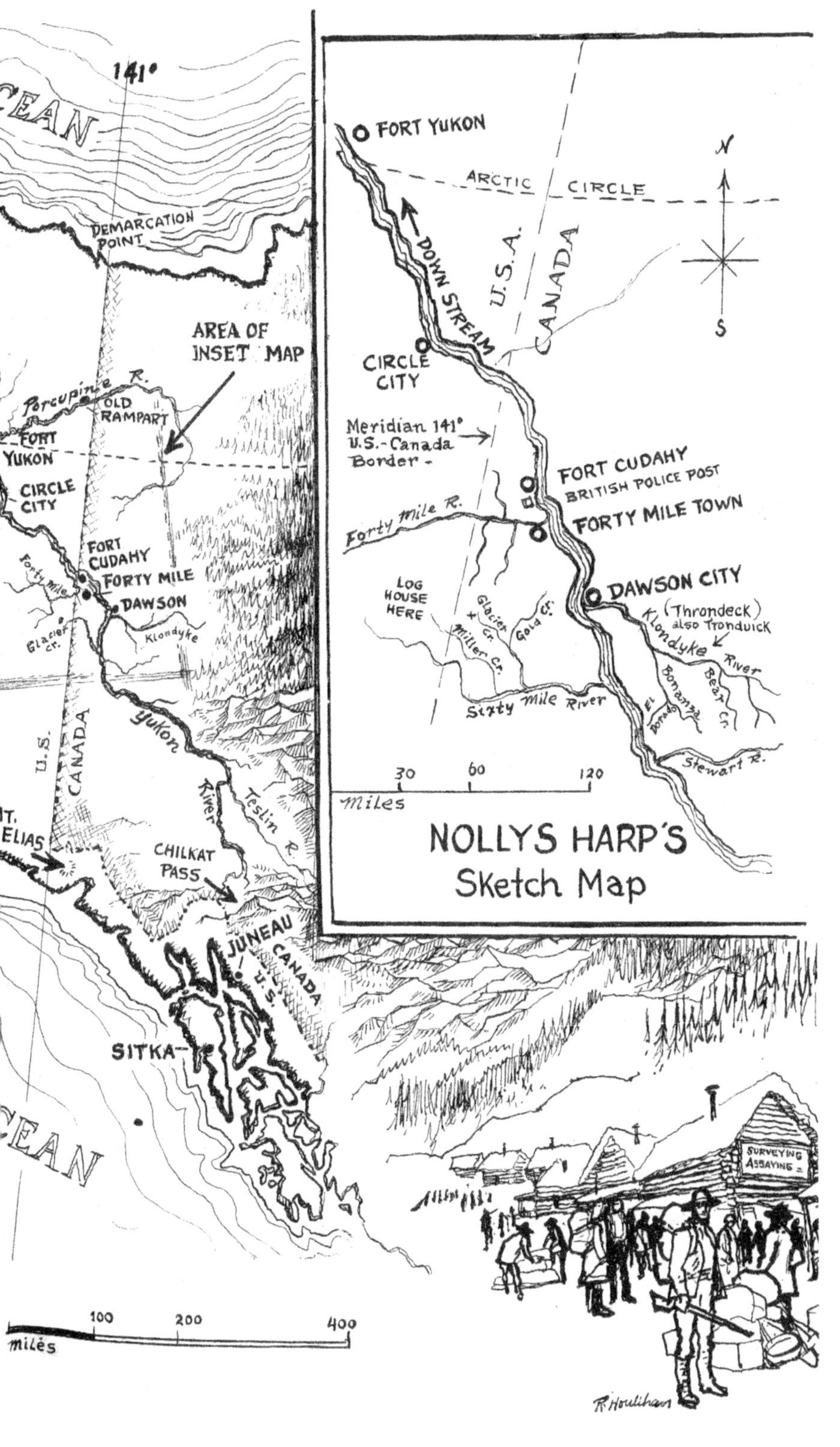

141°
OCEAN
DEMARCATION POINT
AREA OF INSET MAP
Porcupine R.
OLD RAMPART
FORT YUKON
CIRCLE CITY
Forty mile
Glacier Cr.
FORT CUDAHY
FORTY MILE
DAWSON
Klondyke
U.S.
CANADA
Yukon River
Teslin R.
MT. ELIAS
CHILKAT PASS
JUNEAU
CANADA
U.S.
SITKA
OCEAN
100
200
400
miles

FORT YUKON
ARCTIC CIRCLE
DOWN STREAM
U.S.A.
CANADA
N
S
CIRCLE CITY
Meridian 141°
U.S.–Canada
Border –
FORT CUDAHY
BRITISH POLICE POST
FORTY MILE TOWN
Forty Mile R.
LOG HOUSE HERE
Glacier Cr.
Miller Cr.
Gold Cr.
DAWSON CITY
(Throndeck) also Tronduick
Klondyke River
El Dorado
Bonanza
Bear Cr.
Sixty Mile River
Stewart R.
30
60
120
Miles

NOLLYS HARP'S
Sketch Map

SURVEYING
ASSAYING

R. Houlihan

THE GOLDSEEKERS
LIST OF CHARACTERS

ALOYSIUS (GABE) WINDHORN:
about forty; born in London, England; steward, cook, seaman

LLOYD GRACEY:
twenty-four; born in Seattle, Washington; shipping clerk

HOXIE THICKE:
twenty-five; born in Roxabelle, Ohio;
blacksmith's helper, farmer, longshoreman

NOLLYS HARP:
sixty-three; veteran of the Mexican and Civil wars;
soldier, seaman, longshoreman. Birthplace unknown

JAMES HARDY:
twenty-four; born in Roxabelle, Ohio; farmer, shipping clerk

SEATTLE: 1896
The Start of the Quest

As Lloyd and Jim negotiated the steepest part of 3rd Street, panting a little from the climb, they saw Hoxie coming toward them from the harbor, with his blue cotton workshirt heavily sweated and his long-shoreman's hook hanging from his shoulder. They stopped at the crest, opposite their boardinghouse, and waited. Hoxie saw them, waved, then came on.

He was big and oddly made, with wide shoulders, a heavy chest, and long, rather thin legs. His face was swarthy and showed blue where he shaved; his hair was dark, coarse, and curly. He'd been a blacksmith's helper in Ohio and bragged that longshore work on the Coast was "getting it the easy way." He was very proud of his strength and often demonstrated it by bending a nail with his fingers, then straightening it out again. He'd come to Seattle with Jim five years ago, in 1891, was well satisfied with the move, and was always saying: "They can have Ohio with all that farming and horseshoeing. I'll take the Coast." In fact, Hoxie was pretty well satisfied all around; not only with the Coast but with himself as well, particularly with himself.

"Hi, fellows," he said. "How'd you like to get rich?"

They looked at him and laughed.

"What do you think I came West for?" asked Jim, who was about six feet tall and husky, with a fair, almost girlish complexion but with a look in his pale eyes that seemed old for his twenty-four years.

"How do we do it?" asked Lloyd, a little slim slight fellow the same age as Jim, with dark auburn hair and dark eyes. He was dwarfed by his companions, but liked it that way. Their physical strength, strangely enough, did not remind him of his own weakness but helped him to forget it. Ever since the arrival of Hoxie and Jim at his mother's board-inghouse, Lloyd had felt safe. What could happen to a man with friends like these?

"Tell you what," said Hoxie, "I'll answer both questions. Jim, you come West 'cause you was sick of that there Old Hardy farm and all them brothers, with you next to last in line. Getting rich... well, now maybe that was a second thought. How do we do it? We ship out for

Alaska and we pick big nuggets up right off the ground, or else we get us a miner's pan and in two days we pan enough gold dust to keep us in comfort the rest of our lives." Hoxie laughed and slapped his leg. "I been hearing about it for the last week. It's this old fellow I been working with lately. Name of Harp. Big as hell. Past sixty and can work right along with me on the dock, longshore. Ought to see him swing that hook and sling them bales. He's been to Alaska and back, he claims; brought in a pile and spent it. I think he's a first-rate liar, but very amusing."

"I never heard anything about gold in Alaska," said Lloyd, who was native born and thought he knew everything about the Coast and its subsidiary points.

They were climbing the sagging wooden steps of the old frame three-story boardinghouse now, side by side.

"I never did either," said Hoxie, "till this old bird got talking to me. But since then other fellows have told me there's some gold mining way up north. Been getting out dust since around '85. But they say it don't amount to nothing much, and ain't worth the trouble. Me, I don't like to get froze and live in an igloo with an Eskimo girl. I'll get mine the easy way, down on the docks. Hey, that reminds me...." But he broke off as Lloyd opened the front door and they went into the dark, narrow hallway of Mrs. Gracey's boardinghouse.

The house was built at the end of the street on a steep hill. It was strangely shaped as there was only one story in the front, but three in the back, and you had to go downstairs to the bedrooms. It was one of the few frame houses on the street that had escaped the destruction of the terrible fire of the eighties, and it still showed the black scorch marks on the east wall, under the cracked and peeling paint.

The front hall always smelled of damp mustiness and cooking. And almost always, around suppertime, there was the scrape of Mr. Gracey's violin or the tinkling of his piano. Mr. Gracey gave music lessons. "That is," as Hoxie said, "he loafs around while his wife and daughter wear themselves out running the boardinghouse."

Mr. Gracey, Lloyd's father, was a slim, slight, inoffensive little man who drank quite a lot of "patent medicine" for his perpetual cough and hid behind a closed door as much as possible. His manner was apologetic. Hoxie disliked him and showed it. Jim merely felt sorry for him. Lloyd kept out of his way, tried to pretend that he wasn't around, and that on no account was little violin-playing and piano-tinkling Mr. Llewellyn Gracey his real father.

Lena, Lloyd's sister, came in from the back. She always came in from the back at this time of the evening. She was slender and pale, with dark reddish hair and big sad eyes, which Jim always found himself avoiding.

"Hello, Lloyd," she said to her brother. "You're a little late tonight. Evening, Jim. Hoxie."

"What's for supper?" asked Hoxie, eying Lena with ironic amusement. Just let Jim show his face in the door and there she was!

"Corned beef and boiled potatoes, I'm afraid," said Lena.

"Oh gosh, not again," cried Hoxie with a grimace of disgust. "Come on, Jim. Let's wash up."

Jim started to follow Hoxie to the stairs, but paused as Lena asked: "How did it go today, Jim?"

"Oh fine. Same as ever. We're shipping out a lot of lumber these days."

Lloyd had got him the job with the lumber company and now he was a sort of straw boss in the shipping office, with Lloyd as one of his assistants.

"You like your job then," said Lena, relief showing briefly in her eyes, then quickly repressed.

"Oh sure. Yes. Fine," said Jim, shifting about uncomfortably.

"Come on, will you, Jim?" cried Hoxie impatiently.

"I guess I'd better..." Jim began, then broke off, smiled at Lena, and followed Hoxie down the stairs to their bedroom.

Lloyd started to follow them, but Lena held him back. "Did you get paid today?"

"Of course I got paid," said Lloyd impatiently. Lena, with her pale remote ways, her ineffectuality, was not his *real* sister either (in his secret thoughts); she irritated him almost unbearably. And the way she was always standing sadly around waiting for Jim Hardy to notice her was disgraceful and ridiculous!

"Give me five dollars for Pa," said Lena. "He has to play at the Masonic benefit tonight and he ought to have money in his pocket."

"What about the lessons?"

"They've been slack lately, and then some of them don't pay and Pa won't ask them. You know how Pa is."

"Yes," said Lloyd, "I know how he is." Grimacing slightly, he counted off five ones and handed them to her; then he hesitated for a moment and counted off a sixth. "That's for you, Lena. You ought to have some money in your own pocket."

"Oh thank you, Lloyd," said Lena, rather abjectly. "Thank you very much."

In their room Hoxie and Jim took turns at the washstand, then stood combing their hair and getting ready for supper.

"That poor girl," said Hoxie contemptuously. "It might as well be you as somebody else. She'll get it sooner or later. Twenty-seven years old and still mooning around. Why don't you do her a favor, Jim?"

"Why don't *you?*" asked Jim, a slight edge to his voice.

"Now don't go getting sore at me, Jim Hardy, over a poor woebegone girl like that. You used to get around quite a bit back home. I remember you taking them Johnson girls buggy riding over at Roxabelle. And the old horse, he up and come back to the livery barn by himself. What was you doing out in the woods with them two wild redheaded Johnsons?"

"Hunting possum," said Jim, starting to laugh.

"Yeah," said Hoxie. "And I'll bet you found some possum. Two of 'em."

"All right, Hoxie," said Jim. "But this Lena... well, she's different. A nice girl. Ought to been married long ago and had kids."

Hoxie snorted in derision. "'Nice girl!' You still believe in that 'nice girl' stuff? Hell, girls are all alike that way. Ever hear the definition of rape? 'Wrong man.'" Hoxie threw back his head and roared with laughter. "That's a hot one, ain't it? Sadie, down at the Front, told me that one. Sadie knows."

Jim knotted his tie in silence and slipped on his coat. Was he changing? Or was Hoxie getting coarser all the time? Jim couldn't quite make up his mind about this. Why, hell, he and Hoxie had been friends since they were kids playing around Old Man Thicke's blacksmith shop back in Ohio. Old Man Thicke was Hoxie's father and a stern, churchgoing man. Hoxie must have been quite a disappointment to him. In fact, the Old Man had finally kicked Hoxie out of his house.

"That reminds me," said Hoxie, "Sadie's got a couple of new girls, one French from up in Canada, and you know what *that* means! Let's waltz down and see 'em tonight."

"No," said Jim.

"What's the matter with you lately?" Hoxie demanded, looking at Jim narrowly. "You just dreaming about it now?"

"That last time cured me," said Jim curtly.

"Well, you didn't have to look, did you? Aw, come on, Jim. We used to have real big times."

Jim said nothing and stood staring out the window. A gentle rain, hardly more than a mist, was now falling in the spring evening, and the waters of Puget Sound far below looked dimly gray and wrinkled in the fading light.

Hoxie glanced at Jim, then shrugged and turned away. No use arguing with him—he'd learned that long ago. Like all the Hardys, Jim was stubborn as a mule. No man could run him. It was impossible. He went his own way. If you didn't like it, avoid him. Young as he was, Jim seemed as stubborn and, at times, as wrongheaded, as old Theo Hardy himself—Jim's grandfather—who'd had the name as the most cantankerous old bastard in Clark County.

The door opened and Lloyd came in, washed and combed for supper. His auburn hair was slicked down and parted in the middle. Hoxie looked at him askance. Always a-riding on Jim's shirttail. The whole Gracey clan would have taken Jim over if Jim had been a different type of man. No fear of that, however.

Jim and Lloyd stood looking out the window together.

"The Sound sure looks pretty tonight," said Lloyd. "All silvery. Look at the lights coming on. Nothing in the world prettier than lights on water in the twilight."

Hoxie shrugged and grimaced. The whole Gracey family was silly and bughouse like that, except the Old Lady. Now there was a real woman, like his own womenfolk back home. No nonsense about lights on water and stuff like that: cooked, sewed, washed, cleaned, minded her own goddamned business, and kept her mouth shut. The whole Gracey clan would have been in the poorhouse if it had not been for Old Ma Gracey.

All at once Hoxie snapped his fingers at a sudden thought, hurried to the window, pushed Lloyd aside, and looked out.

"By God, that's her, coming down the Sound!" he cried. "See that white tramp? That's the *Osaka Maru*, first Japanese ship ever to hit port here. I heard she was in the Straits this afternoon. By God, that's her!"

Lloyd's eyes lit up. "You mean all the way from Japan?"

"Yep," said Hoxie. "And pretty soon more'll come, shipping out from the Orient, and that means lots of work for us on the docks and higher pay all around. They'll pay us or else they'll be sorry."

"After supper let's go take a look at her," said Lloyd, his excitement rising. He had exotic visions of Fujiyama, and tiny little Japanese women in kimonos, waving fans, upcurved bridges and cherry blossoms—visions of remote beauty, as far away from Pa, Lena, and the boardinghouse as possible.

"How about it, Jim?" asked Hoxie.

"Fine. Sure," said Jim.

The others at the boardinghouse—a woman teacher, an old postal clerk, a silent man from the city solicitor's office—were hardly more than anonymous faces to Hoxie, Jim, and Lloyd; all gray-haired, all over the hill and of no interest whatsoever as far as the three young men were concerned.

Lena kept trying to get Jim to eat more corned beef, timidly insistent, making Lloyd grimace and Hoxie shrug. Ma, a large comfortable woman, beamed benevolently from the head of the table, saying little, hearing nothing, worn out from the day's grind but not wanting to show it.

Pa, who was feeling "porely" and had drunk considerable "patent medicine" that day, was having his supper on a tray in his "study."

During a lull, Hoxie began to talk about the *Osaka Maru*, and the three older boarders listened with interest. They seldom listened when Hoxie talked; they were "white collar," he "workman," and they could not get easy with him and took no interest in his ideas or viewpoint. The young man, James Hardy, was different; seemed to them very well mannered and polite and was working at a respectable job, head shipping clerk. Lloyd, well, Lloyd, a nice enough lad, was just Pa Gracey over again, futile, futile, futile, like his pale sister, Lena, who was always making eyes, sadly, at the handsome Hardy boy!

"Very, very interesting," said the old postal clerk. "Means a lot to Seattle. We're forty thousand or better now and growing all the time. We'll be the metropolis of the Northwest before we're through."

"Very interesting," echoed the schoolteacher, who always found herself in agreement with Mr. Stebbins's ideas. "Means a lot to Seattle."

The three young men swallowed their apple pie in a hurry and finally got away.

"They might have taken Lena to see the Japanese ship," said Ma Gracey, in mild protest.

"Oh Ma, I don't mind," said Lena.

The three older boarders looked at Lena in silence. In a moment she rose and hurried out to the kitchen.

Quite a crowd had come down to Wharf 7 to see the huge foreign tramp freighter, and it took the three young men some time to inch their way forward to the railing. Finally they made it and stood looking up at the tall, weathered white hull. It had stopped raining now and a grayish-lavender twilight had settled down over the harbor. Lights showed on the bridge of the *Osaka Maru* and at many of the portholes.

Lloyd stood staring up in happy awe at this strange visitor from a strange land. He noted the barbaric-looking lettering—strangely resembling the markings on a Chinese laundry tag, but much larger—apparently spelling out the name of the ship, dead black on the glaring white of the hull. He noticed the alien white flag with its huge red-rayed sun in the middle. And in a moment several little brown men with slanted eyes came to the rail, peered down at the crowd, grinned, talked what sounded like gibberish to each other for a moment, then lit cigarettes and leaned on their elbows.

"She's come a long ways, boys," said Jim, his voice sounding a little strange to them.

"Yep," said Hoxie. "Ten thousand miles across the Pacific, and that's no joke. I hope they treat 'em good. I hope they keep coming. I'm already booked to unload this baby tomorrow morning. Money in our pockets."

Lloyd glanced at Hoxie but said nothing. It was a viewpoint he was unable to understand. How could a weird and beautiful visitation like this be measured in dollars and cents? And he felt pretty sure that Jim Hardy was having feelings similar to his own. There'd been an odd, new note in his voice.

"Shipping out for Tokyo?" asked a deep, slightly cracked voice behind them and they all turned to find themselves confronted by an extremely tall, rawboned old man, with a grim, lined, leathery face, cold gray eyes that seemed to look out from the ambush of shaggy white eyebrows, and a wide, straight, thin-lipped mouth. There was a gray stubble on his cheeks, as if he'd forgotten to shave, and the creases in his bronzed, leathery neck seemed deep enough to hide a penny. He was wearing a clean blue cotton shirt, open at the neck and with coarse white chest hair curling out, and an old gray jacket that had seen better days.

"Well," said Hoxie, "it's my chum Harp. If I knew his first name I'd introduce him."

"First name's Nollys, but don't bother with it. Just call me the Old Man. That'll do."

"Oh, we couldn't do that, Mr. Harp," said Jim, shaking hands.

The Old Man laughed. "I'm right proud to be mistered, son. But let's make an end of it. Just call me Nollys, if that suits you better. This fellow here," he went on, indicating Hoxie, "he just yells 'hey' at me."

Hoxie laughed easily. Lloyd shook hands with the Old Man perfunctorily, nodded, said nothing, then returned to his contemplation of the *Osaka Maru*. He heard faint music coming from aboard now, stringed instruments playing something fantastically weird and as if from another world entirely—a world he'd like to be in: a world where there was no talk of corned beef and boiled potatoes, of pocket money for Pa, of manifests and bills of lading.

"Say," said the Old Man, "how about we wet our whistles and listen to some music. Got good steam beer and a new piano player over at the Sailor's Rest."

"All right," said Hoxie. "Jim?"

"Sure. Fine," said Jim.

Nobody asked Lloyd if he'd like to come; he always did, as a matter of course, the original tagalong. But tonight he surprised them.

"Think I'll stay here for a while, fellows, and look at the ship," he said. "May drop over later. If not—see you tomorrow."

"Ain't you seen enough of that dirty old tub yet?" Hoxie demanded. "It's just another tramp. You've seen plenty of 'em."

Lloyd merely looked at him, said nothing.

"Well I'll be damned," said Hoxie, as the three of them walked off toward the Sailor's Rest, "first time he ain't dogged us."

"Who's he?" asked the Old Man. "Don't look like your kind of fellow, Hoxie."

"Lives at the boardinghouse with us," said Hoxie, as if explaining the incongruity.

But Jim said, "He's a friend of ours. Works with me," and the Old Man turned and studied Jim's face for a moment.

The three of them sat at a window table with their steam beer in front of them in thick glass steins and listened to the music. The piano player was a little red-faced man in a yellow shirt and wearing purple sleeve garters; he had a gray derby tipped to the back of his head, and occasionally he took time out to stroke his waxed mustache. He played erratically, using half a dozen notes where one would have done, and he sang the choruses in a high, cracked tenor.

No matter what he played or sang, the crowd kept yelling for "Waltz Me Around Again, Willie," and when they broke him down and he played it again, perhaps for the twentieth time, they all joined in on the chorus.

"I'd like to hear some older tunes, like 'The Vacant Chair' and 'Tenting Tonight'; them's real songs. But that little squirt wouldn't know 'em," said the Old Man. "'The Vacant Chair' was the big Civil War song. All the women cried over it."

"He fought in the Civil War," said Hoxie, winking at Jim.

"I sure did," said the Old Man. "And in the Mexican War. I been around, boys, I been around."

The crowd finally wore the piano player out, then showered him with pennies, nickels, and dimes as he moved away to take a breather.

"He's been to Alaska, too," said Hoxie, winking at Jim again, making him very uncomfortable.

"I sure have," said the Old Man. "And it's my dream to get back. I lay in my bed and see it at night. Yes, sir. And I'm saving my money. Boys, I took thirty-five thousand dollars in dust out of a little claim in the Forty Mile Creek area. That was in '86, ten years back; and I never even scratched the surface."

"That's a lot of money, Harp," said Hoxie. "What happened to it?"

"I spent it on women and riotous living," said the Old Man. "I was young then—early fifties—and full of vinegar. Now it's different. I get my hands on a pile now and women's dark beckoning eyes won't mean a thing. I'll laugh in their pretty faces."

"Aw, come on now, Harp," said Hoxie. "Bet you'd like a roll in the hay right now. I was figuring to take you over to Sadie's later, since my friend Jim won't go."

"No, thank you," said the Old Man. "My rolling's over. All I want to roll in is gold dust. And I'm saving for it."

"How much will it take?"

"About a thousand dollars."

Hoxie stared in unbelief, then burst out laughing. "A thousand dollars! If a man's got a thousand dollars, cash, what's he want looking for more?"

"Why, he wants wealth," said the Old Man. "He wants mansions and private railroad cars and trips to Europe and champagne and hobnobbing with the great and being a big man himself, with maybe a stable of thoroughbreds and a yacht."

"Harp, you sure are dreaming," said Hoxie, shaking his head.

"It's no dream," the Old Man said; then: "This young fellow here's listening; this polite Jim boy. He's listening. Ain't you, Jim?"

"Yes," said Jim, and Hoxie gave him an odd look.

"Tell you what," said the Old Man. "You fellows save your money and I'll take you along. If we could get up a party of five, maybe we could risk it with five hundred apiece and supplies. I been there. I know the ropes. I'll get you in with no trouble at all, right up the Yukon on a steamboat a-setting at your ease. In one year we could pull out with a fortune, maybe fifty thousand or better apiece—and what we could get for our claims besides."

Hoxie had stopped baiting the Old Man. Now he didn't know what to think. Jim was listening, really listening. Could it all be true and not just a waterfront pipedream? Hoxie felt a sudden constriction in his chest. Fifty thousand dollars! Hell, he could go back home, buy the biggest house in town, and laugh at all the fools who'd scorned him after the trouble over Letty. Even Jim hadn't taken it too well. But how could he help it if the damned fool girl overturned the boat and then couldn't find her footing in less than five feet of water? Sure, he walked out and left her. He was sore at her spoiling his new pants. Sure, he never looked around. But, hell, the water'd hardly come up past his chest, and Letty was a big girl, nearly as tall as himself. Drowning in less than five feet of still water—that took some doing!

"Lots of fools," the Old Man went on, "they try to cheat, go in from the south across Chilkat Pass, to save that long boat ride up the Yukon. But Chilkat's a man killer, even in the summer, even in good weather. You get up a storm and if you don't find shelter you're dead. And then you have to pack in boat-building tools, and them portages are rough even for the Injuns. Fools go that way. Most men, in other words. Wise men go up the Yukon."

"It's easy, you say?" asked Jim.

"Is setting on your haunches riding a steamboat easy?" said the Old Man. "Of course it is. You take a tramp boat out of Seattle for St. Michael in Alaska; at St. Michael you get on board a paddle wheeler and you ride in style up the big Yukon. Nothing to it."

"Why don't more go then?" asked Jim.

And Hoxie, deeply absorbed, nodded quickly.

"Don't know about the gold," said the Old Man. "You ever hear tell of it?"

"No," said Jim.

"Yet you been in Seattle quite awhile, I take it. Besides, Alaska seems like the moon to most people, too far away. But mark my word. Some day there'll be a strike; a big strike. And men'll pour in from all over the world and then it'll be too late. But if a fellow would happen to be on the ground at the time...." The Old Man waved his hands in a gesture of finality.

There was a brief silence; then Hoxie leaned forward. "Jim—you considering it?"

"Well," said Jim, after a moment, "I'm at least thinking about it."

Later Hoxie said you could have knocked him over with a feather.

"Just start saving your money, boys," said the Old Man. "You're a couple of big strong fellows, the kind I need. Be proud to have you with me."

Hoxie didn't quite know whether he was coming or going. What had started out as a weak joke seemed to be turning deadly earnest. Fifty thousand dollars...! He wouldn't let himself think about it any longer.

He ordered another round of steam beer, then yelled to the piano player, who had just come back: "Mister, how about 'Waltz Me Around Again, Willie'?"

The piano player grimaced, but there were cheers from the other tables, so the little man sat down and obliged. The men in the bar roared out the chorus, banging on the table tops with their heavy steins.

Lloyd heard Jim out in silence, shocked and excited. He'd beaten Jim home and had sat on the front steps waiting for him. Jim had arrived smelling strongly of beer and strangely agitated.

When Jim had finished, Lloyd said: "But maybe the Old Man is crazy."

"This Old Man is not crazy," said Jim firmly.

"Maybe he's just a... what do you call it?... a dreamer, a visionary, like Pa. He was always going to go on the concert stage, and here he can't even get a job in an orchestra."

"This Old Man is not like that. He's already been there and brought back thirty-five thousand dollars."

"Then maybe he's a plain ordinary liar."

"Maybe," said Jim.

"But you don't think so."

"No, I don't."

Lloyd sighed and fell silent. This wouldn't do at all, not at all. Suppose Jim and Hoxie would get the gold fever and leave? It would probably be forever. Lloyd gripped his fingers tightly together and sat rigid. Then there'd be nothing but Ma, and Pa, and Lena, and the damned lumber company.

"I'd think it over carefully," he said.

"I intend to," said Jim.

All at once, surprising himself almost as much as he surprised Jim, Lloyd blurted out: "If you and Hoxie go, I'm going. I got a little money saved."

And then, as Jim, too astonished to speak, said nothing, Lloyd found himself unable to stop the torrent of his own speech. He talked about the *Osaka Maru* and about the rising-sun flag and about the lure of distant places and his desire to see the world. It began to rain gently. Lloyd talked on.

Finally Jim broke in. "Hey, we're getting wet."

"Is it raining again?" asked Lloyd, and Jim gave him a puzzled look.

They went inside. Lena appeared from the parlor, her hair newly arranged.

"It's raining," she said. "I saw it on the windows."

"Yes," said Jim.

Lloyd took off his wet coat and went down the hallway to put it in the closet. Jim stood shifting.

"Jim," said Lena with an effort, "why don't you ever talk to me any more? We used to sit in the parlor and talk."

"I work pretty hard, Lena," said Jim, keeping his eyes lowered. "I don't have much time. I go to bed early, get up early."

"If you only knew how much it means to me to talk with you, Jim," said Lena hastily, glancing over her shoulder to see where Lloyd was.

Jim cleared his throat uncomfortably. "And I enjoy it, too," said Jim.

"Do you really?" Lena demanded.

But Lloyd saved him by coming back. "How about a game or two of seven-up before we turn in, Jim?"

"Sure. Fine."

"My room okay?"

"Fine."

Lena was already effacing herself, fading back into nowhere. Jim felt a pang of pity, which he tried unsuccessfully to resist. "Your hair looks nice that way, Lena," he said.

Lloyd shifted impatiently, wanting to play cards and talk with Jim.

Lena flushed to the roots of her hair. "Oh thank you, Jim. I'm glad you like it."

"Oh come on, Jim," cried Lloyd.

As they went down the backstairs, Lloyd pulling at Jim's arm impatiently, Jim was thinking: "Whether I go to Alaska or not, pretty soon I've got to go some place away from this boardinghouse." Lena was a nice girl. He liked her. But he had no other emotion at all in regard to her. Too bad, but there was nothing he could do about it.

Jim woke with a start. He'd been dreaming about Buckwheat Creek and a school picnic, with painted rowboats and the quiet water and kids playing tag in the bushes; only it had been all mixed up and fantastic, with intrusions from his present life and an uneasy touch of nightmare.

Hoxie was undressing in the dark, swaying slightly in the moonlight.

"What time is it?" asked Jim.

Hoxie started and dropped his pants. "You awake? Hell, I was trying to be quiet. It's after midnight, maybe twelve-thirty."

Jim sat up. "Moon sure is bright."

"Yeah. Big wind came up about eleven and blew the clouds away. You can read a newspaper out on the street right now. Bet the Sound's rough as hell."

With a groan of weariness, Hoxie rolled into the little narrow bed across from Jim's.

"I've been dreaming about Buckwheat Creek," said Jim, with a laugh; then suddenly he remembered! Hoxie remained silent. Jim went on hastily: "When we were kids, you know, Hoxie—the school picnics."

There was a long silence, punctuated by the blat of a boat whistle on the Sound. "Wasn't my fault, goddamn it," Hoxie burst out suddenly. "Only four feet of water."

"I know, I know," said Jim. "I wasn't thinking about that."

"They can have Buckwheat Creek and the whole of Clark County," said Hoxie bitterly. "I don't even want to think about it any more. I'll take the Coast. That's the place."

Jim lay back and stared at the ceiling with its faint pattern of reflected moonlight.

"You sure surprised me tonight," said Hoxie finally. "Listening serious to old Harp. Maybe it was all that steam beer and music."

"Maybe," said Jim.

"But you don't think so."

"No."

Hoxie flopped over and raised up on one elbow. "You suppose we could cut the mustard, Jim? Come back with fifty thousand dollars? I'm game for anything if you say so."

"I want to think about it," said Jim mildly.

Hoxie sighed and lay back. That was Jim; a damned deliberate fellow. Hell, at times you'd think he was fifty years old instead of not quite half that age.

Silence settled down over the little boxlike room. Hoxie dozed, then woke himself with a start—snoring. He began to laugh. "That Sadie," he said, and laughed again. "Know what she said tonight? 'If "maybe" was money we'd all be rich.' Now that's a right sharp saying for an ignorant woman. Not stupid, ignorant. She never went to school. And the new French girl—she's got blond hair, natural. I thought all French girls had black hair. Her name's Alberte. Now ain't that a hell of a name for a girl? She was so busy I didn't get around to her. Hell, I get just as much fun talking to Sadie. Or almost. You listening?" Jim pretended to be asleep. Hoxie grunted in irritation, then rolled over with his face to the wall.

Ma Gracey's boardinghouse was now dark and silent. The schoolteacher, the man from the city solicitor's office, and the old postal clerk slept heavily, worn out by the day's duties. In the main bedroom, Ma and Pa, huddling in the big bed with their backs to each other, wandered by way of dreams into worlds more suitable to their spirits and to their former aspirations.

Mice nibbled in the wainscoting, making tiny scraping sounds, and big rats skittered about in the total darkness of the basement.

Of all the people in the house only one was awake—Lena. She'd read for hours in Stanley Weyman's *Chronicles of Count Antonio* and had put the book down with confused visions of splendor and intrigue. Somewhere life was interesting and glamorous! At midnight she'd put out her light. The flood of moonlight surprised her, after the misty evening and the rain.

And now she was sitting on the floor, with her elbows on the window sill, looking out at the silvery sparkle of moonlight on the Sound. The mood engendered by the book was gradually dissipated and she found herself back once more in Ma Gracey's boardinghouse, with the mice nibbling in the wainscoting. If she could only get away. If Jim would only *take* her away.

Jim leaned forward on his elbows to listen, while Hoxie swayed back in his chair and smoked a cigar, unable to concentrate on details, leaving all that to Jim; and Lloyd paced restlessly about, pulling nervously at his underlip.

They were in the Old Man's shack on the waterfront. A coal-oil lamp with a badly smoked shade burned in the middle of the table. Strong odors permeated the shack: of oil, tar, new rope, and deep water. A constant babble of sounds rose from the harbor nearby: the groaning of worn timbers, the sawing of hawsers, the clank and rattle aboard the tramps, the tolling of ships' bells, and the loud moaning of whistles.

The Old Man had a map spread out before him. "Them that's going in at all," he said, "are going the south route. And like I said, a big passel of them will never get there. It takes tough, knowing fellows to make them portages. And you may end up on snowshoes. A couple hundred miles of that and you'd be done. Fools! No. We just ease in."

"How far is it from St. Michael to where we're going—if we go?" said Jim, and the Old Man glanced up at him and smiled. "Quite a piece. Eighteen hundred miles."

Jim was startled. "Eighteen hundred miles from the Coast! Alaska is sure a big place."

"Sure is. Ain't all been mapped out yet by a damn sight, but it figures to be about half the size of the United States. But Jim—don't let that eighteen hundred miles bother you. It's all by steamboat right up the Yukon. If we're smart we'll ketch the first boat in—that'd be around July 1, so's we'd have to leave here about the first of June. I got my eye on a tramp. The North American Trading Company's going to charter it to get supplies in and they'll take passengers—a few. Shall I put our names in—the three...?" The Old Man hesitated, glanced round at Lloyd.... "The four of us?"

Jim said nothing, thinking. A little scared, Lloyd turned away and stood looking out the window at the harbor lights. Hoxie puffed calmly on his cigar, humming to himself. Whatever Jim said went with him.

"We don't have to go just because we put our names in," said the Old Man. "We each put down ten dollars, that's all. If we don't go, we lose it. Forty dollars, that's nothing."

"All right," said Jim. "We'll go that far."

"Good," said the Old Man. "I'll look after it. Hand me your money."

The three young men did so and the Old Man put the bills carefully away in his wallet. Then he got out another map and spread it over the table. "Here's where we're headed for. The Forty Mile Creek area. That's where I took out my pile. None of them side creeks have ever been explored, as far as I know. Rich in gold. Up north here—that's Circle City, right on the Arctic Circle...."

"Arctic Circle!" cried Hoxie, waking up at last. "Why, she'll be froze up tight."

The Old Man laughed. "In July? Hell, it gets up to eighty; hot as blazes. Gnats and mosquitoes all over the place. Like the Middle West."

Hoxie was flabbergasted. "At the Arctic Circle!"

"That's right."

Hoxie now stared at the Old Man suspiciously. "You sure you been there? You sure you just ain't dreaming all this up to get a stake and take out?"

There was a brief dead silence. Then the Old Man spoke carefully. "Hoxie—I'm just going to pretend you didn't say that. We been getting along pretty good together. As a rule I don't let a remark like that pass. But I want to keep it friendly."

Jim studied the Old Man. His wide mouth was drawn into a harsh straight line and his gray eyes glinted out coldly from the ambush of his shaggy white eyebrows.

Hoxie, red with anger, said nothing. The Old Man took out his wallet and put the bills on the table. "Tell you what," he said. "I'll pay the forty dollars and if we don't go I lose it."

"Fair enough," said Hoxie, partly mollified.

"No," said Jim, shoving the money back. "I trust you, Nollys. I believe everything you say. Don't mind Hoxie. He gets a little hot over nothing at times."

The Old Man smiled quickly at Jim, then turned back to Hoxie. "All right?"

"All right if Jim says so."

As they were leaving, the Old Man called Jim back on the pretext that he wanted a further word with him about signing the passengers' book on the chartered tramp. Hoxie and Lloyd waited out in front.

"This little fellow," said the Old Man. "This Lloyd. He might not make it up north."

"Why? If it's so easy getting in."

"Oh that ain't it. A young girl could get in, my way. It's staying. Some men just get scared when they see that country. Once you get in, you're in. Can't get out till the next summer. River freezes tight."

"What do you do all winter?"

"Do! You work. Most all the mining's done in winter."

Jim stared at the Old Man in amazement.

"In the winter? How cold does it get?"

"Around fifty below. I've seen it seventy-five, but then you stay in the shack and stoke the stove. Maybe one-two days a year like that."

"I thought the mining was done in the summer."

"So do all the hoosiers, and they try to make the trip from the south in winter to get in for summer work and so they get froze and et by wolves in Chilkat Pass or on the Lakes. You listen to me, boy. I know."

"Maybe I'd better talk to Lloyd."

"Maybe you'd better. I got my eyes on another fellow: Steve, a longshoreman. Ain't said anything to him yet. You and Hoxie are my kind, young and strong. Hoxie needs leading, but he ought to do. But that other boy...! And then the work's pretty hard and he looks scrawny."

"I'll talk to him."

When the three young men had gone, the Old Man made himself a pot of strong black coffee and then sat at the table studying the maps. He knew them by heart and could have drawn the Forty Mile Creek map with his eyes closed. But they weren't just maps to him; they were vivid reminders of the Great North Country and called up visions of the endless tundra with the jagged mountains in the blue distance, of the immense Yukon, like an inland sea, of squat Indians in furs, fishing through the ice, and of gold dust shining in the pan by a rushing stream... always of gold dust.

All day, all night—every day and night—the Old Man had to struggle with a never-ending fear—*the* Fear: that he would never get back, that fate had tied him to Seattle harbor, and that he would finish his days there and be buried in the hillside cemetery overlooking the Sound.

The Old Man pushed the maps aside suddenly and cursed to himself. "That Hoxie—talking to me like that. Could've wrung his neck. But I got to take it. Yes sir, Nollys, you got to take it. Just keep remembering. Take it. Get back."

Lloyd and Jim dropped Hoxie off at the Sailor's Rest, then went on up the hill toward the boardinghouse.

"Hoxie doesn't seem to be saving *his* money," said Lloyd, gesturing back toward the saloon.

"He's got to drink beer and he's got to have a woman—that's Hoxie," said Jim, trying to figure out a way to change Lloyd's mind about going to Alaska without hurting his feelings.

"I'd think he'd get mighty sick of those women," said Lloyd, wrinkling up his face in distaste.

"Hoxie's got a strong appetite," said Jim.

"It's something I just can't understand. It's like animals."

"Yes," said Jim.

Lloyd turned to look at him. Jim stared straight ahead. They dropped the subject.

Near the crest of the hill, Jim spoke. "Gets to fifty below up there."

Lloyd turned to look at him. "Alaska?"

"Yes. Sometimes seventy-five. And you work all through the winter."

"I know," said Lloyd. "I've been reading about it. And there is a perpetual night, sort of a twilight. And in the summer the sun never sets. It's always day. The Midnight Sun, you know. Oh, I've been reading all about it. Wonderful!"

He sounded very excited, very enthusiastic. Jim could think of nothing to say.

"Ever since I saw the *Osaka Maru* I've made up my mind I'd get away and see the world—Europe, the Orient. But Alaska first, and how lucky I am that you and Hoxie are going!"

The next night Jim went alone to see the Old Man.

"It's no use," he said. "Lloyd's more eager than we are. He's reading up all about it."

The Old Man shook his head and stroked the gray stubble on his chin. "Well," he said, "I just don't think he'll do. He'll panic. Mark my word. But... maybe it ain't right to deny him the opportunity."

"He's anxious to get away," said Jim. "Wants to see the world."

"I sympathize with that. I really do. Like myself. I wanted to see it and I did. Mexico, Canada, Alaska, Hawaiian Islands—I've been around. I fought two wars. I was on a ship that foundered off the Galápagos Islands. Damned lucky to be saved, we was. All right, Jim. I guess a man has got to take his chances, even when they're slim."

It was the middle of May. But Jim still hesitated. Hoxie was getting impatient with him, and Lloyd was little by little sliding back into the sea of futility he'd been wallowing in before the miraculous arrival of the *Osaka Maru*. He was sure now that they'd never get to Alaska; that they'd never get to any place at all, except maybe to Victoria across the Straits in Canada for an "outing." That was as far as he'd ever been in his whole life.

One night Hoxie and Jim had an argument and Lloyd looked on in silence, worried and uneasy. It was on the front steps of the old boardinghouse, with the gas lamps, few and far between, flickering down along the steep hilly street that led to the harbor.

"It's not something you just jump into," said Jim. "If you go you're stuck for a year. You can't get out."

"All right," cried Hoxie. "Let's either go or stay. I'm goddamned sick and tired of thinking about it."

"How much money have you saved?"

"Well, I... not so much."

"Then shut up your talk of thinking about it."

"Don't tell me to shut up, Jim Hardy."

"I already told you," said Jim.

Lloyd was badly scared. He was sure there was going to be a fight and that might mean the end of the friendship between Jim and Hoxie. And if they broke up and went their separate ways, what would happen to him?

There was a pause, then Hoxie laughed easily. "All right, Jim," he said. "You told me to shut up, but I won't. Let's go, Jim. Let's go."

"I'm thinking about it," said Jim.

Lloyd heaved a sigh of relief as Hoxie burst out into a torrent of comical swearing and then laughed again. Telling Jim and Hoxie to "hold their horses," he went inside to get them some lemonade. There was always a big pitcher of it in the icebox, spring and summer.

In the dark hallway, Lena grabbed his arm, startling him so that he broke out into a sweat.

"What's up, Lloyd?" she asked. "What are they shouting about? Where does Hoxie want to go?"

"Lena, it's none of your business."

"But it is; it is. I want to know."

"If you don't stop pestering me, I'll tell you. But you won't like it after you hear it."

He pulled away from her and went out into the kitchen, stumbling into the chairs in his agitation and feeling lost and disoriented until he'd got the gas jet lit. It threw a flickering yellow light over the huge kitchen where his mother spent most of her waking life. As he moved to the icebox to get out the lemonade, the door opened behind him and Lena came in.

"What are you doing?"

"Oh my God!" screamed Lloyd. "Can't you let me alone?"

"Lloyd!" Lena showed a shocked face.

Lena's expression of panicky dismay steadied him. He immediately became contrite. "I'm sorry, Sis. I didn't mean to yell at you like that. I'm going to take some lemonade out to the boys."

"I'll get it, Bub. I'll bring it out."

They stood looking at each other in surprise. He had called her "Sis," she had called him "Bub," as in the happier time of their childhood when there'd been laughter in the house and Pa used to play the piano in the evening just for them and they'd sing and dance.

Lena and Lloyd started to laugh. "You haven't called me 'Sis' for years," she said. "You go on out with the boys. How about some cookies? They're fresh made this afternoon."

"All right, Lena."

He started out, but she called to him. "Lloyd—you wouldn't want to tell me what they were shouting about?"

Lloyd hesitated. They'd all agreed to keep it a secret. But, after all, Lena was "family" and she'd have to know in any case—that is, if they ever decided to go, which seemed very doubtful now. Still….

"It's supposed to be kept secret," he said. "Between Hoxie, Jim, and me."

"Did you swear?"

"No."

"Then you can tell me. I won't let on I know—to anyone."

"Are you sure? It might be a shock."

Lena paled slightly, but said: "I'm sure."

"Don't tell Ma or Pa now. They'd think I was out of my mind. We're going to Alaska for gold."

A glass slipped from Lena's hand and shattered on the floor. It was much worse than she'd suspected! "Alaska? Gold? When?"

"First of June—if we go."

"If?"

"Yes. Jim can't make up his mind, and we're waiting on him. If he says 'no,' we don't go. At least *I* don't. Not to Alaska."

"But it's insane," said Lena, appalled by the idea. "You'll freeze to death. The wolves will eat you. You'll never get back."

"We haven't *gone* yet," said Lloyd, the old irritation returning; then he whirled and went out.

Lena swept up the broken glass, talking to herself. "They'll never go. It's preposterous. It's only what men do in books. Jim's got too much sense for anything like that."

By the time she went out front with the lemonade and cookies, she felt very calm and reassured. After all, it was just like Pa, always talking about going to New York and starting over in the music business. Men all had these aberrations, perhaps. Lloyd and Pa surely did. But it seemed odd in a rough, animal-like man such as Hoxie Thicke, and in levelheaded Jim Hardy. It would come to nothing. She was certain of it.

But Jim's hand was forced. A few nights later at about nine o'clock Hoxie came up panting from the direction of the harbor. Lloyd, Lena, and Pa were sitting on the front steps, enjoying the cool, mild evening, with its faint tang of salt air from the Sound.

"Where's Jim?" asked Hoxie abruptly.

"Sleater came and got him," Lloyd explained. "He's at the plant, working. Something about straightening out some orders on a big shipment to San Francisco."

Hoxie was appalled. "Working? At night? And no overtime? They can't do that."

"Jim doesn't mind," said Lloyd.

"No," said Pa. "Jim is very energetic."

Hoxie looked at him askance. "It's not a question of 'energetic,' Pa. It's a question of a man getting paid when he works. Jim's still a farmer at heart. They handle damned little money, farmers. It's all barter and what the land's worth. Jim just don't know about money, and I can't teach him. Got to find him."

He turned and hurried off. Lloyd rose and ran after him.

"Those boys," said Pa, sighing. "They make me tired to watch them. Oh well. They'll stop all this rushing around sooner or later. It's futile."

Lena was not listening to him. "I wonder what Hoxie was in such a state about?"

Pa groaned slightly as he rose. "My back! Got to get it looked at. Hoxie? Oh, nothing important you can bet. Nothing important."

Lloyd was so eager to know what was going on that he grabbed Hoxie's arm, stopping him. "What's happened?"

Hoxie shook him off and started on. "No use me telling it twice. Let's find Jim."

And they found him much sooner than they had expected. As they reached the foot of the hill, they saw him coming up a side street from the lumber company, which stretched for blocks along the northern reaches of the docks. He passed under a gas lamp and they heard him whistling.

"Right cheerful—Jim," said Hoxie. "Now what in hell has he got to be whistling about? No girl. A two-bit job."

"He's got a good job," said Lloyd. "And he'll keep moving up. Jim's that kind."

"I make more money," said Hoxie disdainfully.

"But he'll make more later."

"Maybe. Maybe not." Hoxie laughed, then called to Jim: "Hey there, hayshaker. Where you going?"

Jim looked up in surprise, then came over to them. "What's up?"

"Get down to the harbor with me. Old Man wants to see you."

They found the Old Man with a short, slight, hatchet-faced fellow, with dark, greasy-looking curly hair, and the improbable name of Windhorn. He'd worked as steward on some of the big liners in the East and was now a sea cook on the West Coast, working intercoastal. He'd just got back from Alaska.

"You talk, we listen," said the Old Man.

Lloyd, Hoxie, and Jim took seats around the table and Windhorn paced the floor as he talked. He seemed to have quite an opinion of himself, Jim thought.

"Up to Juneau and back," said Windhorn, "quite a jaunt of maybe two thousand nautical miles, and all I heard about coming and going was gold. She's been hit, boys, way up at Circle City on the Arctic Circle, I hear, and men are trying to get in across Chilkat and then down the Yukon in homemade boats. We had two stokers jump ship; short-handed coming back."

"It's been hit, you see," said the Old Man. "This ain't the big one, believe me; 'cause I prospected Circle, hit plenty, but it was coarse and cheap. I went on upriver to Forty Mile Creek. The big one will explode thereabouts. Take my word for it. But the point is, they're coming. Next year will be too late. It's now or never. The *George B. Schoonover* sails on the fifth of June and if we ain't on it, there's no use going at all."

"That's the truth," said Windhorn. "I hear talk all over the harbor. Once the fever starts you couldn't get a passage for love or money. I'm in."

"And he's valuable," said the Old Man, as the three young men said nothing, but merely stared. "He can cook and he's been around the world and is used to taking the rough with the smooth."

"I'll take the smooth," said Windhorn smirking. "But the rough don't bother me none."

Although Windhorn was not quite forty, he'd been knocking around the world on his own for over twenty years. Born in London, he'd shipped out of Liverpool as a cabin boy at the age of fifteen and he'd been rolling ever since, as seaman, steward, and cook. He'd even been to the Solomon Islands, where they still ate people—long pig—back in the bush, so he said.

He tossed a little gold crescent onto the table; it was attached by a gold cord to his watch chain.

"It's took me through typhoons and earthquakes. A weird old character give it to me in Gaza. A kind of medicine man, I guess you might say. I been lucky ever since. Nothing can happen to me when I'm wearing it. Nothing."

Lloyd stared with his mouth open, taking in every word. But Jim and Hoxie were regarding Windhorn with some skepticism.

"I got the money right here on me," said Windhorn, tapping his chest. "And I'm ready to ship out—for the moon, if you say so, Nollys. You see, Nollys and me are friends. We been around a long time."

The Old Man turned to Jim. "Any objections to Gabe?"

Jim stared. Windhorn tapped his chest again, laughing. "That's me," he explained. "Gabe. Gabriel. Get it? Windhorn's my family name so my shipmates call me Gabriel. Stretching it maybe a little, but it's a kinda nice idea."

Jim said nothing. Hoxie and Lloyd waited for him to speak; then Hoxie grew impatient. "Nollys," he said, "Jim ain't give us the word to go yet."

The Old Man turned. "Jim?"

Jim roused himself and cleared his throat. His face looked a little pale, Lloyd thought. "Gabe's all right with me," said Jim. "And I've made up my mind. We go."

The Old Man jumped up, almost upsetting the lamp, and, waving his arms, let out a few triumphant yells that made the windowpanes rattle; then he turned to get the beer.

"We go," he said, as if to himself. He needed Jim. He'd known it for a long time. The others were mere supers, assuring a large enough stake. But Jim he needed; money or no money.

The strident yelling of the Old Man had unsettled Lloyd. A cold fright gripped at him; and he felt sweat trickling down between his shoulder blades. Alaska—ice, snow, remoteness, an irrevocable commitment....

Hoxie was slapping Jim violently on the back. "He come through. I knew he'd come through. Damn, he's a Hardy from back home. All tough men."

Windhorn poured the beer with his practiced steward flourish, then raised his own glass.

"Gentlemen," he said, "to wealth, by God. To wealth."

They clinked glasses and drank in solemn silence.

Lloyd lit the gas jet in his room, started to undress, then paused in the middle of taking off his vest and stood staring, lost in visions of what the future might bring. He felt both frightened and exhilarated. His hands were ice cold and his heart was beating unevenly, worrying him. Could he make it? Or would he disgrace himself in the eyes of Hoxie and Jim? Could he stand the waiting at the start? Things would be much easier to bear if they were leaving that morning. He groaned at the thought of all he must go through before they could get away: explanations at the lumber company, explanations at home... blank astonishment all around, then arguments, warnings, pleas—days of wrangling....

There was a quick light tap at his door; then it opened and Lena stepped in, wearing a flowered wrapper over her nightgown. Lloyd gave a wild jump, then turned white with anger.

"What do you mean coming in here like that, scaring the daylights out of me!" he screamed.

Lena showed a shocked face. "Lloyd! What's the matter? Are you all right?"

"Of course I'm all right," cried Lloyd impatiently.

"You don't seem all right. You look awful, Lloyd."

Lloyd wagged his head and turned his back on her. "What do you want, Lena?"

"I couldn't sleep," said Lena. "I kept wondering why Hoxie was so anxious to find Jim and why you ran off after Hoxie so fast and never came back."

Tonight Lena's pale, melancholy face irritated him more than usual and his nerves were stretched so taut that he could no longer control them. "So you want to know, do you, Lena? You can't mind your own business. You have to pry. All right. We're going to Alaska—Jim, Hoxie, *me!* And we're leaving June 5. Now, are you satisfied?"

Lena gave a gasp, then controlled herself. "It's not true. You're just saying that because I walked in here and scared you. It's just not true."

"It's true, all right. I swear it. Ask Jim tomorrow."

Lena stood looking at him for a long time, her eyes dilated, then she whirled and, leaving Lloyd's door open, ran back down the hall. In a moment Lloyd heard her knocking on his parents' door; then there was a confusion of voices, lights sprang on, showing pale reflections in the dark hallway, and there was thumping and trampling, dominated by Lena's hysterical-sounding voice. Lloyd sat down on the edge of his bed and waited. The trouble he'd been anticipating had started already.

In a little while he heard them coming. First Lena appeared, then Pa, then Ma. They stood in the little bedroom looking down at him.

"What's this I hear?" said Pa. "Are you young fellows crazy?"

"No," said Lloyd.

"Taking off like this! What do you think we're going to do without you, Lloyd? Not to mention losing two good boarders. You can't do this to us, Lloyd."

"It's just insane," cried Lena.

"I'm going," said Lloyd. "You can't stop me. I want to see the world before I die. You think I want to stay in one place forever and get old without ever seeing anything or going any place?"

"It's all right about the boarders," said Ma calmly. "I've got a waiting list, on account of all the new people coming in. I put our names in at the Methodist church and the Masonic Temple, just in case I might have vacancies."

Lena and Pa looked at her in consternation.

"You encouraging him, Ma?" Pa demanded.

"You never did what you wanted, Pa," she said. "Got married too young. Let Lloyd have a try at it."

Lloyd stood with his mouth slightly open, staring at his mother as if he'd never seen her before. He'd expected opposition of all kinds, but especially from her. After all, when you came right down to it, Ma was the boss—she ran things.

But his emotions were very mixed. It would be impossible for him to back out now, no matter how he felt later. Ma wanted him to go—to have his chance. He'd have to take it now, no matter what!

"But Ma, you don't understand," cried Lena. "It's an awful country, thousands of miles away. They'll never come back."

"Other men go farther and come back," said Ma. "Come on, let's go back to bed."

"But Ma... how can you...?" cried Lena, appalled.

But Ma cut her off. "Lena, go to bed. I'm 'fraid it's not Lloyd you're making all this fuss about."

Lena started slightly, lowered her eyes, then went to her room without another word.

"Well, Lloyd," said Pa, "as long as Ma thinks it's all right...." He coughed reflectively, then tested his back by bending over and wiggling about. "Gosh, I think that kink's gone. What do you know about that?"

Shaking his head in wonder, he went out and walked slowly back to the bedroom.

Ma and Lloyd stood looking at each other.

"Thanks, Ma," he said.

"Don't thank me," she said. "I'm just glad you've got the gumption to try it. We've been a little short on gumption. Get some sleep, Lloyd. You got to get up and go to work."

She smiled at him briefly and left. Lloyd stood staring after her in unbelief. Perversely, he felt abandoned.

Meanwhile, Jim and Hoxie, exhausted by the excitement of the evening, slept on, oblivious. The earth turned slowly in the night and finally dawn began to show palely on the hilltops to the east. Then light crept down from the hills, dew sparkled on the lawns, and little by little the Sound turned from a dull lead color to gun-metal blue, then to greenish blue. The lighthouse beam flicked off for the night. A sea wind sprang up, and clouds started to race in from the west. Now flocks of gulls began to fly over the houses, complaining in harsh voices that sounded like the creaking of rusty gates.

A new day dawned.

The five of them were grouped round the table at the Old Man's shack. The coal-oil lamp flickered in the draughts blowing in through the cracks and cast tall wavering shadows over the clapboard walls.

The Old Man had a pad and pencil in front of him and talked as he wrote down various items.

"A man's got to be ready, you see," he was saying. "Up north, equipment's half the battle. Two–three pair of heavy blankets apiece. A Mackinaw suit. Two–three suits of wool underwear—the heaviest. Maybe three heavy flannel shirts. Rubber thigh boots and a pair of lace-ups to rest your feet now and then. Them rubber boots really pucker you up if you stick to 'em; and then you'll have foot trouble—and that's bad."

"He knows, this Old Man; he really knows," said Gabe Windhorn, smirking and cocking up his perky face.

But there were no longer any doubts about that. Even Hoxie was convinced.

The Old Man looked about him, smiled grimly, then went on:

"Bacon, beans, lots of canned stuff—we got to take our own, see? Supplies are short up north and you can't live off the country. All them whooping miners have chased the game away—although maybe you can get a moose now and then—and it takes the patience of hell to fish in the Yukon. Even the Injuns have their troubles—fishing—except in winter. Come prepared; that's the motto up there—and them that don't stick to it don't last it out. It's a strange place, boys; and you've got to understand that. Supplies get short and you can't get anything for love or money. You can have all the gold dust in the world and it will get you nothing. Come prepared."

"With the Old Man looking after us, we'll be prepared all right," said Gabe; then he smirked: "But maybe I can tell him a thing or two at that."

"Wouldn't doubt it," said the Old Man mildly. "Wouldn't doubt it for a minute." Then he resumed: "Then we got to have a pick per man, long-handled shovels, gold pans, axes, and three augers, one-half inch, one inch, and one and a half inch. With an ax and an auger a man can build most anything he needs, except maybe sluice boxes. Oh yes. Wire nails. Plenty of wire nails. It's the only kind worth a damn up there...."

He talked on. The list grew. Lloyd was overawed and sat staring, like a little boy at a grown-up party. Jim showed marked interest. But Hoxie's attention wandered, he began to hum "Waltz Me Around Again, Willie," and finally he rose to get a bottle of the Old Man's beer.

"... that's the lot, I think," said the Old Man finally. "If I missed anything I'll think of it later. Now, boys, we got to talk serious, so let's get it over once for all. With five of us all working together we got a big advantage and tell you why. If we hit a likely spot in them creeks around Forty Mile we can just about take over the whole damned section. A claim runs five hundred feet, taking in both creek sides to the base of the rise or to the end of the beach. The man who makes the strike can file one more claim for himself as discoverer; then the other four could file a claim apiece. That way we'd have three thousand feet of the creek in a good spot; over half a mile of prime diggings. You see? Now as to labor. It's hard to come by and when I was there you had to pay your help ten dollars a day. It's probably higher now. With five of us a-working, we'll need damned little help. We'll just skim off the cream of all our claims, salt our dust, sell or lease our claims, and get out."

"You make it sound easy," said Gabe.

"Then I'm talking crazy," said the Old Man. "It ain't easy. It ain't easy at all. It's tough and back-breaking. But it can be done. And if it can be done, we can do it."

"Yay!" cried Hoxie, who'd hardly been listening.

"Now," said the Old Man, looking all around him, "this, you might say, is an expedition, and an expedition has got to have a leader. I been there before, I've got the experience, so I figure I ought to lead. All right with you, Jim?"

"Yes, sir," said Jim. "Suits me fine."

There were no protests, so the Old Man continued: "This is the way we do it. I handle the money. I have the say-so. And you men obey, within reason."

"Aw, come on, Harp," said Hoxie. "What the hell is this—the Army?"

"I agree," said Jim, looking hard at Hoxie.

"All right. Okay," cried Hoxie, waving the beer bottle. "If Jim agrees, I agree."

"And me," said Lloyd.

The Old Man glanced at Lloyd in surprise as if he'd forgotten that he was there.

"As for me," said Gabe, "I'm with the Old Boy a hundred per cent, beings as I know Nollys from way back. He's a good man, boys. Tough, but good."

The Old Man took a big money belt from a drawer. It was made of dark, thick, strong-looking leather and the pouch had a lock and key and was studded with brass and heavily sewn with tough waxed cord.

"This'll be round my waist," said the Old Man. "Our stake will be under lock and key and safe from harm. No thieves can get at it, no bank teller can run off with it, and it can't get lost unless I do, which is very unlikely. You all trust me?"

"Yes," said Jim.

"Then it's done," said the Old Man, slapping the table; but he paused at a sudden thought and went on: "About thieves. Better tell you about them, so you men will understand the North. There is really no law and order at all in the Yukon country. And there is no trouble neither. Why—with all that gold dust around? I'll tell you. When I was in Forty Mile working my claim two no-goods come down river in an Injun canoe without supplies, without nothing. They hit a miner over the head with a pick handle and took his savings of gold dust, then tried to get away. But we caught 'em, took 'em back to Forty Mile, strung 'em up in front of the general store, and left 'em swinging there for a week as an example. Birds pecked 'em to pieces. But we never had any more trouble."

There was a brief silence, then Hoxie laughed. "Served 'em right," he said. "Stealing a man's money."

"Oh, it wasn't that so much," said the Old Man. "We hung them fellows to *stop* the stealing once and for all, and we stopped it. Stealing here in Seattle is one thing; stealing in the North Country is another. Them no-goods could take over with a little encouragement, then no man would be safe. Them fellows really begged for mercy, said they'd mend their ways. We couldn't take the chance."

Lloyd counted out his money to Jim, while Hoxie looked on. They were in Lloyd's room and they'd just got home from work.

"Six hundred, right," said Jim. "One hundred for supplies; five hundred for stake. I'll get it to the Old Man tonight."

"You think it's all right, him carrying all that money?" asked Hoxie. Jim merely glanced at him, said nothing.

"Does the passage money come out of the five hundred?" asked Lloyd.

"Yes," said Jim. "It'll cost us seventy-five apiece to St. Michael. Except for Gabe. He signed on as cook on the out voyage, saving us his passage money. Then it'll cost us seventy-five to a hundred apiece to make the voyage up the Yukon from St. Michael to Forty Mile."

"Pretty steep," said Hoxie, "Couldn't we do better?"

"The Old Man says not," said Jim with finality.

They left Lloyd washing up and returned to their room. "Where's your money, Hoxie?" asked Jim, after he'd closed the door.

Hoxie shifted about uncomfortably before he spoke. "I meant to talk to you about that."

"How much have you got?"

"Well, I... I've had some bad luck lately, Jim. You know how it is. I ain't got but three hundred and thirty-eight dollars."

Jim's gray eyes turned cold. "Goddamn it, Hoxie; here we've been planning and talking for weeks and you haven't got spine enough to save your money. No, you got to throw it away on whores at Sadie's."

"Now wait, Jim, wait," Hoxie pleaded. "I thought I'd have it. Swear I did. Last week I counted it wrong. Thought I had five hundred, but it was only three hundred. One of them damned girls—maybe it was

Alberte, that little French tart—must've stole some of it off me...."

"Stop lying."

"Don't you call me no liar, Jim Hardy," cried Hoxie, bristling and shoving his big chest forward.

Jim pushed him back roughly. "That's what you are. A liar. A god-damned liar."

Hoxie turned very red in the face, his dark eyes glaring, then he deflated his chest and began to laugh. "You're right, Jim, boy; you're right. It's them tarts. I can't resist 'em. The trouble with you is... well, I don't know. You just can't understand a man's weaknesses. You ain't got any. Or you're too damned stubborn to admit you have."

Jim said nothing. Hoxie began to plead. "Couldn't you lend me the money, Jim, boy? I figured maybe you would."

"I know you did, damn you."

"But hell, we're going to be rich, Jim. Fifty thousand apiece. What's a few hundred dollars?"

"All right," said Jim, finally, in disgust.

Hoxie whooped and waved his arms, then he grabbed Jim in a bear-like hug and tried to dance him around the room. "That's my Jim," cried Hoxie. "That's my Clark County boy!"

II

TO UNALASKA

The last day had finally come. All the dunnage had been taken aboard and the Old Man had already made himself at home on the ship, looking it over from top to bottom. Windhorn, as second cook a member of the crew now, had nothing to do at the moment and spent his time with the Old Man, who finally took him down to the cabin.

"Not bad," said Gabe, looking about him at the cramped, musty little place. "Not bad at all." Then he opened a porthole. "How about some air? Got a strong smell of bilge, Nollys."

"Snug cabin, eh?" said the Old Man. "Gabe, we got four bunks here. One of 'em's a big one. Why don't you move in?"

"No," said Gabe. "I like my quarters on deck. Stinks 'tween decks. Bilge!"

"Ain't them deck quarters temporary—jerry-rigged?"

"Yeah," said Gabe. "The ship brought back quite a few passengers on a run to Sitka. Put up them quarters."

"Gabe," said the Old Man, "you listen to me. Them northern waters are rough, nothing to monkey with. A big wave might wash over and carry them jerry-rigged quarters away."

Gabe laughed easily, then held up the crescent charm on his watch chain. "Nollys, you forget. As long as I wear this I'm safe. It's took me through typhoons and earthquakes. Strikes me you're more cautious than I thought, Nollys."

"It ain't caution," said the Old Man. "It's just that I believe in leaving as little as possible to chance."

But Gabe laughed and wouldn't listen. Later they went on deck and leaned on the rail, smoking. It was a misty day with the spring sun trying hard to shine through. Gulls were everywhere, screeching and swooping.

The Old Man slapped the rail. "Gabe," he said, "you'll never know what it means to me being on this ship, ready to sail for the North. It's a dream come true."

"Just so the gold ain't a nightmare," Gabe replied, laughing.

"Oh, the gold's there, all right," said the Old Man mildly. "And we'll get it."

"Them young fellows you got—that Jim; wouldn't want to cross him. Hoxie, he's a blowhard but strong as a bull. But that little one...!" Gabe shook his head and whistled dolefully.

"Had to take him to get the others," said the Old Man. "I figure he'll panic sure, once he sees that country. It ain't for everybody, Gabe. Just the size and the space and the distance scares some men—and that river; my God, what a river! However, you never can tell. I've seen the biggest, roughest men fold on the Yukon, and the little skinny ones come through with flying colors."

"I'm on the small side myself," said Gabe, a little put out.

The Old Man laughed. "You? Why, hell, Gabe; you're a veteran of rough times. You've earned your spurs over and over. Who worries about *you?*"

Mollified, Gabe laughed and slapped the Old Man on the back. Then they stood for a long time in silence, leaning on the rail, smoking, and idly watching the gulls.

Lena was in her room, with the door locked. She had refused to come to the table for supper and Ma had calmly explained that she was not feeling very well. But Lloyd knew the truth. The night before, Lena had waked up out of a nightmare and had had a fit of hysterics. Pa, with his suspenders hanging, had run for the doctor, who had given her a shot of morphine that had knocked her out.

Jim and Hoxie had slept through the whole uproar and knew nothing about it. But Lloyd had been unable to sleep the rest of the night. And now it was almost time to go and he was sweating with nervous apprehension. He glanced at Jim and Hoxie with something not very far from hatred. Jim was explaining calmly to the man from the city solicitor's office that they should be out of the Juan de Fuca Straits by morning of the next day and in the open Pacific, while Hoxie kept laughing and making jokes.

Now supper was over. Hoxie had eaten two big pieces of Ma's famous apple pie and, laughing, had let out his belt a notch. The old school-teacher surprised everybody by presenting all three young men with embroidered handkerchiefs as going-away gifts. "See," she said, "'J' for James. 'H' for Hoxie. And a special one for Lloyd because he is Mrs. Gracey's only son. 'L.G.'" To his further astonishment Lloyd noticed that his father was crying. Unable to stand the sight, he jumped up from the table and left the room.

"Pa!" Mrs. Gracey admonished mildly, and Pa took out his handkerchief and blew his nose.

Jim and Hoxie said good-by all around, and Hoxie hugged Ma. "Will you marry me when I get back with all that gold, Ma?" he cried.

"I'll consider it, Hoxie," she said, laughing.

They found Lloyd pacing in the hallway.

Jim hesitated for a moment, then said: "Shouldn't Hoxie and me say good-by to Lena, Lloyd?"

"She's in her room, ill," said Lloyd. Then: "Pa had to get a doctor for her last night."

"Oh! I'm sorry to hear that."

"Come on, Jim," said Hoxie impatiently; but Jim turned and went back into the dining room.

They all looked up in surprise.

"Ma," said Jim, "will you please tell Lena good-by for Hoxie and me? Sorry to hear she's so ill. We'll send her something, first port, if we get the chance. You tell her that."

"I will, Jim," said Ma. "And thanks."

As the three young men started down the hill to the harbor, a window in the boardinghouse was banged up and Lena leaned out.

"Good-by, Jim. Good-by, boys," she cried. "I should have come down but I couldn't."

Her voice sounded very strange. They all eyed each other uneasily.

"Good-by, Lena," called Jim. "I already told Ma—we'll send you something from first port, a souvenir."

"Oh, will you, Jim? Good-by, good-by, good-by...."

The wind caught her voice and carried it away. They turned and went down the hill toward the harbor, where twilight was falling and hundreds of lights were winking on. The beam from the lighthouse began to sweep around, shining for a moment here and there on the dark water,

"Well," said Hoxie, "here goes nothing!"

The first sight of the cabin appalled Lloyd. There was hardly room to turn around, and once the door was closed they'd be like rats in a trap. But Hoxie flung himself into one of the bunks, leaned back at ease, with his hands under his head, and exclaimed: "Ah, this is the life! I hope I never see that goddamned hook again."

Jim looked a little pale. The Old Man kept glancing at him, wondering. "What's that smell?" asked Jim.

"It's bilge," said the Old Man. "You've got to get used to it."

"I got a lot to get used to," said Jim. "I never been in anything bigger than a rowboat before."

Lloyd glanced at Jim in surprise. Was he nervous, too? Obviously; and Lloyd began to feel better at once. If a man like Jim could feel nervous, there was certainly nothing disgraceful about it.

Now Gabe poked his head in. "Hi, mates," he cried cheerfully. "We'll soon be on our way. To the Aleutians, Dutch Harbor, Pribilof Islands, St. Lawrence Island, and St. Michael. Punch your transfers?"

Hoxie roared and took up the old refrain. "'Punch, brothers, punch with care; punch in the presence of the passenjaire!'"

In a moment, Gabe, Hoxie, and the Old Man were howling out the jingle, beating out the time on the steel sides of the cabin. Jim and Lloyd looked on in silence.

"What we need is beer!" cried Hoxie, leaping up. "Hold the fort and I'll run up and get a sack full."

"No time," said Gabe. "You want to get left?"

And at that moment a bell rang some place, there was a roar, and the ship began to quiver with the stroke of the engine. More bells rang. Running feet could be heard on the deck overhead. Then there was a loud blast on the whistle, almost deafening them in the little iron prison.

Hoxie leaped out the door, calling: "Got to take a last look at that goddamned waterfront where I've hustled so many bales."

They all followed him up to the rail. It was a quiet June night and the harbor lights cast a glassy sheen over the unusually still water of the Sound. They slipped slowly past boat after boat, all with lighted portholes and men moving about above. The lighthouse beam swept the water, with monotonous regularity, and far out in the Straits a ship's whistle moaned faintly.

"Can't believe we're really on our way," said Hoxie; then he slapped Jim on the back. "Hot dog! Boy, here we go."

"Rides nice," said Jim.

The Old Man and Gabe laughed, and the Old Man said: "Won't always 'ride' this nice, Jim. Lucky we're heavy laden. These tins really bounce when they're empty."

"And they wallow if they're overloaded," said Gabe. "I figure the *George B. Schoonover* is sailing just about right."

Lloyd felt more and more at ease. Why, hell, there was nothing to it. Only one thing. Why did the boat have to be called *George B. Schoonover*? It should have been named the *Corsair* or the *Nautilus*. He turned to the Old Man.

"What's the name of that steamboat we go up the Yukon in?"

"Well," said the Old Man, "if it's the same one, and likely it is, it'd be the *Nils K. Jensen*."

Lloyd sighed, but made no comment.

At midnight Lena slipped out the back door of the boardinghouse and hurried down the hill toward the harbor. The wharves were deserted. She stood for a while looking at the ships at anchor, then she burst into tears and covered her face with her hands. Little by little she moved over toward the water. It fascinated her with its blackness, its slow gentle motion, and the glassy sheen of its reflected lights. Music was playing faintly somewhere on a moored ship. She listened; then suddenly she had an almost overpowering desire to throw herself into the dark cold water and sink down forever. She moved closer to the edge of the wharf, stared down. It was very still now, with the water slapping gently at the piles. It would be so easy; one little movement, and then all of her pain and desperation would be wiped out, done with, forever.

Heavy stumbling footsteps and loud voices brought her up short, made her turn. Two huge men, staggering against each other at every step, were coming down the wharf toward a small dark steam launch moored at the side.

Terror gripped Lena. Turning, she ran frantically back along the wharf the way she'd come, passing the two men like a streak of light.

"Hey! Hey!" one of them yelled after her; then to his companion: "Did you see what I saw? I hope."

"Sure did. A lady woman."

"What you suppose she's doing down here all alone?"

"Maybe brought her better half down and pushed him in."

"Yeah. She was sure in a hurry when she seen us."

"Let's go see if there's a hat floating."

The *George B. Schoonover* was moving as smoothly as a little excursion boat on an inland lake. Gray showed at the portholes of the cabin, but the men slept on. Both Hoxie and the Old Man were snoring loudly. Lloyd, curled into a ball, had his knees braced against the wall and his head under the blanket. Jim was dreaming.

.... it was a Sunday. Church bells rang all over town. Jim and Hoxie and Red Mather were sneaking down an alley toward the creek, hiding their fishing tackle under their coats.

They'd cut willow poles later. Suddenly Hoxie's father appeared out of nowhere and began to whale them with a blacksnake whip, which little by little turned into a real black snake that eventually slid away from Hoxie's father, took its tail in its mouth, and rolled like a hoop toward the boys, chasing them back toward town....

Jim woke with a start and couldn't figure out where he was for a moment. Then the cabin gradually came into focus. In the bunk above him Hoxie snored and occasionally kicked. In the upper bunk across the way the Old Man had begun to stir and groan. But in the lower Lloyd lay very still.

Jim noted the worn, scoured look of the naked steel walls, the big rivet heads, the coal-oil light above moving gently in the gimbals, the gray at the portholes. A bell tinkled faintly. He heard footsteps on the deck overhead. Then for a moment he lay remembering the crazy dream about the black snake. What did it mean? Anything at all? Did dreams ever mean anything? His grandmother had thought so. She could always "interpret" them, she had insisted, irritating the men of the family but impressing the womenfolk. Women sure set much store by dreams and such oddities!

Jim sighed and sat up. The Old Man's eyes were open and he seemed to be looking off at the portholes.

"Morning," called the Old Man.

"Morning," said Jim.

"Well, so far so good."

"Yes. And she still rides easy."

"Don't figure we're out of the Straits yet. I'm hungry. Let's wake the others and go get us some breakfast. How about yourself?"

"Starved," said Jim; then he began to pound on a stanchion.

Lloyd woke at once, sat up, stared about him blankly, then lay back and stretched, But Hoxie snored on. In a moment Jim reached up and tickled his foot. Hoxie howled, writhed, squealed, and tried to kick Jim in the face. Jim laughed.

"Always was like that," he explained to the Old Man. "Ticklish as a girl."

"Goddamn you, Jim Hardy," cried Hoxie, turning over and settling himself once more for sleep.

But Jim reached up and pulled him out of the bunk by his legs. Hoxie lit fighting mad, grabbed Jim around the neck and tried to throw him down, but Jim pulled away, hit Hoxie a sharp blow in the belly, doubling him up, then pushed him hard with both hands. Hoxie went flying into Jim's bunk, his legs in the air.

The Old Man looked on calmly, but Lloyd was wincing, wanting them to stop. The struggling, the heavy blows, hurt him in the pit of his stomach.

Hoxie came charging out of the bunk like a mad bull, but Jim stepped quickly aside and tripped him. Hoxie fell heavily, rolled over on his back, and lay looking up at Jim. Finally he began to laugh. Jim roared.

"Goddamn you, Jim Hardy," cried Hoxie, "some day I'll get you—even if it has to be from the back. I've put up with this too long." Then he got to his feet, punched Jim hard in the belly, and said: "You old bastard."

"You boys play a little rough," said the Old Man.

"Been doing it for years," said Hoxie. "Ever since we was knee high. You see I'm too strong for him. Jim's puny. I just don't want to hurt him."

"He's strong all right," said Jim. "But you can't think with your muscles. I'm too smart for him."

"Ho, ho, ho," jeered Hoxie.

They dressed and went up to the saloon, a battered little cubbyhole with the long table fastened to the floor. The bleary-eyed first mate, Hansen, was having a cup of coffee and staring drearily out of a porthole.

"Hi," said the Old Man heartily.

The mate winced. "Don't speak above a whisper. I got a blinding, bloody, roaring beaut of a hangover."

Joe Portugee, man of all work, hustled their breakfasts in to them—toast, bacon, jelly, and coffee; then in a moment Gabe Windhorn appeared in the companionway door, smirking.

"Hi. Happy sailing. We'll soon be out of the Straits, Cape Flattery's up ahead. Come on deck. Take a look after breakfast."

"Who wants to look at that goddamned cape?" growled First Mate Hansen.

They stood at the rail watching as the *George B. Schoonover* passed Cape Flattery, land's end, and headed out into the immense gray solitudes of the open Pacific. The wind freshened sharply, and the bow rose and dropped away, cutting a white V through the heavy green water.

Fear stabbed at Lloyd as he looked ahead into the wilderness of water, into nowhere, and for a moment he envied a lone sea gull he saw heading for land.

Hoxie and the Old Man merely stared. But Jim looked up at the sun, which was showing faintly through a light mist, then off at the land to the south. "We're heading almost due west," he said.

"That's right," said Gabe.

"I figured it would be more like due north."

"You're wrong," said Gabe. "Unalaska's west of Seattle, a little to the north, that is, and that's our first stop."

"How soon do we get there?"

"With a lucky run, we'll make it in nine days. But don't hold me to it. This old tub just ain't got no schedule at all. It's a tramp. Getting there is all the captain's interested in."

"How about we play cards?" Hoxie broke in. "We got the whole damned day to kill. Gabe, has the skipper got his daughter aboard?"

Gabe laughed coarsely. "If he has, she'll be too old to count. Skip's right at sixty, maybe as old as Nollys."

Nine days! Jim said nothing, putting a brake on his worries and fears. He'd committed himself. Regrets were useless. He turned. Lloyd was looking at him. Jim smiled and Lloyd smiled back.

"Sea wind smells good," said Jim, with an effort.

"Yes," said Lloyd. "Very good."

It was late afternoon and the four of them were playing cassino in the cabin when the headwind hit. At first they paid no attention as the ship gave, a desultory series of exaggerated pitches and heaves; but little by little they began to look at each other. Overhead the lamp started to bang in the gimbals and the ship creaked, strained, and groaned.

"Storm?" Jim asked the Old Man.

"Don't think so. Headwind maybe. Be rough for a while." Jim got to his feet. "I'll go on deck and see."

The Old Man started to protest but before he could speak the ship gave a wild leap and Jim was flung backward into his bunk with his feet in the air.

Hoxie roared with laughter, throwing back his head, but the ship righted itself, heaved in the opposite direction, and Hoxie was flung suddenly to the floor of the cabin.

Without a word, Lloyd climbed into his bunk and lay braced, staring in silence at the bottom of the bunk overhead.

Jim managed to get to a sitting position in his bunk and Hoxie picked himself up from the floor.

"You stay below, Jim," said the Old Man, "with a roll like this. You're a landsman with no sea legs. You might get flung overboard."

"Yes," said Lloyd with an effort, "stay below, Jim."

The thought of Jim being thrown overboard terrified him. He'd never make it without Jim. That was a dead certainty. He'd just never make it.

The ship continued to pitch and heave with what at times seemed like purposeful malevolence, and there was a continual banging, rattling, and creaking. White frothy spray began to blow past the portholes and now and then a wave would hit the hull with a violent concussive sound, like the slap of a giant hand.

Lloyd began to pray silently and his prayer called up a tranquil vision of the interior of the bare little Methodist church on the hill a block up from the boardinghouse, where he'd gone to Sunday school as a boy. The Reverend John Fenstermaker, in his black suit, was telling them the story of the Passion. Jimmy Wallis kept pinching Lloyd and giggling. The preacher gave them a tired look, but said nothing. Lloyd had gone to the preacher's funeral last spring. Was it true what he'd been taught? Was there a Benevolent Presence? Was He aware of the fall of a sparrow? Lloyd had never been quite able to believe it. But now with all his heart and soul he hoped that it was true.

"Jesus Christ," cried Hoxie suddenly, "I'm sick. I got a hell of a bellyache."

Moaning, Hoxie climbed into his bunk and lay back.

Jim and the Old Man sat on, saying nothing. The violent pitching continued, growing worse at times, then slacking off for a spell. Finally the Old Man noticed how pale Jim's face was and said: "Take the horizontal, son. It sails easier that way."

"How about yourself?"

"Oh, I'm ready for it," said the Old Man, after studying Jim's face again.

But Jim sat on, his mouth grim, gritting his teeth. Smiling to himself, the Old Man finally climbed up into his bunk and lay back. Jim waited, then followed suit.

A little later the door opened and Gabe looked in, grinning. "Well," he said, "I see we got some sensible sailors aboard. Joe'll bring you some coffee later."

"No! God no!" gasped Hoxie.

"Oh, it'll taste good. You'll get used to this. Just a bit of weather. Good thing she ain't empty, though, or this roll would be nothing but a touch and tickle. Sail easy, mates."

He left, carefully closing the door. Hoxie cursed him for a full minute, then rolled over with his face to the wall, moaning.

"I'm dying," he yelled finally. "Jim, I'm dying."

"Shut up," said Jim coldly.

"It'll pass," said the Old Man soothingly. "We'll all get our sea legs."

"Wish I was back on the waterfront," cried Hoxie. "Wish I had my hook over my shoulder. Wish I'd never met you, Nollys Harp!"

"Will you shut up!" Jim shouted.

Though Lloyd was sick and scared he lay congratulating himself. It was hard to believe, but he was doing better than big tough Hoxie. Much better. Maybe his prayers were working.

Evening fell, but the pitching did not abate. Now the portholes showed black, and the light overhead, swinging in its gimbals, cast a flickering sickly light over the little cabin.

"I hope she sinks," yelled Hoxie. "I hope to Christ she sinks."

"I'm coming up after you in a minute," said Jim, in a weak voice.

"Get out the moose gun and shoot me," said Hoxie. "I can't stand this."

Lloyd remained silent. In a moment the Old Man climbed down from his bunk and put on his coat, bracing himself against the heavy roll.

"Boys, I'm going up," he said. "I'll be back shortly."

The Old Man had been hungry for hours and was unable to stand it any longer.

"Ain't you sick at all, Nollys?" asked Hoxie, in disgust. "Well...." said the Old Man. "I figure a breath of sea air might do me good."

He went out quickly.

"He's crazy," said Hoxie. "Never get me up on deck on a night like this."

"We haven't eaten since morning," said Jim. "Nollys went up to get his supper."

"His supper!" screamed Hoxie. "Oh, for the love of God! Oh Jesus! His supper!"

Lloyd choked and struggled with himself, then lay back and remained silent. He'd show them!

A little later Joe Portugee arrived with steaming hot black coffee. Lloyd and Jim drank a little, but Hoxie turned his face to the wall and held his hand over his nose so he couldn't smell it.

"Good, no?" said Joe, grinning. "She strong. We like strong. Wind she move. Pretty soon calm."

"How soon?" yelled Hoxie.

"Pretty soon," said Joe, grinning.

They were four days out from Cape Flattery now. The sky was heavily overcast but the lead-colored sea was flat as a plate and the *George B. Schoonover* steamed northwestward effortlessly with hardly a movement of its deck. An odd grayish lavender light showed at the edge of the western horizon, then little by little turned darker till it was a deep thunderhead blue.

The three young men lounged at the rail at their ease, looking down at the water. Lloyd had acquired the beginning of a sea tan and was smoking a pipe. Already he felt like a veteran adventurer. Hoxie had a mug of black coffee in his big right fist and occasionally took a sip. Jim was smoking a cigar First Mate Hansen had given him.

Hoxie shifted his heavy shoulders and grinned at Jim. "Nothing to it, once a man gets the hang of it," he said. "Great, eh, Jim? We ride this tub to St. Michael, then we ride that other tub to where the gold is. The Old Man was sure right, wasn't he?"

"Looks like it," said Jim.

There was a shout from the bridge and they all looked up. It was Hansen and he waved his arms, then pointed.

"What's he saying?" asked Lloyd.

Gabe came hurrying up behind them. "Whales off the port bow, fellows. Hansen thought you might like to see 'em."

They moved up farther along the rail, Gabe following them. "Thar she blows!" he cried, laughing. "And sparm at that!"

"What?" Hoxie demanded.

"*Moby Dick*, a real seaman's book. Ain't you fellows ever heard tell of *Moby Dick*?"

But none of them had.

"Read in every English-speaking fo'c'sle on the Seven Seas."

But he'd lost their attention. Jim gestured with his cigar. "See! Over there. Look at that spray."

"Yeah. He's blowing," said Gabe. "Look! There's another one."

The ship was moving toward the whales on a course that would bring them directly across their path. The whales came on lazily, blowing from time to time. Now they could be plainly seen. And the three young men were staggered by their size.

"Jesus," said Hoxie. "Damned near as big as this ship."

Lloyd was shaking with excitement and could not speak for the moment. He'd seen two whales in the open sea—with his own eyes he'd seen them, not *read* about them!

The ship drew closer and closer to the whales. Their enormous, rubbery-looking bodies, only partly submerged, slid effortlessly through the water. Now a tremendous head was raised; a little, wise, elephant-like eye peered for a moment at the smoking, alien object cluttering up the bosom of the sea; then both whales sounded.

"Gone," said Lloyd, astounded by their sudden disappearance.

The three young men looked at each other in amazement, then laughed.

"Good luck seeing whales that close," said Gabe, rubbing the crescent charm on his watch chain. "Damned good luck."

Hansen tooted the whistle; then as they all looked up he waved to them and grinned.

"Too bad Nollys missed it," said Jim.

"Oh, he didn't miss it," said Gabe; then he jerked his thumb toward the bridge. "He's up sitting with Hansen."

They all stood at the rail, talking. Gabe kept glancing off to the west and finally said: "Looks like a little weather could be making up."

The three young men turned to him and he pointed. "You think it might storm?" asked Jim.

"Might blow a bit," said Gabe. "Or we might miss it altogether. Seems to be moving southeast. In any case it won't be any worse than that damned headwind."

Jim, Hoxie, and Lloyd were not worried about "weather making up" now. They'd been thoroughly initiated on their first day out and no longer considered themselves to be lubbers.

The five partners were all playing poker in the cabin. It was after eleven o'clock. The portholes showed black, and the light swung with monotonous regularity overhead, as the ship had quite a roll. But it was not a bouncing, pitching, shuddering roll as on the day of the headwind. There was something almost soothing about it.

The men ignored it and concentrated on the game, playing as if their lives depended on it, although it was only penny ante. Gabe kept winning hand after hand, laughing at them, and occasionally shining up his crescent charm.

"I told you seeing them whales up close was good luck," he crowed.

"We seen 'em, too, didn't we?" Hoxie demanded sourly.

"Sure, mate. But you ain't got my little crescent charm to rub."

They broke up a little before midnight. Gabe pocketed his winnings, laughing and baiting the others; then he said: "Off to the galley. The skipper has a big meal about twelve—takes the night watch; part owner of this ship. Don't want to lose it. Good news, eh, boys?"

He went out, laughing, but in a moment put his head back in: "Boys, she is really blowing out. A whistling, screaming wind. If you keep real quiet you'll hear it. I think we're ketching the tail end of that weather. Ain't raining yet. Sleep snug, boys. I'll give you a chance to get even tomorrow night."

The four men stripped down to their underwear and climbed into their bunks. Now rain began to lash at the portholes and from time to time, even over the creaking and groaning of the ship and the throb of the engine, they could hear the howling of the wind.

"Snug is right," said Hoxie sleepily. "I'm getting so I kinda love this damned old tin tramp."

At a little after three they were all awakened by a shuddering crash; the ship staggered slightly, then righted itself and moved forward with the same long, easy, monotonous roll. They all lay listening.

"What the hell was that?" asked Hoxie, after a moment.

"Don't know," said the Old Man.

Now they heard the thud of feet on the deck above, then trampling, and what sounded like heavy hammering, long drawn out.

"Something must have carried away," said the Old Man. "I don't know what else."

"What?"

"I don't know."

In a moment the door opened and Joe Portugee stepped in, looking pale, almost ghostly, in the overhead light which was kept on all night.

Something about Joe's manner warned the men that there had been a catastrophe. They all sat up and stared at him. "You podna—Gabe," stammered Joe. "He gone."

"Gone?" said Jim, not sure he had understood.

"Gone. Overboard. Lost. Big wave like have eyes—whap!—wood house, gone. Gabe sleep inside."

There wasn't a sound in the cabin except for the creak of the ship and the throb of the engine.

"We circle back. We look now. No use. Never find. Gone." Joe lowered his head and crossed himself. "You like good black coffee now?"

"Yes," said Jim.

Joe left. They all got up and dressed, then sat as if in a stupor on the two lower bunks, waiting for the coffee.

Lloyd was cold with fright. Seasoned adventurer, eh? What a joke! Merely because he'd lasted out a few tame days at sea! And what had happened to the Benevolent Presence? Hadn't Gabe been worth as much as a sparrow? Wiped out—just like that, with his penny-ante winnings in his pocket, likely, and his crescent charm from Gaza on his watch chain. Lloyd winced away from the picture his imagination called up—the sleeping man swept overboard without warning into the cold dark sea, lost, abandoned, hopeless, with the ship moving on away from him into the howling darkness.

"Strange thing," said the Old Man finally. "I warned him about sleeping up there. But he wouldn't listen."

"How did you happen to do that?" asked Hoxie.

"I could see them quarters were jerry-built, and I've been in some rough seas in my time. Man's a fool to take a chance like that. But Gabe—well, he was hipped on that charm. Me, I don't believe in charms. I believe in leaving as little to chance as possible. That's what I told him."

"Do you believe in prayer, Nollys?" asked Lloyd in a shaky-sounding voice.

The Old Man hesitated before he spoke, studying Lloyd's tense face for a moment. "Yes, for them that believe."

"You think it helps?" Lloyd persisted.

"Son," said the Old Man, "if you believe, you believe. You'll never hear a word from me against the Christian religion, nor any other."

It was a very unsatisfactory answer, but Lloyd did not pursue the point.

"He should have listened," said Hoxie. "Me, I'm going to listen to you—*hard*, from now on."

Joe came with the coffee and had a cup with them.

"Cap'n put about again. No find," he explained. "Gabe lost at sea."

Jim had been stubbornly silent all day. Very early he'd gone above to examine the work that had been done on deck where the jerry-rigged quarters had been torn away by the big wave. At breakfast he'd sat by himself, then later had gone up on the bridge with Hansen.

Hoxie managed to corner him during the afternoon. "What's the matter with you, Jim?" he demanded.

"I hated losing Gabe," said Jim bluntly. "I hated it like hell. I don't want to talk."

He turned and walked away. Hoxie knew better than to go after him, so he went back to the galley to chin with Joe Portugee, who broke out some choice tins from England: spiced meat, water crackers, and orange marmalade—all intended for the table of the skipper.

"But he like sowbelly—beans. Always sowbelly—beans," Joe explained, giggling. "Pancakes, black coffee, sowbelly—beans."

They talked about the waterfront. Joe knew Sadie's. In fact he'd had a whirl with the Frenchy, Alberte.

"Nice girl," said Joe. "All white, pink, and gold. Very nice."

"Stop it," said Hoxie. "We don't hit land for four–five days."

Joe roared with laughter. "Hit land! Unalaska? No Frenchies there."

Hoxie stared; then he said: "Guess I can hold out. Tell you something, Joe. When *you* begin to look good to me, get worried."

Joe laughed so hard he almost fell into the stove.

On the way back to the cabin, Hoxie observed to himself philosophically: "Well, it ain't all bad. The Old Man's got Gabe's money. And we may need it."

Four days passed in the pleasantly boring semi-stupor of fine sea weather and the effortless eating up of mile after nautical mile by the little tramp steamer—one thousand-ton burden—*George B. Schoonover*. The partners loafed and read in the cabin, took turns on the bridge in the daytime with First Mate Hansen, lounged and smoked at the rail, keeping an eye out for whales or for anything else that might break the monotony of the endlessly rocking, white-flecked gray sea, and usually concluded the day with a game of hearts or cassino, which almost invariably ended in a half-serious argument between Jim and Hoxie, with Hoxie flinging the cards around the cabin and yelling that he'd never play with that cantankerous hayshaker, Jim Hardy, again.

The arguments amused the Old Man, but unsettled Lloyd, who liked things to run smoothly among friends. The relationship between Hoxie and Jim puzzled him greatly. He always expected it to flare out into open dislike, maybe hatred, even; but it never did. One minute they'd be cursing each other, the next minute they'd be laughing together and talking about Ohio. Lloyd wanted to be one with them, but could never quite feel that he was. They'd known each other too long; they had a common reservoir of associations and memories; they'd been little boys together. When they talked about Ohio, Lloyd felt shut out, completely excluded. And little by little he began to realize that he could never hope to play more than a secondary role in the drama of Jim and Hoxie; he'd come too late on the scene; to them he no doubt represented merely the "Seattle" sequence of their saga.

As for the Old Man... how could anyone get close to *him?* Always reasonable, good-tempered, completely approachable in the way of ordinary human intercourse, basically he seemed as remote as an utter stranger, ironically amused by his own thoughts, imperturbable, somehow very disturbing to Lloyd. Jim and Hoxie seemed to take him at face value. But Lloyd, more acute, sensed something cold and implacable behind the Old Man's friendly, open, simple ways and manners.

Lloyd had not missed the Old Man's reaction to the death of Gabe Windhorn. After all, Gabe had been the Old Man's friend, and yet Jim Hardy had taken his loss deeply to heart while the Old Man had not. He'd hardly turned a hair, and, to Lloyd, had seemed merely irritated with Gabe for being a fool and not listening to the advice of an Elder, One Who Knew.

A feeling of loneliness began to nag at Lloyd as the days passed and the ship steamed northwestward into the watery gray wilderness of the Pacific, taking him farther and farther away from home, from all that was easy and familiar and manageable, from all rules of thumb and landmarks, into... what?

Although the morning was fine, with a bright sun, big white harmless-looking clouds at the horizon, and with the gray-green waters rocking gently, an occasional gust from the north brought a touch of iciness and the partners shivered and got out their Mackinaw jackets.

"We're getting up there," said the Old Man, grinning. "Them gusts are coming off the Bering Sea. Yep, we're getting up there."

Jim was on the bridge with First Mate Hansen. They sat at a little table talking, while a silent hard-faced seaman manned the wheel.

"Landfall by tomorrow morning," Hansen was saying; then he added dubiously: "I think."

"You *think?*" said Jim, wondering.

"Boy," said Hansen, "you ain't traveling on a luxury liner in the steamer lanes. We got no chart for them islands—the Aleutians. No lighthouses. No pilots. Navigation is tough as hell, and the Skip leaves it to me. He's only made this here run once before. I been twenty times.

That's why he signed me on. Yep, I been twenty times. And I been lost twenty times." Hansen laughed and hit the table.

"You lost now?"

"Mislaid," said Hansen, laughing. "Just mislaid, son. Oh, don't get scared. We'll make it. But it just ain't easy." Hansen gave Jim a cigar and they lit up; then Hansen went on: "Used to work for A. C. Company—American Commercial, you know. They've got a post at Unalaska-town. And another smaller one at Dutch Harbor. Boy, what a place! Don't know how them Russians stuck it out. They used to own all of Alaska, you know. We bought it—cheap. Turned out to be quite a buy. There's a Russian church at Unalaska—what is it they call it? Greek Orthodox, something like that, though how the hell the Greeks got in it, I don't know—real pretty, that church. Sure looks funny as hell stuck out there on that damned stinking island."

"So you think we might get in by tomorrow?" asked Jim, far more interested in arriving than in Russians and Greek Orthodox churches.

"Davy Jones willing," said Hansen, laughing. "Hey," he cried suddenly, standing up. "Gulls. See 'em? Land around some place. Guess I ain't such a bad navigator. One tramp, trying for the Aleuts, wound up in Japan." Hansen slapped the table and laughed.

On the afterdeck the Old Man was showing Lloyd how to rig line for cod fishing.

"We may get a chance," the Old Man explained. "Cold-water cod—best eating in the world. Personally I'm getting pretty sick of all that pork. How about you?"

"Yes," said Lloyd. "I couldn't eat mine at dinner. Even had to struggle with the beans."

"You wait. We'll get us some cod and eat like kings. Cods are rough-going ordinarily, but these cold-water kind, for some reason once they are hooked, they come up easy. Big ones. Real big. Meat's solid, like beef. Ever eat fresh cod?"

"No," said Lloyd. "Just the cured kind, I guess. You know. Codfish balls."

"They ain't bad. But fresh cod—you just wait."

They worked on now in silence, the Old Man showing great patience with Lloyd, who was very inept when it came to any kind of manual labor.

Hoxie lounged in the galley with Joe Portugee, drinking black coffee and smoking Joe's black Mexican cigarettes.

"Get 'em at Monterey," Joe explained. "Pretty strong. You like?"

"Taste like the bottom of a parrot's cage," said Hoxie, "but they keep me waked up. Hell, it's got so I don't want to do nothing but sleep and eat. I'm getting bone lazy. The thought of swinging a pick in Alaska curls my hair."

Joe laughed, not understanding half what Hoxie was saying but laughing just the same, because he considered Hoxie one very funny Anglo. And sympathetic. Hansen, now, always screaming: "Joe! Joe! Where's that goddamned spig?" But Hoxie, now, he was friendly, a pal.

"You sure enough going to get me a girl when we get to Unalaska?" asked Hoxie.

"Sure," said Joe. "Breed. Kinda dirty."

"All right. Don't keep saying that. By the time I get there an old lady wouldn't be safe."

Joe almost fell into the stove laughing.

The portholes of the cabin showed gray, then yellowish, but the partners slept on. Finally there was a faint tapping at the door; then Joe Portugee came in bringing a tray loaded with big mugs of steaming black coffee.

"Land ho!" said Joe, waking them up. "Land!"

They leaped out of the bunks, dressed in a hurry, and carried the coffee up to drink at the rail.

"First leg," cried the Old Man, grinning. "Right on schedule."

Hansen tooted the whistle, waved from the bridge, then pointed. There were a lot of gulls about now, flying around the ship, screaming and fighting over scraps from the galley, some of them resting on the gray bosom of the sea, rocking gently in the long swell.

Far off to the north there was a dark uneven penciling on the horizon—land! Hoxie took off his hat and waved it, cheering. Jim and Lloyd slapped each other on the back. The Old Man continued to grin.

The island came nearer and nearer—rocky, desolate, bleak. An icy wind was coming in weak gusts now, making them shiver, but they stayed at the rail, all anxious to land, stretch their legs, and get a look at this mysterious northern outpost which was practically unknown to the world outside.

Blankhart, one of the seamen, stood at the rail with them, peering. "We don't find Priest Rock we don't get in today," he explained.

"What do you mean?" asked the Old Man, turning.

"Only mark you can go by to make the channel into the harbor," Blankhart explained. "I been here, oh, many times. It's rocky as hell. Can't take chances the wind might shift. Anything happen to your engines—pow! Right into the rocks. Many whalers have been lost around this island. It's a sea graveyard. Davy Jones—he's done a good business hereabouts."

Lloyd, Jim, and Hoxie turned away from the dreary-looking old seaman with distaste. What could happen when you were this close to land? But the Old Man's eyes narrowed and he looked off at the elusive island as at an enemy he'd eventually have to cope with.

Quarter of an hour later the fog came, suddenly, inexplicably, blotting out the entire world. The island disappeared, the sea disappeared, and the partners were advised by Blankhart to go below and forget the island for the time being.

"We're going no place in this fog," he explained. "We're going no place till it lifts, and I've seen fog hang on for days around the Aleuts." Gesturing cheerfully, he turned and left them, walking aft.

Hoxie cursed the old seaman till he ran out of epithets; then he said: "Bad luck, with that ugly old mug of his! Why don't he mind his own goddamned business!"

"I'm going up to talk to Hansen," said Jim.

He hurried off without another word, disappearing at once into the fog. The others groped their way forward, then below, Hoxie still cursing.

"Nollys," he said, "how about the Yukon? Fog there, too?"

"No," said the Old Man. "Clear as a bell. You can sit in your shirt sleeves on the deck all the way and take the sun."

"Okay. But from the Aleuts to St. Michael?"

"Oh, there's fog now and then."

"How the hell do you find your way in stuff like this?"

Lloyd waited for the answer. He'd been wondering the same thing himself.

"Fog don't last forever, you know," said the Old Man. "No more than rain back in the States. Sometimes you steam right on; sometimes you heave to and wait it out."

"Just sit there?" Hoxie demanded.

"You fish," said the Old Man. "Passes the time."

And now Lloyd understood why the Old Man had been rigging the cod lines. He'd anticipated fog. It was almost uncanny to Lloyd. He began to feel a little afraid of the Old Man.

"Fish, for the love of God!" cried Hoxie. "I want to get there; I don't want to fish."

"Ain't you tired of pork?" asked the Old Man mildly.

"Damned right I am."

"Well, if the fog holds, which likely it won't, we'll ketch us some big cod and eat like kings."

"Do!" Hansen exclaimed to Jim's question. "What the hell is there to do? We alter course and steam back and forth, taking soundings, till this goddamned fog lifts. I ain't taking no chances on them rocks, boy."

"Then we can't get to the island now?" asked Jim, disappointed.

"How?" cried Hansen. "Tell me how and I'll do it. Only mark I know is Priest Rock and how the hell can I see it in this fog? I can't even see that goddamned stinking ocean!"

"All right, Hansen," said Jim, a touch of coldness in his voice. "I'm only asking."

Hansen wagged his head, irritated at himself, then slapped Jim on the back. He liked this kid. "Sorry I yelled. But I got the whole responsibility for this ship. Skip don't know nothing about these waters. It's all on me. Just go play cards or something. Sleep. Anything. We'll get in when we get in—no sooner."

The fog was worse than ever. On deck visibility was about five feet, but the Old Man and Lloyd were fishing for cod over the port rail, while the *George B. Schoonover* steamed slowly and restlessly back and forth roughly parallel to the elusive island, with a seaman in the bow singing out the soundings at short intervals. Jim stood by, watching the fishing. He considered it a futile occupation. As a boy he'd fished for bass and crappies with a bobber in small streams, but the northern sea seemed so vast to him that he considered it an impossibility really to hook anything out of this nothingness.

Hoxie lounged in the warm, cheerful galley, chinning about girls with Joe Portugee, who knew the brothels of every port from Ensenada to Dutch Harbor.

The fog abated slightly, enough for Jim to catch a glimpse of gray waters which had a pewterlike sheen and looked extremely cold, uninviting, and deep. Suddenly there was a shout. Jim turned. The Old Man was landing a huge writhing fish which seemed to come up easily over the railing. Just as the Old Man got it aboard, it came off the hook and flopped about the deck, gasping and goggle-eyed. Lloyd waved his right arm in triumph. The Old Man stomped the fish into quietude, then said: "There's your supper, boys. Fresh cold-water cod; pounds and pounds of it. Let's ketch some for the crew, eh, Lloyd, boy?"

"All right, Nollys. Wish me luck."

Jim stood looking down at the immense cod. The fish had thoughtlessly grabbed the hook, been pulled up out of its natural element, and was now dead. Jim somberly began to wonder if he himself wasn't a little bit like the dead cod.

The fog was worse than before. Skip had taken over on the bridge in exasperation, as if a sea captain's mere presence might bring clear weather; it was cold and dismal out, with a weak, chill breeze blowing huge thick white strands of the fog about the ship; but in the saloon it was bright and cheerful and Hansen and the partners had stuffed themselves to repletion with cod and were now sipping black coffee, smoking, and talking.

With the aid of a stubby pencil and a piece of oiled butcher's paper, Hansen was trying to explain to the four lubbers the exact position of the *George B. Schoonover* as it steamed slowly back and forth through the fog.

"See this series of dots I just made?" he was saying. "Them's the Aleutian Islands. They continue out from the Alaska Peninsula, like steppingstones, all the way out to Attu—that's the last of 'em. We're right here, east and a little south of Unalaska. The Aleuts are a kind of barrier between the North Pacific and the Bering Sea, between parallels 52 degrees and 55 degrees and are stretched from about meridian 165 degrees to 185 degrees. I guess them figures don't mean much to you fellows, but here we are, goddamn it, right here."

"God, we're really getting up there," said Lloyd, very much impressed with Hansen's knowledge.

"Sure are," said Hansen. "When we leave Unalaska we head due north, in the direction of the Seal Islands, the Pribilofs, for St. Matthew Island, then to St. Lawrence Island, then to port on the mainland at St. Michael."

"How far from Unalaska to St. Michael?" asked Jim.

"Oh," said Hansen, "let me think. Maybe fifteen–sixteen hundred miles."

All the partners were staggered, except the Old Man. "But it's pretty clear sailing all the way," he added quickly.

Hansen threw him an ironical glance, but said nothing.

"How long will it take?" asked Lloyd.

"Maybe a week with a little luck," said Hansen.

Jim glanced off at the befogged portholes, but made no comment. Lloyd was silent. Hoxie groaned and said: "Hansen, couldn't we smuggle just one little Eskimo girl aboard for the trip to St. Michael?"

Hansen laughed and slapped Hoxie on the back. "No, son. Skip's a religious man. Besides, if we did, would you help me fight off the crew every night?"

Hoxie sighed and sipped his black coffee.

"You'll just have to make up for past and future in Unalaska, Hoxie," said Hansen. "That is, if you've got a strong stomach."

"Oh, he's got a strong stomach, all right," said Jim.

It was Sunday. Church bells were ringing all over Seattle. Ma stood at the living-room window, with the lace curtain pulled aside, watching Lena going down the front steps in her good dark-blue dress, and with her prayer book clasped in her gloved hands. Ma nodded to herself, as if in satisfaction, then went back to Pa's study, where Pa was "resting," in his big leather chair, with a sheet of newspaper over his face to keep out the light.

"Pa."

He gave a start, pulled the newspaper aside, peeked out at her. "Just resting my eyes, Ma. Been using them a lot lately."

Ma sighed, sat down, and got out her mending. Sunday was just another day to her, as far as work was concerned, except that the evening meal was eaten cold.

"Lena's on her way to church," said Ma.

Pa grunted.

"I was getting pretty worried about her, afraid she might go off her head the way she was acting, but I think she's resigned since I had the minister talk to her. Nice young man. I think Lena likes him, and he needs a wife."

"Marrying a preacher?" cried Pa, sitting up. "Preachers never have a cent, not a cent."

"Pa," said Ma, "the main thing is to get Lena married. She'll be twenty-eight this fall. It's not natural, not good for a woman. She needs a husband."

"Oh, that's all bosh," said Pa, "woman talk. Some of the happiest women I ever met were old maids."

"They might have seemed so," said Ma mildly, "but they weren't. It's a woman's business to marry and raise a family. That's what they were put on earth to do. What else?"

"How do you know what they were put on earth to do?" asked Pa.

"Stands to reason," said Ma. "Otherwise it makes no sense. Life is not easy for women. There must be some purpose."

"But suppose there's no purpose at all," said Pa peevishly.

There was a pause. Then Ma said: "Llewellyn, I think you'd better start going to church again. That statement you just made... well... it's blasphemous."

Pa sighed and sank back. He wanted to doze. He did not want to be bothered with problems. Ma was always bothering him with problems.

There was a long silence. Pa's eyes were just closing when Ma said: "I wonder what Lloyd's doing and where he is. I wish I could see him in my mind's eye, but I just can't, he's so far away in a foreign land."

"Alaska is not a foreign land," said Pa. "We own it."

"Well," said Ma, "it's so far away it seems foreign. Sun never sets, they say. Can you imagine?"

Pa did not want to try to imagine. He wanted to doze. Ma worked at her mending. A fly buzzed against the windowpane. Then, after a while, rain began to fall softly past the window.

"Oh my goodness," cried Ma, starting up, "Lena's good dress! Pa...!"

Pa jumped and sat up."

"... put your collar and tie on and take Lena an umbrella. It started raining all of a sudden. She'll ruin her dress and hat."

Pa groaned. "She's in church by now."

"But she's got to come out."

"Maybe it'll stop."

"Llewellyn Gracey," said Ma severely, "do as I tell you."

Pa rose, groaning. "Guess you don't care if *I* get wet. I got to come back, you know. I'm not sitting through any long-winded sermon."

"For goodness' sake," cried Ma, "can't you take two umbrellas?"

Suddenly the fog lifted and Skip saw to his astonishment and dismay that the *George B. Schoonover* was less than a quarter of a mile away from a beetling cliff of naked black rock. Shouting along the tube for Hansen, he altered course at once and called down to the engine room for full speed ahead.

Bells rang. The whistle tooted. Feet pounded across the deck. Awakened from their afternoon naps by the commotion aboard, the four partners grabbed up their coats and went up on deck.

At the head of the companionway they stopped for a moment, unable to believe their eyes at the harsh bright glare of sunlight; then they continued on and went to the rail. A huge rocky island was slowly receding astern. Gulls were everywhere. Reflections on the water were so full of glitter that they all kept flinching and half closing their eyes.

"Where the hell are we going?" cried Hoxie. "There's the island back there."

Blankhart appeared. "Damned near piled up the ship, the old Skip did," he explained. "We're coming about. Hansen's already sighted Priest Rock. We'll soon be in now, gents; soon be in."

Hoxie cheered and waved his hat.

"Wouldn't mind a little terra firma myself," said Blankhart. "It's been a damned dull voyage."

They were steaming into the roadstead now, a perfect little landlocked harbor, with the still water the color of indigo under the glare of the northern sun. They passed two American Revenue cutters anchored in the bay, the flag of the United States whipping in the brisk offshore wind. Then they saw the town and Hoxie moaned.

"Jesus, the jumping-off place," he said. "Lousetown, back home, looks like a metropolis compared to this."

"Stop complaining," said Jim. "We're here, aren't we?"

Lloyd stared, gripped by an apprehension the cause of which was not apparent to him. Was it just the barren ugliness of this far outpost, with its low, storm-beaten wooden shacks? Was it a premonition of disaster? Or was it because the feeling of loneliness had been growing on him the last few days and now the sight of this sordid huddle of hovels only served to increase his sense of separateness, his sense of distance from home and from all that was familiar?

"A place is a place," said the Old Man calmly. "One very like another, some bigger, some smaller—just a collection of people."

"And what a collection!" cried Hoxie, pointing to the small crowd waiting for this unscheduled tramp, this wanderer of the northern seas—good old *George B. Schoonover*—to dock.

The crowd was dominated by short, squat, dark-faced men, Indians, Eskimos, Aleuts—who could tell? There was a sprinkling of tall Anglos, in Mackinaws, all dirty and with bristling whiskers.

"Good Christ!" cried Hoxie, pointing at a group of short, squat giggling squaws or breeds, waving wildly at Hansen on the bridge. "I just don't know if I'm that hard up or not. I'll have to experiment, like."

Jim remained silent, fighting back his fears and regrets. God, he was a long ways from the hometown! A damned long ways!

"From here on we put away our razors for good," said the Old Man. "Raise ourselves a fine crop of chin furniture."

"Now, by God, that's an idea," said Hoxie, grinning. "I get so damned sick of shaving twice a day. Wait'll you see my black whiskers, boys. You'll be calling me Blackbeard. But I don't know about Jim and Lloyd. Still look kind of fuzz-cheeked to me."

Jim ignored him. But Lloyd smiled weakly. Two years ago he'd tried to raise a mustache but had finally shaved off what little there was of it in disgust, sick and tired of listening to his father's joke about the boy with the "feebly growing down on his upper lip."

"What's that glinting over there?" asked Hoxie. "Looks like a church."

"That's right," said the Old Man." A Russian church. Used to be all Russian here."

"Hell of a place for a church," said Hoxie, "and a damned pretty one, too." He turned and hit Jim on the back. "Matter with you? Got the bellyache or something? You come along with me. I'll fix you up with one of them lovely Injun princesses down there—Jesus, are they dirty! Joe was right—and that'll take your thoughts off your pain."

Jim shoved him away. Hoxie turned and studied Jim, then subsided. Something was biting that Ohio boy, and when something was biting him, let sleeping dogs lie. He could be an ugly customer at such times.

III

TO ST. MICHAEL

They were twelve hours out of Unalaska now, steaming due north through the Bering Sea. Although it was nearly midnight the sun was just setting, casting a pinkish golden glaze over the glassy green water. Jim, standing at the rail with Lloyd and the Old Man, kept looking at his watch and shaking his head.

"Top of the world," said the Old Man, grinning at him. "We're really getting up there."

Lloyd felt slightly dizzy, decided to go below, then remembered that Hoxie was in the cabin snoring like a grampus, smelling like a distillery, and sleeping off a three-day drunken carouse. He steadied himself at the rail and looked about him. As far as the eye could see, there was nothing but flat green water, with reddish pale glints and reflections. The sea showed no movement whatever; it was like a pond, but a sinister pond, cold, menacing, completely alien. And yet actually the weather was fine and warm, with a faint lukewarm wind blowing up from the direction of the Aleutians from time to time. It was the unnaturalness of the scene that bothered Lloyd, he decided, and made him dizzy and apprehensive: the big red sun setting at midnight, the frigidly cold-looking water, the feeble gusts of warm wind.

"Halcyon weather," said the Old Man, rubbing his hands in satisfaction. "It's often like this in the Bering Sea in the middle of June. What's the date, Jim, you know?"

"Yes," said Jim. "It's the nineteenth."

"You see?" said the Old Man, a note of triumph in his voice. "We've only been on the way fourteen days, and we're on the last leg to St. Michael."

Jim stood shaking his head in wonder. Fourteen days! It seemed to him that he'd always been on the *George B. Schoonover*, sailing through the northern seas, chasing the horizon.

Lloyd was remembering Unalaska. While the Old Man renewed acquaintances at the American Commercial Trading offices, and the longshoremen of the town unloaded freight and supplies from the ship, and First Mate Hansen, Joe Portugee, and Hoxie "went out on the town," as they said ironically, Lloyd and Jim had gone to look at the

Russian church, had tramped the hills beyond the settlement, and bought curios of walrus ivory for Pa, Ma, and Lena, which they entrusted to Skip—Sea Captain Lars Petersen of the good ship *George B. Schoonover*—who said that he would see the presents safe into Seattle eventually, God willing.

Lloyd and Jim had exhausted the town in one afternoon and did not know what to do with themselves for the remaining two days in port, so they went back aboard ship, played seven-up and dominoes in the saloon, drank black coffee till "it ran out of their ears," and chinned with various seamen, especially old Blankhart, who'd got his fill of fleshpots fast and sat in the saloon all day long with a mug of coffee in his gnarled fist and talked cheerfully about marine disasters in the northern seas.

On the last night Jim disappeared. Lloyd was worried about him, looked for him all over the ship, then scoured the town. The Old Man came aboard at ten o'clock; he'd been drinking and there was a mellow, kindly light in his pale gray eyes. Lloyd grabbed him anxiously, asked if he'd seen Jim.

"No," said the Old Man. "But I guess he couldn't hold out any longer."

"What do you mean?" Lloyd demanded.

"Oh, he's a stubborn youngster," said the Old Man, laughing. "And he's got high ideals, too. But he's human, Lloyd; he's human."

Lloyd was thunderstruck. "You mean... with those... with those...!" He broke off, unable to continue.

"Why, they're women... just women," said the Old Man. "Human people, just like us. A dog's a dog, Lloyd; and a man's a man. I'm going to bed."

Jim came into the saloon around midnight. He looked pale and grim. Blankhart and Lloyd were playing dominoes, with Grimsby, sea cook, looking on. Jim sat down. No one made any comment. In a few minutes Jim got up and went out.

"He sure looked wrung," said Blankhart, giggling. "Some of them young klutches... they'll wring a man, and no mistake." At 4 A.M. Hoxie came roaring into the cabin, helped by Hansen and Joe Portugee. They tossed him into his upper bunk and went out, singing and laughing. Hoxie took off his shoes and threw them at the lamp, missing; then he began to sing and holler. Jim told him to shut up. Hoxie merely laughed at Jim, defied him; then when Jim insisted, Hoxie yelled: "Don't you take no high tone with me, Jim Hardy—I seen you sneaking off with that little dark young one. I seen you. Old Hoxie seen you, boy. So don't take no high tone with me, boy, because I seen you...." And so on and so on.

Jim never said another word. Hoxie sang and yelled himself to sleep....

Lloyd stood at the rail remembering, still shocked, still unbelieving. Not *Jim!*

Day after day passed and the good weather continued. The ship moved northward at a steady rate over a sea as flat as a billiard table and under a sky a-glare with light till after midnight. There was hardly a cloud, not even on the horizon.

Hoxie spent his time now in a sort of stupor and slept from twelve to fourteen hours a day. Lloyd read book after book from the ship's library, played seven-up and dominoes in the saloon, and tried hard to fight off acute and recurring attacks of loneliness, which became so unbearable at times that vague ideas of suicide lurked at the back of his mind late at night when the others were asleep and the ship was as silent, except for a faint tinkling of bells, as the *Flying Dutchman.*

He kept remembering Gabe Windhorn. Over the side and down, down forever to quiet oblivion! At least Gabe was not lonesome now.

Once he had felt close to Jim. But no longer—not since Unalaska. Of a sudden he'd seen a new Jim, a Jim that baffled and dismayed him. And he realized that he'd never really known him at all; he'd only had rather romantic ideas about him... like Lena! Jim, the hero! But he was, of course, no hero at all. But just a man, just another man, like Hoxie and Gabe and Hansen, and the rest. Lloyd knew vaguely that he himself was some way different. How or why was completely beyond him.

They had left the Pribilof Islands astern days ago and had seen hair seals and fur seals in abundance. It was getting colder, day by day, and occasionally a gust of wind came down out of the north, which was so icy that it almost took their breath away.

In the saloon with a mug of coffee in his hand Hansen shook his head over the gusts. "They're too cold," he explained. "Unseasonable. Hell, we're getting on for July."

Later, Jim asked the Old Man what Hansen meant, but the Old Man said soothingly: "Oh, Hansen's worried about everything, naturally. He's got to get the ship where it's going. The skipper depends on him, so he worries about the weather. Like a farmer. You ought to know about that, Jim. Spent half your time worrying about the weather, did-n't you?"

"My father did," said Jim. "So did my grandfather. I never was much of a farmer. All I wanted was out!"

"You see," said Hoxie, "they made a big mistake with Jim, the Hardys. They took him to Columbus to the state fair when he was about sixteen. He seen a girl in satin pants in the cooch show and he's never been the same since. No more farm for that boy."

To Lloyd's surprise Jim laughed quietly. Hoxie, pleased by Jim's docility, leaned over and patted his shoulder. "Well, here we are, kiddo," he said. "A long, long ways from Clark County. Did you ever figure you'd see the sun hanging in the sky at eleven o'clock at night? Boy, that would sure louse up them roosters back home. They'd go plumb bughouse trying to figure it out."

The Old Man encouraged Jim and Hoxie to talk about Ohio and the past, and this did not escape Lloyd's notice. Why? Was it like rigging up the cod lines in anticipation of the fog off Unalaska?

One morning they woke to a gray day. Thick, heavy, low, grayish-black clouds blotted out the sun; and the water, with a long easy swell running, looked as thick as molten lead and was of the same color.

They went up to the saloon for breakfast and found Hansen tossing down a cup of coffee, standing.

"This keeps up long, won't know where I am," he grumbled.

"Why?" asked Jim.

"Can't take observations in this weather, can I? We're somewhere off St. Matthew. That's all I can tell you. We may bypass it. Nothing to stop for. Nothing important, that is." He glanced out the porthole. "God-damn those clouds."

When Hansen had gone on deck, the Old Man grinned and said: "You hear that, boys? St. Matthew, then St. Lawrence Island, then St. Michael, port. We're getting there."

The next morning when they woke, the day was darker than before and the ship seemed to be drifting. They dressed hastily and went up on deck. Before they realized what had happened, Hansen shouted at them from the bridge and waved both arms wildly. Then they saw the ice floes—all about the ship, and as far away as the eye could see, acres of white snowy ice, hard as crystal, drifting in the lead-colored water.

"Good God!" cried Hoxie. "What do we do now—walk?"

Lloyd shrank back, then went below to wrestle with his terror. This was the end—the *end!*

Jim and Hoxie turned to the Old Man. "Ever see anything like this before?" Jim demanded, eying him suspiciously.

"Yes," said the Old Man mildly. "Floe ice. It's common. But usually not this late in the year."

"What happens?"

"It drifts on. We get out of it, to open water."

"Why aren't we moving then?"

"Pretty thick right now. This ain't no ice cutter, boys. You leave it to Hansen. He's been up this way for years; knows all about it."

Hoxie grunted. "You sure Chilkat Pass is worse than this, Nollys?"

"Boys, boys; you don't know what you're talking about. We're warm; we're comfortable; we got food. Just a little patience, boys; and we'll get there safe and sound."

"And then eighteen hundred more miles up the Yukon—Jesus!" said Hoxie; then he turned to Jim: "We must have been crazy."

Jim hesitated, as if about to speak, then said nothing. The Old Man got out the cards and they began to play cutthroat seven-up over their coffee.

The day went on. The ice floes continued to drift past the almost stationary ship and the sky remained cloudy.

The Old Man slipped out to talk secretly with Hansen, who showed a grim face.

"Oh, we got trouble, Old Man, trouble," said Hansen. "And it's coming in bunches. First the ice; now we find some of our drinking water is foul; oil has got into it. I guess you could drink it at a pinch. But Skip says it will make everybody sick. We got to get ashore—water party."

"We'll go," said the Old Man, "along with a few seamen. Might give the boys something to think about." The Old Man laughed easily, undisturbed.

Hansen eyed him in irritation for a moment, then grinned. "You're a tough old bastard, ain't you? Been around. Nothing bothers you."

"Hansen," said the Old Man, "I'm sixty-three. It's my last chance—and I'll get there in spite of hell. I know it in my heart. I'll get there."

"Gold," said Hansen contemptuously. "What'll you do with it?"

"Spend it—like I did before. Only I'll have more this time. Live like a king."

"Kings live uneasy, so I've heard," said Hansen.

"Poor men live uneasier."

Hansen laughed. "That's a true saying, Old Man. A true saying."

They remained icebound all through the night and when morning came the ice was still coming down from the north and the sky was still heavily overcast.

Breakfast was eaten in silence, with Lloyd looking pale and withdrawn. Hansen did not appear. Suddenly the sugar bowl glittered and they all looked up in wonder. A strong beam of sunlight was slanting down into the porthole. Forgetting their breakfast they all ran up on deck.

The whole northern part of the sky was clear, and to the northwest a low-lying rocky island could be made out on the horizon; wide spaces of open water showed here and there among the drifting ice floes.

Now bells rang aboard ship, the whistle tooted, and Hansen waved and grinned from the bridge.

"You see?" said the Old Man. "Just a little patience. Here we go."

Little by little the color began to come back into Lloyd's wan cheeks. Hoxie slapped Jim on the back and laughed.

"It's better than Chilkat, boys," said the Old Man. "This way you've got nothing to wrestle with but yourselves, not snow and hunger and avalanches and wolves."

Lloyd's face brightened more and more. He felt hopeful for the first time since they'd left Unalaska. What the Old Man said was true, very true.

Hansen, elated, came down off the bridge to talk with the partners.

"All open water to the north," he chortled, "as far as I could see with the glass. That's an uncharted island off there; to the east, and a little north, of St. Matthew Island. So we by-pass St. Matthew and go due north to St. Lawrence Island. With a little luck we might make it in twenty-four hours or maybe a bit longer, but not much. Once we get to St. Lawrence we're only two hundred and fifty miles due west of the mainland and St. Michael."

The Old Man grinned and nodded to his partners. "See? Soon be there. Couple days; maybe three."

But in the middle of the night they encountered ice floes again and by dawn the *George B. Schoonover* was drifting, engines off, surrounded by acre after endless acre of floating ice.

The day was clear. The sun was out. The sky was blue. But the ice floes just came drifting down lazily from the north, jamming and pressing hard against the hull of the ship at times, turning it against the current, then slewing it around erratically.

"Could it freeze up tight?" Jim asked Hansen.

"No," said Hansen. "No chance, in June and July. Air's too warm."

"Why don't it melt then?"

"It *is* melting. Where do you think them floes are coming from?"

When they turned in that night the ship was still drifting aimlessly through the sea of ice floes. The Old Man went to sleep at once. Time passed. Silence. Jim, Hoxie, and Lloyd kept turning and twisting in their bunks.

"Jim," called Hoxie finally.

"Yes?"

"Think we'll ever make it?"

"Sure we'll make it."

"Why?

"Because it's Hansen's business to see that we make it. He's been up around these waters for twenty years."

"There's a first time for everything, Jim."

"Shut up and go to sleep."

Lloyd remained relatively tranquil, remembering what the Old Man had said: "Nothing to wrestle with but yourselves." They were in no immediate danger. They were dry and warm and there was food and water aboard. Presently he drifted off to sleep with a smile on his face.

They were awakened by the throbbing of the engines. It was day. They dressed and hurried up on deck, then stared about them in unbelief. No ice. Nothing but the endlessly rocking green sea stretching away to vast horizons.

About noon rocky islands appeared off their starboard bow and the ship changed course slightly and headed for them. Hansen came into the saloon, grinning, and yelled for his dinner.

"See the islands?" he asked. "Them's the Penuncks. Uncharted. St. Lawrence is just beyond. One of the Penuncks has got a good spring. Eskimo village there—but they don't mind us watering. Plenty for all. You fellows like to go with the watering party—sight-seeing maybe?"

Hoxie jumped up and waved his hat. The table would have been upset if it hadn't been fastened to the floor. Hoxie had a heavy, curling black beard now and looked like a pirate. The Old Man's beard was scraggly and snow white. Jim's was thick and brownish, streaked with blond. Lloyd had a silky, reddish excrescence on his face that was neither one thing nor another. Hansen said that he looked like a dissipated saint.

"Ashore! Ashore!" yelled Hoxie. "Anything to get off this goddamned ship."

Blankhart, senior seaman, was put in charge of the watering party. The longboat was raised on its davits, the men climbed in, the boat was lowered slowly to the choppy green water, and in a short time they had left the *George B. Schoonover* astern and were headed for what looked like a beach, with big ugly rocks just beyond. There were twelve in the party, all told, with Blankhart handling the rudder in the stern. Tall, heavy, ironbound wooden casks were heaped in the bow.

The Old Man pulled an oar right along with the seamen, but Jim, Hoxie, and Lloyd sailed as supercargo.

The boat was beached with little trouble, the men hardly getting their feet wet. The "beach" consisted of tundra moss and was covered with driftwood and thousands of coarse yellow and blue flowers. It looked like nothing the three young men had ever seen before, even in dreams. It was a "new" place, as if they'd been landed on an alien planet.

The seamen shouldered the casks and picked their way up through the rocks to a place where a crystalline stream of water was gushing up, filling a huge rocky basin, then spilling over. The Old Man helped with the work of filling the casks, while Jim and Lloyd looked on, suddenly thirsty at the sight of this beautifully clean, pure-looking water, after the muck they'd been drinking aboard. But Hoxie wandered up to the crest of a low, moss-covered hill and stood looking off toward the interior of the island.

"Hey," he yelled. "I can see the village. A lot of little houses, look like mounds. But there's nobody around."

Blankhart looked up from his work.

"Any smoke?"

"No smoke."

"That's goddamned funny," said Blankhart.

Hoxie kept looking. The work continued and finally all of the casks were filled.

"See any smoke yet?" called Blankhart.

"No," said Hoxie. "Tell you what I think. I don't think there's anybody there. It's a ghost town."

"Couldn't be," said Blankhart. "Been people there for years. I seen 'em with my own eyes three summers ago, a raft of 'em, all fat and happy."

"Why don't we take a look, commodore?" called Hoxie, and the old seaman grinned.

"All right. I guess there's no blasted hurry for us to get back. We can put in at St. Lawrence any time now."

None of the seamen were interested in the project. Ironical looks passed between them; then they got out their pipes and sat down among the casks to wait.

"Commodore" Blankhart and his party of explorers set off across the rolling tundra toward the collection of little low mud huts, barely visible in the distance.

"By God," said Blankhart, "I don't understand this. Nobody around. These people hunt the walrus and the whale in the summer, live off the blubber all winter; sell walrus ivory and whalebone and maybe seal furs in the spring to the traders. Always been a prosperous little place, for Eskimos."

They were almost to the village now. There seemed to be a deathly stillness in the air. Blankhart stopped short, looked about him. "I don't like this, men," he said. "I just don't like it."

"They probably moved on," said the Old Man.

"Moved on? Where? Away from their hunting grounds? What ship would take a whole village aboard?"

"Well, hell," cried Hoxie, "let's go see."

Lloyd's flesh crawled slightly. He liked it even less than Blankhart.

"Maybe they're on another part of the island," Jim suggested.

"There ain't no other part," said Blankhart, "at least not for a village, too rocky all around the shores."

Hoxie shrugged with impatience, then went on to the first hut. It was a big low mound, built like an igloo, but of mud. A long zigzag passage led to an entrance that was partly underground. Hoxie got down on his hands and knees and tried to look in, as the others came up slowly behind him.

"Deserted," said Hoxie, rising. "All blocked up."

Blankhart stared. "All blocked up? That's the way they block themselves in, in the winter, and live on blubber till spring. It's not fit for man nor beast out here, in the wintertime. Wind blows a gale. Everything freezes up."

"Well," said Hoxie, "if that's true they're still in there."

They went from hut to hut. The passages of all of them were blocked up with debris.

"Something terrible has happened here," said Blankhart. "But I'm damned if I know what."

"Let's dig off a roof," said the Old Man. "Then we can see. If the place is deserted, where's the harm?"

Jim and Lloyd backed away, but Blankhart, Hoxie, and the Old Man grabbed up sticks and began to dig at a low, rounded mud roof. In a short time they'd made quite a hole and Hoxie was lowered into it. They heard the scratching of matches; then Hoxie finally gave a shout and climbed out, carrying an armload of loot—blubber lamps, walrus-ivory fish hooks and harpoons, some odd-looking ivory utensils or tools, and the skull of a man.

"Where did you get *that?*" cried Blankhart, pointing to the skull.

"Down there," said Hoxie. "There's four skeletons—three humans and one dog. I brung up this skull so you couldn't say I was seeing things."

"Good God," cried Blankhart, "what happened here?"

They dug into hut after hut, Lloyd and Jim helping now. Every place it was the same. Some unlooked-for catastrophe had wiped out this prosperous Eskimo village. They returned to the spring in silence, glad to get away from this Village of the Dead, but carrying armloads of walrus-ivory tools and weapons.

When the longboat was taken aboard and Hansen saw what they'd brought he was livid. "You thieves! What's this? Take all that stuff back to the villagers. Don't kid me. They don't trade their weapons and fish hooks."

Once on deck, Blankhart explained, and Hansen stood staring in unbelief, with his battered first mate's cap off, scratching his head.

"Got to talk to Skip," he said hurriedly. "Maybe he's got some idea what happened."

That night the seamen crowded into the saloon to hear a firsthand account of the Village of the Dead.

"In one hut," said Blankhart, proud to be the center of attention, "there was two dog skeletons with their jaws locked together; died fighting or trying to eat each other. I think them people starved. Some of the skeletons were all screwed around—contorted-like—as if the people'd had a hard time dying. Pretty gruesome, mates," he added, with what sounded like satisfaction.

Hansen came in, banging back the door. "Skip's got the explanation, I think," he said. "Some of them goddamned traders have been carrying casks of cheap whisky. Maybe a couple of springs ago the villagers traded their stuff and took whisky as part payment. They got to drinking it and stayed drunk when they should have been hunting. When they got round to hunting it was too late. Winter came. They couldn't get out. So they blocked themselves in and starved. Maybe ate each other. It's happened before, Skip said."

Lloyd repressed a shudder, but said nothing.

"Yeah," said Blankhart cheerfully. "Sounds reasonable."

They climbed into their bunks in silence as the ship steamed off for St. Lawrence. In their various ways they were all preoccupied with thoughts of the Village of the Dead. To the Old Man it was a perfect illustration of what could happen to those who insisted on leaving too much to chance; the time to drink was *after* everything else had been taken care of. To Lloyd it was a startling and horrifying example of the malevolence of nature. To Jim it was a reminder of how far away from home he was and how unlikely it seemed that he would ever get back. While Hoxie was thinking: "Too bad we couldn't've made one more trip back to the island and got us some more of them walrus-ivory doodads. I'll bet we can peddle 'em in St. Michael, pick ourselves up some extra dollars. Extra dollars might come in handy."

St. Lawrence village, a bleak outpost as depressing as Unalaska, had been left far astern and the *George B. Schoonover* now headed due east across the Bering Sea for St. Michael on Norton Sound.

Hoxie lay in his bunk, staring happily at the lamp in its gimbals, while Lloyd read and Jim and the Old Man played seven-up in the bunk.

"Soon be in," he said. "By dawn sure. So you see, boys...?"

"We see," said Hoxie, laughing. "After all the yelling and carrying on and wishing we were home, we are damned near there, like riding a horsecar to church down the street."

Lloyd, gradually shaking off the pall of the Village of the Dead, was feeling hopeful again. He'd made it. He'd won the battle with himself. He was looking forward with eagerness to St. Michael and the Yukon.

"You know," said Jim, "it's a funny thing, but we've hardly once mentioned the gold."

The Old Man laughed. "That's right. Don't believe I've heard it mentioned except once—by Hansen; and in derision at that."

"Well, here we are," said Hoxie, laughing. "All safe and sound."

"Not quite," said Jim. "We lost Gabe."

"Yes. But he was never really...." Hoxie checked himself. He'd been going to say that Gabe had never really been one of them, but then suddenly he'd remembered how inexplicably cut up Jim had seemed at his loss. "Yeah," he said. "Poor Gabe."

The Old Man sat nodding to himself, then said: "But Gabe had a good life, boys, and he was no chicken—forty or better. Gabe did just what he wanted to do, all his life. How many men can say that?"

"He didn't want to fall overboard," said Jim bluntly.

"We all got to go sometime," said the Old Man. "It's what's gone before that counts."

The log read: "July 3rd, 1896. Dawn. Landfall, Michaelovski (St. Michael). Day clear. No wind, fog, ice. Visibility unlimited. Down to emergency coal reserve. Cargo sound and ready for unloading. Quiet run except for loss of 2nd cook Aloysius Windhorn."

But the partners slept on in the quiet cabin. Gray showed at the portholes; gulls screamed about the ship. All at once Lloyd woke with a start, sat up, looked about him, then called: "Nollys."

"Yep," the Old Man answered, groaning as he pulled himself up from the dark depths of sleep.

"We've stopped. You figure we're in the ice again?"

Now Jim and Hoxie woke.

"Hell, it's light," said Hoxie. "Maybe we're in."

And at that moment the door was banged back and Joe Portugee came in, grinning, carrying a trayful of mugs of steaming black coffee.

"Michaelovski," said Joe, laughing. "We there."

The partners said nothing. The Old Man had expected to "get there" all along, so he made no comment; but the three young men could hardly make themselves believe that the long and dangerous voyage through the northern seas was over. Land! Terra firma! There a man was safe!

Hoxie jumped out of his bunk with a wild shout. They all dressed hurriedly and rushed up on deck, carrying their coffee mugs, the three young men expecting to land at once, the Old Man saying nothing.

Hoxie pulled up short and stared. "Why, hell, we're way out," he cried, pointing off across the flat green water toward a little village, with a few large wooden buildings, straggling along a flat shore.

Jim stared, openmouthed. "*That*—is St. Michael?" he demanded. It was Unalaska all over again.

"Christ's sake, why don't we land?" Hoxie cried impatiently.

"Too shallow," the Old Man explained. "Can't take most ocean-going ships in there. So the riverboat comes out and picks up the cargo and the passengers." He looked off toward shore, shading his eyes against the glare of sunlight on the water. "Yep. It's the old *Nils K. Jensen*, big as life."

The squat white, double-decked paddle wheeler, wood smoke pouring from its two tall thin stacks, came chugging toward them across the flat green water.

"Is that the boat we go up the Yukon on?" asked Lloyd.

"That's it," said the Old Man. "Nice, big, roomy, and comfortable. See the second deck? Got a gangway all around it. You take a chair and plant yourself there with your feet on the railing. Like riding a trolley car."

"Say! Looks all right," said Jim, starting to smile.

But Hoxie stomped about impatiently. "Nollys, you mean to tell me we got to stay on board while they shift all that cargo?"

"Yes," said the Old Man. "What's the hurry? We'll be on shore by mid-afternoon. Besides, I want to be sure our dunnage is stored right on the steamboat and I want to get out that moose gun and give it a fresh oiling and see if our ammunition's okay. Fresh meat might taste real good later on."

"Goddamn," cried Hoxie. "I want to get on shore. I've had enough of this damned ship."

"Let's go eat breakfast," said the Old Man. "It might be our last meal aboard."

"I hope," growled Hoxie.

They went toward the shore on the *Nils K. Jensen* at a little after two that afternoon. The day was bright and warm, the water still as a pond.

While the Old Man made sure of their cabin bookings as far as Forty Mile, the young men wandered about the steamboat, looking at everything.

"We got two cabins right off the gangway here, I think Nollys said," Jim explained. "This is all right, eh, boys? No more rolling and pitching and fog and ice."

"Yeah," said Hoxie, "this is the life, I guess. But I'll tell you later, when we get into the town. White women up around here, I hear tell."

As they neared the shore, Hansen, who was making the trip in to supervise the unloading of the cargo, joined them.

"Hi, boys."

"Some town," said Hoxie, gesturing off toward the low cluster of shacks and long wooden company buildings.

"Yeah," said Hansen. "Some town."

"But there's white women here, I understand," said Hoxie.

Hansen laughed at him. "Yeah. They're here, all right. Wives of the company officials and the clerks. Stick to the natives, boys; the natives."

"You're joshing," said Hoxie, his face falling.

"I'm not joshing. I'm warning you. No nonsense with married women up here, and all the white women are married. A man could get strung up."

Hoxie sighed and looked off toward St. Michael. "Town," he said, "you are already a great disappointment to Hoxie Thicke."

The Old Man joined them, rubbing his hands in satisfaction. "Everything's fine. Dunnage loaded right. Moose gun in perfect shape. Got fine cabins, and I made arrangements for us to sleep aboard till we sail the morning of the fifth."

"Good work, Nollys," said Jim. "We must seem pretty useless to you."

"Oh, there will be plenty of work for you young fellows later. Plenty. Eh, Hansen?"

Hansen laughed and ran his eyes ironically over the group. "Wait till you start swinging them picks," he said. "That ground is hard. Frozen solid a foot down under the moss, even in the summer. Oh, there'll be plenty for you boys to do, all right."

There was a small crowd to watch them land. Hoxie noticed a group of laughing white women in summery-looking dresses—but they were guarded, well guarded, by tall, bearded Anglos. Off to one side was a semi-circle of Indians, short, squat, dark, dirty-looking, all in felt pants and moccasins, all with long hair in braids. You couldn't tell the men from the women. Hoxie groaned to himself.

Hansen laughed. "Wait till you get close to them Injuns. What an aroma! They live on seal fat, and, boy! do they smell fishy."

"What does a man do?" Hoxie demanded.

"Oh, there's white whores at Fort Yukon and Circle City," Hansen explained. "Just sleep till you get there." He laughed and slapped Hoxie on the back.

The steamboat was warped into the pier where the company longshoremen were waiting to unload the cargo. Hoxie watched them in silence for a moment; then he jeered: "Suckers! Breaking their backs for low wages! I hope I've seen the last of that blasted hook!"

The three young men washed up, combed their hair and beards, put

on clean shirts, and went ashore. The Old Man had preceded them, explaining that he wanted to look up a few old friends who might still
be working for the American Commercial Company at St. Michael.

The three young men wandered down the main street, a muddy thor-
oughfare, as ugly as a back alley in the States. All the buildings were
of frame, sagging, storm-beaten, woebegone.

A group of smiling Indians tried to sell them curios, but they hurried
on, appalled at the overpowering stench of fish that hung like a cloud
over the aborigines.

"Hansen was right," said Hoxie. "Oh boy!"

Not only Hoxie but Jim, too, seemed extremely tense and restless to
Lloyd as they moved from building to building and from store to store.
There was hardly anything said. Hoxie and Jim seemed to be looking
for something and Lloyd had a good idea what it was. Finally, to their
surprise, they were joined by Joe Portugee.

"I stowaway on steamboat," he explained. "Cap'n no know. Okay,
though. Ship shorthanded. He like have me anyway. No worry."

"Got any ideas, Joe?" asked Hoxie hopefully.

"Sure," said Joe. "Always got ideas. You come with me. We drink.
Then see."

"Drink?" said Hoxie. "Yeah. That reminds me. Ain't there no saloons
in this town?"

"No," said Joe. "Government say no drink. Against law. Wrong.
Drink back room. Plenty drink. Then maybe we see."

"Girls?"

"Maybe. We see."

"Come on, boys," said Hoxie. "What are we waiting for?"

"Not me," said Lloyd. "I think I'll go back to the boat." He noticed
that Jim seemed to be avoiding his eyes, so he turned and left hurriedly.
After a moment he looked over his shoulder: Joe, Hoxie, and Jim were
disappearing down a narrow passageway between two low frame
shacks.

Lloyd felt depressed. They'd reached their goal after a long, tortuous,
dangerous voyage and he should have been elated and ready for the rest
of the adventure, but he was not. Loneliness nagged at him like a
toothache. Why hadn't he gone with the others? Was he so saintly then?
Was it so awful for young men to want women, no matter what kind?
Yes! To him it seemed awful, like animals. He couldn't help it. When
he thought of women it was of something sweet and kindly and maybe

a little remote. The few experiments he'd made with the giggling girls of his acquaintance had been both embarrassing and futile.

He just didn't realize how naïve he was in regard to girls. He was confused by their stratagems and withdrawals and took their outward manners and attitudes at face value. His approach was basically romantic, and therefore reality was always breaking in to startle and bewilder him.

Lost in thought, he noticed a little curio store near the head of the pier, stopped, and stood looking absent-mindedly into the window at a collection of Indian wood carvings—small totem poles, animals, gods. The carving was excellent, the general result ugly and unpleasant, at least to Lloyd, as it presented and artistically explored the harsh, savage world of the northern Indians, a world of the fantastic, the grotesque, and the horrific.

Something made him look up from the curios, and he caught a quick glimpse of a small dark face, long, chopped-off black hair, and enormous dark eyes. There was a kind of beauty in this quick glimpse that gave him a sharp pang. He looked away, wondering if he'd actually seen this vision; then he glanced back. The face was turned away now and all he could see was a shoulder and a mass of black hair.

Drawn against his will, he started into the shop, then hesitated. What was he thinking of? What were his intentions? This was obviously a native girl, and very young. He turned away and walked down the pier toward the steamboat, but in a moment he was back in front of the store, looking at the curios; then he went in.

A little old blue-eyed man with a harsh, grayish face came forward, smiling. Out of the corner of his eye, Lloyd saw that the girl was sitting on what looked like a big sack, with her hands folded in her lap, obviously waiting—but for what? As the old man showed Lloyd around, he kept getting glimpses of the girl. Her thick straight black hair was cut off short at the shoulders as if with an ax; it did not really look like Indian hair. Her face was olive. Her big eyes had exaggeratedly long eyelashes.

His hands were cold as ice as he bought a small totem pole and a fright mask, and he fumbled futilely with his pocket money and finally dropped it all over the floor. The girl quickly got down on her hands and knees and retrieved it, to the last penny. Then, on one knee, she handed it to him, as if he were lord and master and she a slave. He looked into her dark eyes. They showed nothing. He thanked her nervously, then turned back to the old man. The girl, who had not made a sound, returned to her sack and sat with her hands folded, waiting.

Lloyd started out, the old man following him to the door. "You off the *Schoonover?*" he asked.

"Yes," said Lloyd.

"Taking the steamer up the Yukon?"

"Yes."

"Big strike at Circle," said the old man. "So we hear. May be all talk. This'll be the first trip this year, you know, so pretty soon we'll have some news. You a prospector?"

"Yes," said Lloyd, with an odd feeling of pride.

"Good luck then."

Lloyd left, but turned and came back. The old man was standing in the doorway.

"It's none of my business, I know," said Lloyd, shifting about nervously, "but who is that girl?"

"Oh, it's a sad case," said the old man. "She's always being left behind. Her parents left her here with an aunt and went off to Fort Yukon last summer. Her aunt got married to a Swede and has gone to Juneau to live. She's been working for Mrs. Brant, as maid. Now she's trying to get to Fort Yukon to find her parents. She's too pretty, that's the whole thing—even if she is only fifteen. I think there was some trouble at the Brants. I won't say more. 'Pears like I'm the only friend she's got. She can stay and work for me for board, if she likes. But she won't. She's stubborn. She's going to find them parents of hers or die."

"What is she? A native?"

"Breed," said the old man. "Name's Adorée Belleau."

Lloyd couldn't believe his ears. The name chimed in his heart like a lovely song. "What did you say her name was?"

"Adorée Belleau. Father's a French-Canadian; mother's a breed, part Indian, part Swede."

"Won't somebody lend her the money to get to Fort Yukon?"

"Are you crazy, boy? Eighty dollars! Dollars are short up here in Michaelovski. I don't take in a hundred dollars a year. Trade and barter. Why, boy, eighty here is like a thousand back in the States, except maybe where the gold is, and the gold may all be talk, although some's been taken out over the years."

"Then what will she do?"

"She says the Indians might run her up as far as Fort Yukon in a yuniak—big canoe. But that's a hell of a dangerous trip, upstream—takes forever. But she's just crazy enough to try it." The old man laughed. "And don't let them pretty eyes fool you; she's got a knife a foot long under that jacket. She won't stand for no nonsense—you see, she's been manhandled some, on account of her prettiness, even if she is only a kid."

Lloyd hesitated, then looked over at the girl. She said something in a low voice and the old man laughed.

"She says she likes your red beard," he said, laughing again. "For my money it ain't much of a beard, son."

The girl spoke again, low.

"Hey, what is this?" said the old man. "She says she thinks you're very nice."

Lloyd laughed nervously, then went out, rather abruptly, but turned back to the old man and said in an agitated voice: "Tell her not to go away—I mean, in any canoe. Tell her to wait."

"To wait?"

"Yes," said Lloyd. "For the steamboat to leave. I... I'm not making any promises. Just tell her to wait."

He hurried away. The old man stood staring after him, very puzzled.

They'd had supper in town at a little American eating house where they'd stuffed themselves so full of king salmon that they were now torpid and half-asleep as they sat on the gangway of the river steamboat with their chairs tipped back and their feet up on the railing. Although it was after six o'clock the sun was still high in the sky; the green water glinted with little diamond points of light, and gulls were everywhere, flying overhead, lighting on the water, screeching and fighting over scraps.

Jim, Hoxie, and the Old Man talked desultorily about the trip up the Yukon and about the endless ramifications of the gold strike at Circle City, their voices sounding sleepy and remote. Lloyd remained silent. He just could not bring himself to speak. He'd tried half a dozen times, but the words simply would not come out. He winced inwardly at the thought of the ridicule and ribaldry he'd have to face from Hoxie, the cold patient opposition of the Old Man. What Jim's attitude would be he could not guess, but there was little chance that it might be favorable. Looked at rationally, the thing was crazy. But Lloyd found himself unable to look at it in that way and kept remembering the pretty, olive-faced girl sitting patiently on the big sack, her hands folded in her lap, waiting.

Far out the *George B. Schoonover*, looking oddly small, battered, and inadequate to Lloyd, rolled gently at anchor, surrounded by gulls.

Whiskered men, in their shirt sleeves, stood on the dock and talked and spat. Apparently everybody chewed tobacco, everybody spat. Hoxie had already acquired the habit and was now spitting over the rail. Patient Indians, short and squat, lounged here and there, talking and laughing, their strong teeth showing very white in their dark faces. Along the strand workers from the American Commercial Company were gathering driftwood; it was the only fuel to be found in St. Michael.

The conversation broke off and Hoxie and Jim rose to go back into the town. The Old Man waved away an invitation to come along and said that he intended to turn in early and maybe sleep ten or twelve hours.

"Conserving my strength," he explained with a grin. "You young bucks don't have to worry about that—yet."

"How about you, Lloyd?" asked Jim, with Hoxie wagging his head impatiently in the background.

Lloyd swallowed hard, then rose. It was now or never. He hesitated for what seemed like a long time to him, his lips working; then he said: "Fellows, before you go I got something I want to bring up."

He seemed both so nervous and so solemn that they all knew something unusual was brewing and turned to study him.

"Well, what is it, Lloyd?" asked the Old Man.

"I want eighty dollars of my money," Lloyd stammered. "I got to have it."

Jim and Hoxie glanced at each other in surprise, but the Old Man said: "Eighty dollars! Why, hell, Lloyd, that's a lot of money out of our common stock. Might mean as much as five hundred to us later. You just don't seem to understand how important it is for us not to get broke up here. Takes a while to get started, you know."

"You want to gamble or something?" Hoxie demanded. "Joe warned us about that. Card sharps up here; take your shirt."

Lloyd shifted impatiently. "Well, Nollys," he said, "let's take it another way then. All right. I agreed to everything, like you said; and I'm not trying to back out. So maybe you can lend me the eighty dollars out of the common fund and I'll sign over a small percentage of my claim to any gold we get later."

"Boy," said the Old Man, "that's still the same thing. Cash money is cash money. Percentages of something we ain't got yet is just so much bookkeeping." He turned to Hoxie and Jim. "What do you fellows think?"

"I'm with you, Nollys," said Hoxie.

"We all agreed, back in Seattle," said Jim.

"Goddamn it, I've got to have that eighty dollars," screamed Lloyd, startling them, "and I'm going to have it one way or another."

"Wait a minute now, Lloyd," said Hoxie, bristling, but Jim shoved him back.

The Old Man gestured placatingly. "Lloyd, you don't seem to realize it, but we're all in the dark. You ain't stated your case. Why do you want this eighty so bad?"

Sweat was running down Lloyd's back and he felt himself wilting. It was crazy, crazy! What had got into him? He just hadn't been thinking straight. It should have been obvious from the first that they wouldn't listen, and when you came right down to it they were right. Once one of them started to withdraw his money, what was to prevent the others from withdrawing theirs and—especially in the case of Hoxie—spending it foolishly; and pretty soon there would be no money left and no partnership and eventually they might all be stranded in this God-forsaken, alien land.

"Forget it," he said loudly; then he turned suddenly and went below.

"He's crazy," said Hoxie. "Alaska's got him already."

"Beats me," sighed the Old Man, scratching his beard.

But Jim gestured for Hoxie to wait and he went below, looking for Lloyd. He found him at last on the ocean side of the lower deck, standing at the rail, looking out across the green water to where the *George B. Schoonover* was anchored.

"What is all this, Lloyd?" asked Jim. "Must be damned important to you."

"It's nothing, nothing," said Lloyd. "I was wrong. I'll admit it."

But Jim felt guilty in regard to Lloyd and wouldn't give up. In Seattle they'd been close friends, but on the voyage up they had drifted apart and Jim was pretty sure that he knew the reason. He'd disappointed Lloyd by his shore antics in Unalaska. Lloyd was still a child in regard to that side of life, knew nothing, expected too much.

"Maybe I can help," said Jim. "What is it?"

Lloyd turned and studied Jim's face for a moment; then hope sprang up in his heart, and, hardly stopping to breathe, he blurted out the whole story, talking so incoherently at times that Jim made him stop and go back.

"She's the prettiest girl I ever saw in my life," said Lloyd, relieved now that he had got the whole thing off his chest and Jim had neither laughed nor protested. "And she's only fifteen. I just can't stand the thought of her sitting there patiently—waiting for nothing."

Jim took out a cigar, lit it, and stood looking down at the water for a long time before he spoke. "Got any money?" he asked finally. "Pocket money, I mean."

"None to speak of," said Lloyd, looking at Jim curiously. "Maybe ten dollars."

Jim unbuttoned his shirt and, holding it open, worked at a safety pin for a moment, then took out a bill and handed it to Lloyd. "There's a fifty. That's the best I can do. That makes sixty. Maybe you can raise the rest some way."

Lloyd's hand trembled as he took the bill; then he turned away to hide his tears. Jim slapped him on the back and said: "You're a good fellow, Lloyd. I like you."

Then he turned and walked away. Lloyd took out his handkerchief and cried into it for a moment; then he hurried down to the hold and began to rummage through his own private sea bag.

Hoxie was pacing the deck impatiently, chewing tobacco and spitting over the side, when Jim returned, but the Old Man was still sitting with his chair tipped back and his feet on the railing.

"Well? Well?" Hoxie demanded.

"All settled," said Jim. "Everything's all right. I made him see he was wrong."

The Old Man nodded, said nothing.

"What got into that mouse all of a sudden?" cried Hoxie. "Why, he's got more vinegar in him than I thought."

"Yes," said Jim, smiling to himself, "he has."

The two young men left. The Old Man sat watching them lazily as they walked down the dock and disappeared around the shoulder of a battered wooden building.

Lloyd waited till the Old Man had gone to the cabin they shared, for the night; then he stole off the boat like a thief with a big bundle clutched under his arm. It contained his own things—a good gold railroad-type watch his mother had given him, a new compass, a small revolver he'd bought to "protect" himself on the voyage, a box of ammunition, and a suit of dark clothes he'd never worn; yes, everything was his own, but he still felt guilty about it and as if he were stealing from... somebody.

At a little after eight he turned up at the curio shop. The door was wide open, and the harsh-faced old man was smoking a pipe just inside. But to Lloyd's dismay the girl and the sack she'd been sitting on were gone.

"Where is she?" he asked.

"Sleeping in the back," said the old man. "I told her you said to wait so she right away went back to take a snooze. She seems to think everything's all settled now." The old man snorted a laugh.

"It is," said Lloyd proudly; she'd been depending on him and he hadn't let her down; then he began to count bills and silver into the old man's hand.

"Wait! What's this?" the old man demanded. "All that money!"

"Eighty-five dollars," said Lloyd. "Eighty for her passage to Fort Yukon and five dollars so she can have something in her pocket."

The old man showed a startled, unbelieving face. "But, young man, you can't buy her. That's all over with up in this country. I'm sorry, but you just can't do it. Besides, she's only fifteen, and under the laws of the United States...."

"Buy her!" cried Lloyd, appalled. "I just want to see that she finds her parents."

"But why? Why?"

There was a slight sound and they both turned. Adorée had come in from the back and was standing nearby, watching them. She looked very strange and barbaric to Lloyd in her beaded sealskin jacket, her felt pants, and her moccasins. She said nothing.

"Will you look after getting her cabin and paying the passage?" asked Lloyd, his voice trembling slightly. "And can she stay here till sailing time on the fifth?"

"Yes. Of course," said the old man, still staring.

"Thank you," said Adorée, her English sounding stilted and as if she wasn't quite sure what the words meant.

"You're welcome," said Lloyd; then he shifted about for a moment, very uncomfortable, nodded to the old man, bowed slightly to Adorée, and went out.

"I don't like this, Adorée," said the old man.

"I like it."

"He's in love with you. He's crazy about you."

"He is a nice man."

"How do you know he's a nice man? You never saw him before. You're a child."

"I am not a child. Ask Mr. Brant if I am a child."

"Adorée! Stop such talk. It wasn't your fault."

Adorée smiled slightly and disappeared into the back. The old man put the money away in a little strongbox; then he carefully locked the front door. When he got to the back room, Adorée was already asleep on the floor, with her head on the sack. He covered her with a blanket; then he went out the back way, locking the door after him, and started uptown to play dominoes with an old crony of his. By God, tonight he really had something to talk about! Rumors concerning Circle City had been chewed over so much they were getting stale and boring. But this weakly handsome young man with the reddish beard... and Adorée...!

Old Gustafson would keep his mouth shut, if he warned him to do so. Gus was real close-mouthed.

It was the Fourth of July and a small crowd lined the jetty, watching the annual Indian canoe race. The canoes were huge and each held sixteen paddlers. They had started in from the sea at a point just to the north of the anchored *George B. Schoonover* and were now heading, in a widely deployed irregular line, for the jetty.

Jim, Hoxie, Lloyd, and the Old Man had got good places at the end of the jetty and had made a complicated series of nickel bets on the outcome.

Hoxie waved his hat and cheered them on; then he said: "Look at them silly guys. No regular stroke. How the hell can they paddle that way?"

"Sure is every man for himself," said Jim, laughing.

The canoes came on in a gradually widening, fanned-out V; the bearded Anglos on the jetty began to scream encouragement; but when the leader was about a hundred yards from the shore suddenly the big canoe seemed to skid, slew around, and then upset, dumping all of the paddlers into the water. The other canoes immediately gave up the race and headed for the sixteen paddlers thrashing around in the cold-looking, choppy green sea.

"All bets off, goddamn it," cried a big brown-bearded man in a plaid shirt; then he turned away and started back toward town, paying no attention whatever to the rescue.

"Having a little trouble out there," said the Old Man, peering.

"Aw, hell," said Hoxie indifferently, "they're just Injuns."

Lloyd turned and looked at him. Hoxie noticed the look, then said:

"Well, they are, ain't they? Just Injuns?"

"They got 'em all but one," said Jim. "God, they're going to upset that other canoe if they don't watch out."

Hoxie roared. "Look at them silly guys diving, their butts coming up like ducks."

Lloyd turned away and started toward town. "Where you going?" cried Hoxie. "Hey, Lloyd—what are you up to lately?" Lloyd shrugged and went on, and Hoxie turned to Jim: "Got a good notion to follow him, see what's doing. That boy just don't act natural any more."

"Let him alone," said Jim, and when Hoxie made a move toward town Jim grabbed his arm and held him back. "Mind your own business."

Hoxie studied Jim's face. "So you know what's up, eh?"

Jim pushed him. "Since when have you started running around after Lloyd? Haven't you got any business of your own?"

Hoxie grimaced and subsided.

"They got him," said the Old Man. "Looks like a bundle of wet wash."

Hoxie roared.

Now one of the canoes headed for shore, the paddlers driving full strength, bringing in the last man fished out, who was lying inert in the bow. As soon as the canoe was beached, the unconscious Indian was laid flat and worked on. The Anglos watched indifferently for a while, then wandered off slowly toward the town, talking desultorily about what a washout the canoe race had been that year.

Hoxie put his arm around Jim's shoulder. "Think it's okay to go to Alushka's without Joe? I think we made ourselves solid yesterday. How about it?"

"Well …" said Jim hesitantly.

"Go ahead, boys," said the Old Man. "We're leaving early tomorrow morning. I'll go take a nap."

Jim and Hoxie moved off toward town, and the Old Man got aboard the *Nils K. Jensen*, climbed to the gangway, tipped his chair back, propped his feet up on the railing, and closed his eyes. The boat rocked gently, gulls flew screaming, and a warmish wind, smelling of rank vegetation, blew in from the interior. The Old Man dozed in the pleasant sunlight, conserving his strength for the struggle ahead.

A harsh-sounding, animal-like wailing brought him up with a start, and he rose and looked over the gangway rail. A squaw (or *klutchmon* as they were called in the North) and three small Indian children were kneeling about the inert figure on the beach. They all had their heads back and were howling like wolves. A big group of Indian men—the canoe racers—stood respectfully by.

"I'll be goddamned," cried the Old Man, astounded. "He drowned."

A huge stoker, known as Alf, came up the gangway stairs and stopped beside the Old Man.

"Too bad," he said. "Steve Tchepatka, the best hunter around here. Brings in fresh meat when there just ain't none. They're going to take up a collection for his family. Mr. Brant's sending the list around. I already give a dollar."

"First time I ever heard of one of them Injuns drowning."

"He must've got hit by the canoe or a paddle or something. He was out cold in the water."

Alf gestured and passed on. The Old Man returned to his chair, tipped it back, and put his feet up. The dismal Indian death wailing went on, but the Old Man dozed in spite of it and in a little while he could no longer hear it.

Lloyd wandered aimlessly about the town. He did not want to talk to Hoxie and Jim and the Old Man; he felt too agitated and worried and was afraid they'd notice it. Anxiety nagged at him, and he was beset by all sorts of petty fears and suspicions. Suppose the Curio Man—who was very old and did not look strong—took ill suddenly and forgot to make the arrangements? Suppose he just kept the money and denied that Lloyd had ever given it to him? He was a long-time resident, Lloyd a drifting stranger; it was obvious which one would be believed. Or suppose the girl would change her mind and decide to go upstream in an Indian canoe after all?

Contrary impulses pulled Lloyd in opposite directions. He wanted to go to the curio store and see for himself, but he was afraid that his anxiety might be too apparent or that he would be suspected of unjust suspicions and maybe of spying. By late afternoon he had exhausted all of his resources and finally wandered down to the beach, at the far north end of town, and sat staring off across the choppy green water toward the gently rocking *George B. Schoonover*, his former home. Gulls moved boldly all about him, walking stiffly through the tundra moss. Lloyd studied them idly: queer birds, so beautifully graceful in flight, so silly-looking and awkward on land.

Lloyd ate alone and barely picked at the king salmon that had seemed like such a treat the night before; then he left the little eating house and took up his wanderings once more. He held out till nearly ten o'clock; then, unable to stand it any longer, he hurried down the muddy street toward the curio store, at the south end of town. But the windows were dark, the front door locked. He ran round to the back but it was the same there. His heart began to pound; sweat broke out on his forehead.

Hardly knowing what he was saying or why he was saying it, he burst out: "I can't lose her. I won't!"

A series of sharp rattling explosions, like a distant fusillade of rifle fire, brought him up short. What was it? Why the firing? Had the Indians...? But at that moment a huge rocket burst directly overhead, showing a sickly greenish pallor in the broad daylight of ten o'clock of the Alaskan evening. The Fourth of July! Even in this faraway outpost of America they shot off firecrackers and sent up rockets!

The zoom and crackle went on. Lloyd wandered aimlessly toward the sounds and in a moment saw a straggling crowd watching the setting off of the fireworks by a few men on the top of a low hillock.

The old Curio Man was standing at the edge of the crowd, smoking a pipe. Beside him was a slight, blanket-wrapped figure. Lloyd could see nothing but the lower part of her felt pants and her small beaded moccasins. His heart turned over painfully. He made a quick move to start back for town but the Curio Man had seen him.

"Hello, son," he said. "Come here."

Lloyd went over to them. Adorée's small face looked out at him from the blanket, as if from ambush.

"Made the arrangements," said the Curio Man. "Here's your receipt. All shipshape. I'll get her aboard sometime tonight. I think it's best I slip her on board. There's been considerable talk around town... about... well... uh... another matter. It will be best."

"Oh yes, certainly," said Lloyd quickly, fighting off a touch of dizziness. "Anything you say, sir."

A big rocket zoomed up with a whistling crash and burst overhead into a shower of pinkish-pale sky flowers. Adorée screamed faintly.

"That was the loudest one yet," she said.

"Adorée is very excited about going," said the Curio Man. "She wouldn't eat today."

"You must eat," said Lloyd.

"She don't eat enough for a bird," said the Curio Man. "First Indian I ever see didn't eat like a Malamute."

Lloyd winced, but the girl ignored the Curio Man's comment and watched the fireworks.

The next rocket failed to rise, hung for a moment, turned sideways, and skittered erratically down toward the crowd, hissing like red-hot iron thrust into water. Adorée screamed and grabbed Lloyd's upper arms as the rocket rose slightly, whizzed harmlessly over their heads, then burst somewhere beyond the buildings of the town. There were outraged shouts and cursing from unseen citizens, howls of laughter from the men on the hill.

"Raise your sights, Jabez!" yelled somebody. "For Christ's sake, raise your sights."

Adorée took her hands from Lloyd's arms and said: "That one was green. I like the red ones better."

"Yes," said Lloyd. "They're the prettiest." Then he started to shift about uncomfortably: "Well, I..." he began.

But the girl asked, in surprise: "Aren't you going to see all the fireworks?"

"Well," said Lloyd, swallowing, "yes. I guess I...."

So they stood side by side in the broad daylight, watching rockets, flowerpots, pin wheels, and Roman candles futilely exploding and wasting their night brilliance on the Arctic evening.

Then the three of them walked back to the curio shop together and Lloyd stopped in front to say good-night.

"Don't worry," said the Curio Man. "She'll be on there tomorrow morning when the boat sails."

"Good. Fine," said Lloyd awkwardly, not knowing quite how to take his leave.

The girl said nothing, just stood there almost completely hidden in the blanket.

"Good-night, Adorée," he said.

"What is your name?" she asked.

"Lloyd."

"Good-night, Mr. Lloyd."

"Not mister," said Lloyd, laughing uncomfortably. "My name's Lloyd Gracey."

"Good-night, Mr. Gracey."

Lloyd was going to protest, but the Curio Man intervened. "No use arguing," he said. "This child's stubborn as a mule."

"Good-night, Adorée."

"Good-night, Mr. Gracey."

"You see?" said the Curio Man. "Might as well learn now."

Lloyd wandered back to the ship in a daze. He found the Old Man already asleep in the lower bunk, stripped to his underwear.

Lloyd was soon in his own bunk and lay with his hands under his head, staring at the ceiling, where wavering watery reflections, coming in from the porthole, made odd patterns and arrangements.

Little by little he dozed; then he slept, fitfully, turning and twisting. Finally Hoxie and Jim came aboard, talking loudly, laughing, and hanging things about in the next cabin.

The Old Man groaned, sat up, and struck a match. It was dark now.

"What time is it?" asked Lloyd.

"After 2 A.M.," said the Old Man.

"When do we move?"

"Oh, I don't know. Seven or eight, maybe earlier. You see, we've got eighty miles of ocean before we hit the river channel. Cap'n likes to get that over with before dark."

"Eighty miles of ocean!" cried Lloyd.

"Yep," said the Old Man; then, soothingly: "But it's right along shore. In weather like this, nothing to it."

"You say the boat might leave earlier?"

"It might. Go to sleep, Lloyd. Tomorrow's another day—and a big one."

Lloyd lay back, realizing with a start that Adorée had driven everything else from his thoughts: the trip, the gold, fear for his own safety. He thought only of Adorée. At once he began to worry. Suppose the boat left very early? Suppose the Curio Man did not realize …? Lloyd wanted to get up and dress and go back to the town, but he dreaded the Old Man's questions and comments. And suddenly a soothing thought calmed him: the Curio Man was a long-time resident and knew all about the *Nils K. Jensen*, its arrivals and departures.

Lloyd said his prayers (he'd got the habit since the day of the big headwind), then he composed himself and in a few minutes fell into a heavy sleep.

IV

TO FORT YUKON

While Blankhart and the other seamen got into the longboat, Hansen and Joe Portugee turned to say good-by. It was a raw morning for July, with low, drifting cloud wracks, a gray sky, and a leaden sea. Gulls were everywhere, complaining in creaking voices. Far out, the *George B. Schoonover* rolled at anchor, smoke pouring from the one thickset stack.

Hansen and Joe shook hands with Jim, Hoxie, and the Old Man.

"We're going to miss you fellows," said Hansen. "Return voyage's going to be damned dull." Suddenly he looked about him. "Where's the little one?"

"Still sleeping," said Jim. "Worn out, I guess."

"He's getting worn out early," said Hansen, and they all laughed.

"Tell the skipper not to forget those letters and curios," said Jim.

"Deliver 'em myself," said Hansen. "You've got my word."

"It's right up the hill from the harbor, top of 3rd Street. Can't miss it."

"Ay, ay, sir," said Hansen, grinning. "Well, here we go."

"Joe," called Hoxie, "kiss Alberte for me when you get back—and be careful where."

Hansen half fell into the longboat, doubled over with laughter; Joe roared, waved wildly, then shoved the boat off and jumped in. The seamen pulled hard for the little tramp freighter; Hansen and Joe stood in the stern, waving, Hansen at the rudder.

Jim suddenly remembered the Village of the Dead and how it had looked that day when they'd rowed to the Penuncks for water. He felt deeply depressed without knowing why.

"Come on," said the Old Man. "Let's get back to the steamboat. She's leaving anytime now."

They started back, Hoxie and the Old Man talking about the voyage out. Jim followed them, then turned to look off at the longboat. It was out quite a ways now, surrounded by flying gulls.

All at once he realized why he felt so depressed, and why he had remembered the Village of the Dead. There went the *George B. Schoonover's* longboat, the last link with home; and it was possible, just possible, that they were moving forward toward a Village of the Dead in which they might turn out to be victims and happier men the despoilers.

A loud blast on the whistle shook the *Nils K. Jensen* and brought Lloyd straight up out of his bunk. The boat was moving; gray showed at the porthole. Lloyd dressed with frantic haste, then hurried out on the deck. It was empty. But thick wood smoke was billowing up from the twin stacks, and a couple of hundred yards of open gray water showed between the boat and the jetty. Lloyd felt panicky. Suppose the Curio Man had not got her aboard in time; what could he do? If he waited too long it might be impossible for him to get back to St. Michael at all. If he acted now... perhaps he might persuade them to put him ashore. He could work; he could find a job, maybe, with the American Commercial Company. He'd heard that educated men were at a premium around St. Michael.... His thoughts buzzed on irrationally....

In his haste to make the circuit of the gangway he collided with the Old Man, and Jim reached out and grabbed him to keep him from falling.

"What's your hurry, boy?" Hoxie demanded. "Thought you were still asleep."

Lloyd said nothing. Jim released him. The Old Man stared at him curiously.

"Look off there," said Jim to Lloyd. "There goes the old tramp, back to Seattle. She sure looks small out on the sea, eh, Lloyd?"

Lloyd did not know how to get away. "Yes," he said, hardly glancing at the outward-bound ship. "Very small."

Close by, near the curve of the stern, a cabin door opened a few inches. Lloyd caught a quick glimpse of a beaded sealskin jacket; then the door was hastily closed. Lloyd heaved a long sigh of relief, then took off his hat, wiped his brow, and lounged easily against the rail. Again the Old Man looked at him curiously, surprised by this obvious change of front.

"How about we sit down now, boys," said the Old Man. "We got a long ways to go, so we might as well get used to taking it easy and being lazy while we can."

They moved around to the landward side of the gangway, got out their chairs, tipped them back, put their feet up on the rails, and sat staring off at nothing, while the *Nils K. Jensen* chugged southward toward one of the mouths of the big Yukon River, which would carry them, by way of the Land of Many Waters, to the Alaskan interior and their destination eighteen hundred miles away across the wasteland of limitless tundra.

The sea was calm and the color of antique pewter; grayish clouds hung low over the land; and the weather had turned warm and muggy.

"Our luck's holding," said the Old Man, smiling as if to himself. "A perfect day to get into the channel. This is not really a seagoing boat, so if it blows or the weather is rough, you have to put back to St. Michael."

"Put *back?*" cried Hoxie, horrified at the idea.

"Yeah," said the Old Man. "But not us. Sea's like a pond. Not a breath of air. As right as if we'd ordered it."

The shore looked almost dismayingly barren. There was not a hill, tree, or rock in sight, hardly even a rise. Mile after mile after weary mile of flat tundra stretching north, south, and east, beyond the margin of the cold-looking, gray sea. Gulls screeched dismally along the endless, inhospitable shore, seeming as alien and out of place in this flat, gray world as the chugging white steamboat and the men aboard it.

"Jesus," said Hoxie finally, "who invented this country! It must've been an afterthought."

"Oh," said the Old Man, "it's not so bad, once you get used to it."

"Is it like this all the way?" asked Jim, secretly appalled.

"No," said the Old Man. "There's quite a bit like this, but it's timbered once we get inside—lots of spruce; and further on she narrows, and there are some hills—kinda low hills—called the Ramparts. The Yukon changes here and there. Quite a river."

"When do we make the channel?" asked Jim.

"During the night, I'd say," said the Old Man. "Then it's just plain chugging. Takes time, but you get there without fuss or bother."

There were three other passengers aboard, aside from Adorée. Two were old sourdoughs, veterans of the eighties, like Nollys Harp, who'd been living in St. Michael for ten years and had decided to go back up the Yukon to Circle City to investigate the only half-believed rumors of the big strike. Their names were Blaik and Dogett, and they were gray, crusty old characters who kept to themselves and sat together in silence, spitting tobacco juice over the railing. The third passenger was a big, bespectacled, middle-aged man named Purdy, who was an official of the American Commercial Company and was on a tour of inspection. He spent most of his time in the wheelhouse with the huge, red-faced skipper, Carl Jensen.

In the hold, sweating stokers endlessly fed wood into the ravenous furnaces, urged on by Rudy Kelpak, the big breed engineer, who had married an Eskimo woman and given up the open sea for the comforts of St. Michael and an occasional run on the White-Smoking-Monster-That-Walks-On-The-Water, as the *Nils K. Jensen* was called in the language of the Yukon Indians.

… the tundra slid past with featureless monotony, remote, barren, alien-looking. The boat was in fairly close to shore and for this reason the lubbers aboard felt safe, although Carl Jensen (and the Old Man) knew better. It was only on the calmest days—such as the fifth of July, 1896—that a skipper could dare to sail so close to disaster, tempting fate. But it saved time, distance, and wood, and Carl, like his father, old Nils, was a very economical man.

Hoxie fell asleep, nodding in his chair; then the Old Man followed suit.

"She's aboard, if that's what was worrying you," said Jim, speaking in a low voice.

Lloyd started slightly. "Did you see her?"

Jim smiled. "All I saw was a blanket and legs walking across the deck."

Lloyd nodded reminiscently. It was almost all he himself had seen last night at the fireworks.

"They'll know sooner or later," said Jim, jerking his head at their sleeping partners.

"It's only Hoxie I'm worried about," said Lloyd.

"I'll handle him," said Jim. "Hoxie's not bad. He's like a big kid. Don't worry. I'll handle him."

Lloyd gave Jim a grateful smile, then rose, put his fingers to his lips, and slipped off down the deck and around the curve of the gangway, with Jim looking off after him, shaking his head, wondering how such a thing would end. But in a moment Jim shrugged, stopped worrying about it, and was soon sleeping along with Hoxie and the Old Man.

Lloyd just could not bring himself to do such a simple thing as tap at her cabin door. Now he was standing at the gangway railing looking off over the sea to where the *George B. Schoonover* was no longer more than a smudge of black coal smoke on the horizon.

He heard a creak finally and turned. The door of Adorée's cabin had opened for a moment, then closed. What did it mean? Did she want to see him? Or had she opened the door to come out, noticed him loitering there at the railing, and fled back in? He did not know what to do or think, and he was sweating heavily, not only because of the muggy day.

The door opened again, after a few minutes of suspense, and a small, graceful, brown hand motioned for him to come in.

The cabin was very small, and very dim in the cloudy gray light from the porthole. Lloyd could hardly believe his eyes and struggled hard to keep the disappointment out of his face. Looking taller, and far stranger, Adorée was standing in the middle of the cabin, as if for his inspection, wearing a cheap blue cotton dress that fitted her like a sack and was so long that it hung in folds and trailed on the floor.

"You don't like it," she said, studying his face.

He hesitated for a long time, touched and not wanting to hurt her feelings.

"I know you don't like it. Say so," said Adorée calmly.

Lloyd stammered, but finally said: "Adorée... I like you better the way you were."

"All right," she replied calmly. "This is the kind of dress the white women wear. You are a white man."

"I like you better the other way."

"Very well, Mr. Gracey," said Adorée. "You go now."

Lloyd hardly knew what to say. She was like an unexplored continent to him, mysterious, unknown, full of pitfalls. He never had the slightest idea what she was thinking or feeling. Had he offended her? Humiliated her? Hurt her badly? "I hope you're not angry with me," he said, coughing a little in embarrassment.

"I—with you, Mr. Gracey? Oh no. You go—and come back, if you like."

"I'll wait by the railing."

She nodded. He went out, closing the door softly. The two old sourdoughs were taking a turn round the deck; they glanced at Lloyd, then looked away quickly before he could speak to them. They had no desire whatsoever to make the acquaintance of this "puny little red-bearded outsider!"

A few minutes later Adorée motioned him back inside. She was wearing her jacket, her felt pants, and her beaded moccasins now; she looked small, slight, and very exotic, as she had the first time he'd seen her at the curio shop.

She sat down on one end of the bunk; he took the other end. She remained calmly, unembarrassedly silent. He fidgeted nervously, looked at her, looked about the cabin, then up at the gray porthole.

"Do you like your cabin?" he brought out, finally, with an effort.

"Oh, very much."

"Did you sleep well?"

"No. I looked out the porthole."

"All night?"

"Yes."

"Why?"

"I couldn't believe it was happening. I was afraid if I went to sleep I'd wake up and it would be a dream."

"Where did you learn to speak English so well?"

"Mrs. Brant thought I spoke it badly. At the American school. I won a prize for English."

"I should think so."

"It was easy. The others wouldn't try. I speak French, too. *C'est la vie. Sacre chien! Nom de nom!* Do you understand French?"

"No, I don't."

"My father is French. But he was too impatient to teach me and he was always away. My mother can speak Swedish but I don't like that language. It's ugly, like Indian. French is pretty. I like English best."

"I went through high school," said Lloyd. "But I never won any prizes.

"Why should you? But we—we should try."

He wasn't quite sure what she meant and he did not want to ask.

"Where will you eat?" he inquired. "I mean, on the ship. There's nothing but men."

"Here," said Adorée.

"But how? Will they bring it?"

"Bring it? But I have my food."

"You don't understand. Food is furnished. Your passage has been paid."

"You mean I get food, too?"

"Yes."

"But I can't eat with all those men."

"I'll arrange it some way. I'll bring it to you myself."

"Oh, but that wouldn't be right, Mr. Gracey, you carrying my food. It would be embarrassing."

Lloyd looked at her blankly. "Why?"

"Oh... it just would."

It suddenly occurred to him that she'd had nothing to eat that day.

"What would you like?"

She stared, then turned away, got something out of a small sack, and held it out in her hand.

"I've eaten already. Here's my food. Pemmican."

Lloyd tried not to show his distaste. It was a kind of Indian jerky, hardly fit for dogs, in his opinion.

"Oh, I see," he said. "But wouldn't you like some tea and maybe some bread?"

Adorée's eyes brightened. "Do they have tea? I've only had tea once—at Mrs. Brant's. Yes. Could I have some tea? Are you sure they have it?"

"I heard Captain Jensen yelling for it on the bridge."

"Oh, if I could only have some," cried Adorée, sounding like a child.

Lloyd hurried out to see what could be done about the tea, relieved somehow to get away.

Jim, Hoxie, and the Old Man had finished their supper and were now talking, smoking, and sipping black coffee; they were alone in the saloon, as the other passengers had eaten earlier. Kobo, a fat, smiling Indian steward, was brushing the crumbs from the table and listening to the conversation.

Hoxie glanced out the porthole, then grimaced in irritation. "Seems like we just keep passing the same place."

Kobo giggled and went on with his work.

"Making great time," said the Old Man. "If this keeps up we'll do better than a hundred miles today; be twenty miles up the river before morning."

"Oh yes," said Kobo. "New boiler."

"That so?" said the Old Man.

Kobo nodded, pleased at the attention he was getting. "Mr. Purdy— he see put in. New boiler. Very nice."

Hoxie jerked his thumb toward the porthole. "That same gull just went past. It's like we were on one of them what-you-may-call-it's...."

"Treadmills," Jim suggested.

"That's it," said Hoxie. "One time I seen a show in Columbus, Ohio. There was this fellow on a horse, and they were galloping on this here treadmill, riding like hell and getting no place, with the scenery flying past. That's us."

Kobo giggled; then he took a small bottle from inside his jacket, held it up, and inquired: "You gentlemen like drink? White whisky, pretty hot. You drink, say nothing. Kobo get in trouble."

They passed the bottle round and drank, all wincing and shuddering as the raw, fiery liquid slid down their throats.

"Kobo," said Hoxie, "you can pour that back in the boiler."

The Indian shook with laughter. Blackbeard was really one very funny Anglo. The Old Man turned and handed Kobo a quarter. "Thanks, son," he said.

The Indian ducked his head several times and carefully put the quarter—silver cash money!—away. "You like drink, you tell Kobo."

"Nollys," said Hoxie, "tell me something. How come there's only six passengers on this here boat—and one of 'em a company officer? With all that gold talk, why ain't there a rush from St. Michael?"

Kobo listened, showing marked interest.

"Oh," said the Old Man, "most of the fellows in St. Michael are old-timers. They've been to Circle City; they've seen the quality of gold taken out—this ain't the first time, you know. It's coarse, some of it not worth working. These strikes die down. This ain't the big one, Hoxie; it's only the kind that brings the crazy hoosiers in."

There was a brief pause; then Kobo said: "Seven."

They turned to look at him. "What did you say, Kobo?" asked Hoxie.

"One more passenger. Seven."

Jim shifted about uncomfortably and lowered his eyes. Here it came. Couldn't be kept secret anyway. Might as well get it out in the open and over with.

"Who's the other one?" asked Hoxie.

Kobo giggled. "Very pretty girl. Breed. Frenchy."

"What?" cried Hoxie, staring. "Sure you ain't been using too much of that boiler juice, Injun?"

Kobo rocked with laughter. "No drink own stuff. Only sell."

"Where is she?" cried Hoxie.

But Jim intervened. "Never mind where she is. Don't tell him, Kobo. None of his business."

Kobo, sensitive to the bewildering moods of the Anglos, darted his little slanted black eyes from Jim to Hoxie, then said nothing, turned away, and picked up his broom.

"Say, what the hell is this?" yelled Hoxie, rising. "Jim Hardy, you stay out of my life. Let me run it. Kobo! Kobo!"

But Kobo, as if suddenly deaf, began to sweep the floor furiously. Jim shoved Hoxie back into his seat.

"Now listen to me, Hoxie," he said, "and listen carefully. This girl is only fifteen. Lloyd is paying her passage to Fort Yukon so she can find her parents."

Hoxie stared. "So that's what the little mouse wanted with his money, and that's why he's been acting so damned funny and sneaky-like. Trust them quiet, mealy-mouthed boys!"

Jim reached across the table, took Hoxie by the shoulder, and shook him hard. "Hoxie! Listen to me. Stay away from her. You hear? Or we're going to tangle. I mean it. I'm dead serious."

Hoxie saw that... whatever it was... shining out of Jim's pale narrowed eyes and felt very uncomfortable. First he blustered and shook off Jim's hand; then he began to laugh. The Old Man looked on imperturbably; he felt that Jim could handle the situation and that it would be well for himself to stay out of it entirely.

"Now looky here, Jim," said Hoxie, "it's a free country. Suppose once that little girl sees me, she don't want no more of Lloyd? Then what?"

"Stay away from her," said Jim, his voice so cold and menacing that even the Old Man turned and took a good look at him.

"Aw, now, Jim," said Hoxie, laughing, "can't you take a joke? Fifteen? I don't rob no cradles. You know me better than that. Sure I'll stay away from her. I was only trying to rile you."

Jim's face softened little by little. Finally he hit Hoxie on the back. "All right," he said. "All right."

Now Hoxie turned round in his chair and began to look out the porthole. "I swear it's the same place, over and over," he said in disgust. "Nollys, you sure we're moving?"

Kobo giggled faintly over his sweeping. All was peace now with the Anglos.

Adorée sat at one end of the bunk, Lloyd at the other, drinking their tea and nibbling at some ship's biscuits Lloyd had found in the galley. Heavy clouds were blotting out the day and it was almost dark in the little cabin, with only a faint, ugly grayish light coming in through the porthole.

"This is better than Mrs. Brant's tea. Very good. Can we have it often?"

"I think so. Till it runs out, Kobo said."

"Oh Kobo!" Adorée exclaimed. "He's a fool."

"Is he? He seemed very friendly."

"Kobo is money crazy. He is always finding ways to get money from the Anglos. Then you know what he does with it? He buries it."

"Buries it?"

"That's what Mrs. Brant told me. He has a little chest buried out in the country some place, full of silver coins."

"But why? You'd think he would spend it."

"For what? He has his keep from the company. He needs nothing. His sister, Elka, used to work for Mrs. Brant. She told."

"What is he saving it for?"

"To play with—Elka told Mrs. Brant. He goes out, digs up the chest, plays with the coins, then puts it back. His sister followed him once. He saw her and moved the chest. She doesn't know where it is now."

Lloyd sat shaking his head. It was a fantastic story. He didn't know whether to believe it or not.

Adorée poured him out some more tea, then filled her own cup and sipped it delicately.

"If I could have tea every day," she said, with a sigh.

"I'll see what I can do," said Lloyd, wondering how he was going to manage it. Kobo had made a great mystery about the tea, carefully unlocking a drawer and taking it out as if it was something very precious. In fact, he'd made such a fuss about it that Lloyd had given him a fifty-cent piece. But he just couldn't do that every day, as there was very little left of the money he'd raised by borrowing from Jim and selling—at a ridiculously low price—the objects from his sea bag.

While Hoxie snored in his chair on the gangway, Jim and the Old Man talked. Thick gray clouds hung low over the shore, blotting out the endless wastes of tundra. The steamboat was very close in, the banks looking like putty, the still water like lead. There was something so aggressively ugly about the scene that Jim lowered his eyes and stared at his boots. God, what a place!

"You think it was wise, helping him, Jim?" the Old Man was asking mildly.

"I don't know," said Jim. "He was pretty much upset."

"The trouble with these expeditions is they bust up," said the Old Man. "For one reason or another—usually damned foolish reasons—they bust up. This girl, Jim—I don't know."

"She's just an Indian."

"Even so. Lloyd's a damned funny youngun. Can't quite figure him out. But we need him, Jim—at least we need his money. I told you all along—it's not easy up here. It can be done, but it's not easy. If men would just stick together...."

The Old Man's voice trailed off. He'd got them all this far with a minimum of difficulty, but now the trouble was starting, as it always seemed to do eventually; and they still had a long ways to go, a damned long ways. In a way he couldn't blame these young fellows too much. They just had no real idea of what they were in for. If luck stayed with them, they'd reach Forty Mile by the middle of July; this would give them time—although it might be a squeeze—to explore the creeks, stake their claims, build their shacks, and get ready for the winter mining season. But things could go wrong, and the last boat left for St. Michael the latter part of August. Pretty soon the frost would come, then snow, then winter, with the big river frozen solid and no way in the world to get out till the next summer. The twilight of the Arctic winter would close down over the silent land with temperatures as low as seventy-five degrees below zero, and a man's life depending solely on the fuel he had stacked and the food he had hoarded.

The picture was clear in every detail in the Old Man's mind, but how could he communicate it to these three young fellows whose blood was hot, whose reason was undisciplined, and whose expectations were unlimited? Their ideas of reality were faulty; they had not learned yet what you could and could not do, with impunity. It was up to him to teach and guide them. But how? How?

For the first time since the departure from Seattle, the Old Man began to have his doubts. "But I'll get there," he told himself grimly. "I'll get there by hook or crook. I'll make it, by God; I'll make it."

Hoxie shook Jim roughly to wake him. It was dark in their cabin. The boat was rocking slightly and there was a heavy pounding of the engines.

"What do you want?" cried Jim sleepily; then suddenly he was wide awake, noticed that Hoxie was fully dressed, reached out, grabbed and shook him. "Where the hell you been? Have you been fooling around with that girl?"

"No, no," cried Hoxie. "Take it easy. But I sure heard a lot about her, I want to tell you. Fifteen years old, eh? Just a child. Oh boy!" Hoxie chortled gloatingly.

Jim punched him hard in the chest. "Did you wake me up just to...?"

"Wait, Jim. Wait. Hell, you can go back to sleep, can't you? I been talking to Kobo in the galley and Rudy Kelpak in the hold. Listen, this little baggage—her name's Adorée Belleau—hey, hey!—you like that?—well, she was working hired girl for Mrs. Brant. Now Old Man Brant's the big boss of St. Michael—I mean, he's head man at the American Commercial Company. Well, this big man, he gets to playing horsey with little Adorée—Rudy says 'she purtiest girl I ever seen'—that's the way he talks—yeah, Mr. Brant gets to playing horsey and the missus catches them in fragrant delecto—man, man, man!—the hasenpfeffer was really in the ice cream. So out goes little Adorée to look for her parents in Fort Yukon. She's through in St. Michael. No more jobs for her. The white ladies just don't want their ever-lovings playing horsey with that pretty little breed girl. How you like that, Jim? How you like that goddamned mouse—Lloyd—ending up with the 'purtiest' girl in the North Countree...?" Hoxie could hardly contain himself and kept bouncing around and chortling as he talked.

"She was fifteen," said Jim coldly. "Mr. Brant's a middle-aged man. Who do you blame?"

"Blame!" cried Hoxie. "I don't blame *nobody!* I'm a hundred per cent for horsing—and so are you, you damned hayshaker hypocrite, only you won't admit it!"

There was a pause; then Jim said: "Hoxie, I meant every word I said in the saloon. You stay away from her or we tangle."

"Don't this change nothing?"

"No."

Hoxie rose with a sigh and began to take off his clothes. "Don't suppose Lloyd is getting any, at that," he said. "Taking tea up to her and biscuits. Can you imagine that? To a Injun?"

"Go to bed. Shut up," said Jim.

The Old Man woke with a groan and gradually pulled himself up from the depths of sleep. In their new quarters, Lloyd—a very polite boy—had insisted that he take the lower and he had agreed. It saved him all that climbing up and down. He must conserve his strength now; he must conserve it, day by day, hour by hour, minute by minute. This was his last chance, his very last.

He went outside to relieve himself. Darkness ruled the world. The air was close and muggy. He could see nothing but still water in the dim blanket of light the steamboat was casting all about itself.

When he went back into the cabin, Lloyd was sitting up.

"I suppose you know all about it by now," said Lloyd, without preamble.

"Yes."

"I guess it was a fool thing to do, Nollys. Wasn't it?"

"Yes."

They said no more. In a little while the Old Man was snoring. But Lloyd, with his hands under his head, lay wondering why it was that committing a folly made a man so happy.

It was day. The boat had stopped. Hoxie and Jim dressed hurriedly and went out on the gangway. Lloyd and the Old Man had preceded them, and they all stood at the rail, looking off eastward across the vast watery reaches of the Yukon River. The land was as flat and feature- less as the top of a table, except for a dense clump of spruce on the right bank. An immensely high gray sky arched over them, accentuating the feeling of limitless empty distances—of infinity.

The steamboat was tied up at the bank; a clanking and hollow bel- lowing came from the hold.

"What the hell's going on here?" asked Hoxie in irritation.

"Getting the sea water out of the boilers," said the Old Man. "Wood party going out pretty soon."

"For what?" cried Hoxie.

"Well," said the Old Man, "this boat uses about a cord and a half an hour; runs strictly on wood. So they got to cut it as they go along. Can't carry enough."

"And stop every time? Oh Jesus," said Hoxie, in disgust. "Why don't we just walk and get it over with?"

Now Captain Jensen went ashore from the lower deck, with an ax over his shoulder, followed by Rudy Kelpak and two huge stokers, Alf and Creeb, all carrying axes. Jensen glanced up, saw the men standing at the gangway rail.

"Any volunteers?" he called. "The more who help the faster we get there."

"Come on, Hoxie," said Jim. "Let's get the kinks out. Haven't swung an ax for years. How about you, Nollys?"

"Nope," said Nollys, and both Hoxie and Jim turned to look at him. Nollys, the tireless longshoreman, Nollys, who had pulled a big oar along with the seamen in the longboat, now refused to swing an ax.

"It's my back," said the Old Man, lying. "And Lloyd better stay along with me. That green spruce is tough going."

Jim and Hoxie ran down the stairs, laughing, got axes from the hold, and joined the wood party.

After the captain had watched Jim and Hoxie swing their axes for a little while, he began to smile at them. Real men, these two young outsiders; real men!

Jensen was huge, with a big grim red face and thick blond eyebrows. He was proud of his strength and held most men in contempt. As a rule he was taciturn and withdrawn, and it was almost impossible for an outsider to make friends with him.

Later, as Rudy and the stokers got the wood aboard, Jensen slapped Hoxie and Jim on the back. "We're going to get there a lot faster with you fellows along. You been loggers?"

"Cap'n," said Hoxie, "you ain't done nothing till you've rassled with stumps on an Ohio farm. I used to hire out to help clear land and my friend here farmed."

"Well, glad to have you aboard," said Jensen.

Days passed. The big squat white steamboat chugged its way laboriously upstream hour after hour, through low flat country with an almost maddening sameness: mud, tundra, king grass, with here and there immense clumps of spruce. They were well into the river now, with the current growing gradually swifter as they moved northeastward toward the Arctic Circle. The sun hardly seemed to set now and beat down, far into the night, with what seemed like tropic intensity. Swarms of mosquitoes attacked the boat from time to time and yells and curses could be heard from deck to deck. On shore, great clouds of small black gnats surrounded the wood parties, and the men came back cursing, fuming, and slapping at the almost invisible, faintly humming insects.

There was very little to break the monotony. One afternoon they stopped at a small Catholic mission and Jensen bought a huge load of wood from the priests. The place, with its low shacks, looked almost as squalid as the Indian villages that dotted the river banks here and there. On the little beach were huge fish traps and many small Indian canoes. Cabbages and other coarse vegetables were grown here, and Kobo traded some steel fish hooks for a barrowful to garnish the meals of the passengers.

Jim, Hoxie, and the Old Man stood at the railing, watching the activity at the mission.

"Jesus," said Hoxie, "how'd you like to be buried here for life?"

"There are worse places," said the Old Man.

"In hell, maybe."

The *Nils K. Jensen* chugged on, fighting the heavy current. The men played cutthroat seven-up on the gangway and took as much time as possible over their meals in the saloon. Lloyd was generally absent.

"Holed up all the time with that Injun," said Hoxie resentfully. "Don't know how he stands it."

Jim looked at him and laughed. But Hoxie did not even smile, did not even realize that he wasn't making sense when he talked. The unnatural heat of July near the Arctic Circle was getting to him; he felt sweaty from morning till night; and the gnats and mosquitoes drove him to a frenzy; and to make things worse, Kobo's supply of "white whisky" had given out.

Often Jim would see Hoxie standing at the rail alone, looking out at the vast nothingness: mud, tundra, king grass, spruce, repeated over and over and over... and little by little Jim began to realize how apt Hoxie's original summing up had been: they were on a treadmill; the scenery went past, but they were going no place.

One day Hoxie said: "What do you think this is like in the winter?" Then: "Ever figure you'd like to be back in the boardinghouse and this all a dream?"

"No," said Jim.

"Wish I had a girl to hole up with," sighed Hoxie. "Pass the time. Got a notion to grab one out of one of them villages, wash her up good."

Hoxie's moods began to worry Jim. In the past Hoxie had never been one to whine; now he was whining around the clock, sullen, sulky, resentful. Jim consulted the Old Man, who said: "I wouldn't worry. It's this trip. Hard on a man because there's nothing to do. Me, I just rest, but I can't expect young fellows like you to do that. We'll play cards more. I'll think up something."

Jim repeated what Hoxie had said about taking a girl out of one of the villages. "I don't know if he meant it," he added.

"He better not mean it," said the Old Man. "In town it's one thing; out here it's different. The Indian men won't stand for any messing with their womenfolks. They got survival problems and every man, woman, and child has got to do his part and is needed. It ain't a question of what's right and morality and all like that, it's merely a question of how to live twelve months a year in a place like this. Tell him to let the Indians be. Other white men don't like it either, and we got Purdy on board and he's a kind of honorary U.S. deputy marshal, got a badge and all, and can act if necessary. Keep him in line."

"All right," said Jim, who was feeling a certain amount of resentment himself.

Why should he be called on to look after others when he was having his own troubles? The farther the steamboat moved to the northeastward away from St. Michael and the coast, the stronger grew his regrets. Why had he left Seattle and gone on a wild-goose chase like this to the top of the world? He'd had a good job with plenty of chances for promotion; friends; a little money—no regular girl, it was true; but that would have come in time. Now look. He was committed, irrevocably committed. They were already hundreds of miles away from the coast and every hour brought them closer to their destination. Once the steamboat left them behind and started its return journey to St. Michael they were stuck for the year. A year—in terrible country like this!

Jim felt a certain sympathy with Hoxie's ugly moods and at times had a fleeting, perverse desire to let him run wild, just to see what would happen. Hoxie was a boy who could really run wild! Once he got started the thought of consequences never seemed to occur to him. But the idea was insane and Jim suppressed it grimly. No. They were committed. All of them. And they'd just have to make the best of it.

Lloyd and Adorée were sitting on the cabin floor, playing seven-up. They'd had their tea for the day (Lloyd, ashamed of himself, was getting it on promises of future largesse now), and they looked flushed and happy.

Beyond the portholes the nightmare of mud, tundra, king grass, and spruce slid slowly by, unregarded. The boat shook and vibrated with the heavy labor of getting itself upstream against the increasingly strong pressure of the current; the whistle blew shatteringly in the stillness of the river but Lloyd and Adorée played on, noticing nothing beyond their own words, contacts, and glances.

Lloyd would often hold her small warm hand now, but it stayed very still, very unresponsive in his grasp, as if imprisoned against its will but ready for flight. At such times she refused to look at him.

"I won! I won! I won!" cried Adorée, crowing and laughing. She had beautiful little white teeth. Lloyd never tired of looking at them. They were perfectly shaped, except for the canines which were a bit pointed, and in the daylight they had a nacreous shimmer that seemed almost artificial. Did Indians use a toothbrush? But then Adorée was hardly an Indian at all and had probably been taught Anglo ways at the American school or perhaps by Mrs. Brant. Lloyd wanted to ask. He had a devouring curiosity about Adorée and all the trivia of her short life. But

Adorée did not talk about herself very much and Lloyd could not bring himself to question her.

"You are a very good teacher," said Adorée. "Look how I am beating you."

After a while they tired of the game, and Lloyd found an old piece of wrapping paper in the cabin and showed Adorée how to make paper hats and boats and how to cut out paper dolls. Adorée was so delighted with this that she could hardly speak, but kept gasping and laughing.

They played on the floor like children, cutting out paper dolls and talking about nothing, while the boat carried them farther and farther up the massive Yukon.

Jim, Hoxie, and the Old Man were sitting at the gangway with their feet on the rail when the Old Man sighted the moose.

In a quiet voice he said: "Look over there beyond that little hillock. See where the spruce clump is? Just to the right of that, back a little."

Jim saw it at once. Except for the big shovel-like antlers it looked like the kind of horse you might see in a nightmare. "What the hell's that?"

"Moose," said the Old Man.

"Yeah, I see it," said Hoxie indifferently.

"Sure is big," said Jim.

"A dandy," said the Old Man; then: "Look at him take out."

"Boy, can he run," said Jim.

They watched the moose till it disappeared over a slight rise. The Old Man got up and started away. "Where you going, Nollys?" asked Hoxie suspiciously.

"To get the moose gun and the ammunition out of the hold. I'll keep it in the cabin. Next moose we see, we'll get. Best eating in the world. Prime venison."

He left. Hoxie grunted. "That old man," he said. "He's beginning to get on my nerves. He got us into all this. Just think, Jim—if we don't get no gold, after all this! I ain't been so bored since my old man used to make me go to church and I had to listen to them hell-fire sermons. Won't this never end?"

"We're getting along good," said Jim, with an effort. To hell with Hoxie! Let him worry about himself and his boredom. "Lot better than we did on the *Schoonover*. Remember the fog? The ice?"

"Yeah. But I also remember Hansen and Joe. Them was real amusing fellows and we had fun. Now Lloyd's always in fumbling with his Injun—you reckon he's got it by now?—and the Old Man is always "consarving" his strength. As for you, Jim Hardy—hell, you're hardly like the same fellow who set out from Seattle."

Jim began to lose his temper. "And you—Hoxie; I guess you think you're all right. All you do is bellyache, from morning till night. It's the heat. It's the mosquitoes and the gnats. No whisky, no girls. Why don't you just keep your big mouth shut for a while?"

Hoxie turned and stared at Jim in consternation. "You mean that, don't you? You mean it. I can tell."

"You're damned right I mean it," said Jim. "It's all right for you to go around bellyaching and boring everybody to death—but the rest of us, we're different, we're not like we used to be—and maybe it's all just to annoy poor little Hoxie Thicke."

"Come on, Jim," said Hoxie, worried. "Cut it out. I'm sorry."

Jim stared off at the tundra sliding slowly past, his mouth grim, his pale eyes narrowed and bleakly unfriendly. An uneasy silence settled down over them. They sat on, saying nothing, staring at nothing, and now hoping for nothing.

Captain Jensen went past them toward the bridge, cursing. "Matter, Cap?" asked Hoxie.

"It's that goddamned new boiler," yelled Jensen, almost bursting with rage. "Wasn't installed right or something. Can't get up the pressure like the old one could. I told Purdy I didn't need any new boiler; the old one had been getting me there for years, but he wouldn't listen. Meddling, meddling—that's what drives a man crazy!"

He hit the cabin door a terrific wallop with the flat of his hand, then moved round the gangway rail and disappeared. In a moment he reappeared on the bridge and they saw him go into the wheelhouse, muttering to himself.

Hoxie sighed, then laughed sadly. "I guess I ain't the only one riled by this trip."

Jim glanced at Hoxie, then laughed, a single snort. "God," he said finally, "you'd think we were going across Chilkat Pass on snowshoes when all we're doing is sitting on our butts riding a steamboat. Let's cut it out."

Hoxie grinned sheepishly. "Jim, you're right. You're always right. We'll cut it out."

In a little while the Old Man returned carrying the big, heavy-caliber moose gun, and with a bandoleer of ammunition over his shoulder.

"I'll put it just inside the door of my cabin," he said. "Next Mr. Moose we see, we'll get, and feast big."

Days passed, with grinding, almost unbearable monotony, as the *Nils K. Jensen* chugged northeastward toward the Arctic Circle. The sun was up nearly round the clock now, shining bright at midnight, and the interminable days sweltered in a muggy, breathless heat reminiscent of the Midwest in August.

"Never knew how much the night meant till now," groaned Hoxie at eleven o'clock one evening, shading his eyes from the glare of the northern sun and wiping the sweat from his face.

The mosquitoes, coming in great swarms, continued to attack the passengers and crew aboard ship, and the little black gnats made it almost unbearable for the wood parties ashore.

"I say give it back to the Russians," cried Hoxie.

One morning they woke to find themselves hemmed in by hills, which formed a sort of low canyon, forcing the river into a much narrower bed, making the current far more swift.

Jim, Hoxie, and Lloyd stood at the gangway rail staring with a sort of awed unbelief at the hills, while the steamboat labored heavily upstream against the current, heat rising all around them from the over-stoked and heavily taxed boilers.

"Them's the Ramparts," the Old Man explained. "We're getting there. Pretty soon we come out into the Flats, with Fort Yukon just beyond. Then we make the great bend and turn south. Oh, we're getting there, boys."

"How much further?" asked Jim.

"To Forty Mile? Oh, maybe four hundred miles, give or take a few."

Hoxie wiped the sweat from his face and spat tobacco juice over the rail. "We come about fourteen hundred miles up the Yukon already then, eh, Nollys?"

"Yep," said the Old Man. "That's about right."

"How long should it take us to get to Forty Mile?" asked Jim.

"Hard to say exactly," the Old Man replied. "Can't tell about the current, may be weaker south of the bend, may not. Say, four–five days."

Jim brightened and looked at Hoxie, who grinned. "That all?" said Jim. "Why, hell, that's nothing at all."

The Old Man laughed and patted them on the back. "See? Told you I'd get you there. And none of us have had so much as a bad cold."

"Except for Gabe," said Jim.

The Old Man studied Jim's face for a moment before he spoke. "That's right, Jim. Except for Gabe."

Later, Lloyd took the Old Man aside. "Nollys, when do we get to Fort Yukon?"

"Day or so. Can't tell for sure till we get out into the Flats. Sometimes there's a contrary wind, holds you back."

Lloyd made no comment, turned and walked aft. The Old Man watched him go, then shrugged. It was obvious that Lloyd was worried about leaving the little Indian girl at Fort Yukon. And the Old Man knew that something serious might come out of this situation yet. But there was no use to borrow trouble. It was a bridge they'd just have to cross when they got to it.

Cheered that the end of the journey was in sight, as you might say, Jim and Hoxie went to the saloon, drank black coffee, chinned with Kobo, and played seven-up for small stakes.

The Old Man went to his cabin, stripped to his underwear because of the heat, got the moose gun out, dismantled it, and spent the better part of the afternoon cleaning, greasing, and oiling it. Then he patted it affectionately as he put it back in the corner. "Keep you in good shape," he said. "May need you later on in Forty Mile. Beans and sowbelly and sour-dough bread can get right monotonous."

Lloyd wandered disconsolately about the boat, tramping from the upper deck to the hold and back again, then all around the gangway, past Adorée's cabin door, then up the front stairway to the bridge, where he stood for a moment watching Jensen at the wheel, battling the river, with set, grim face, then down again and around the gangway and once more to the hold, where the sweating stokers, looking like demons, were throwing wood into the gaping furnaces, fighting, hour by hour, to keep the boiler pressure from dropping beyond a certain point. The boiler room was like a preview of hell and Lloyd shuddered as he climbed back up to the lower deck....

He hardly knew what to do with himself he felt so agitated, nervous, and depressed. He did not even want to face Adorée for the moment, though he knew she was waiting for him. One more day... and then he must leave her, maybe forever. Distances were so great in this vast, empty country, travel so uncertain, and with the bleak menace of an Arctic winter only a few months away... how could you plan? How could you even hope?

Playtime was over: no more tea and biscuits in the quiet twilight of the little cabin; no more paper hats, and boats, and dolls; no more pleasant talk about nothing; no more Adorée....

He just couldn't stand the thought of it!

Finally he forced himself to go to the cabin. Adorée let him in, then took up her accustomed seat at the end of the bunk, but today Lloyd sat down right beside her and held her hand. She kept her eyes lowered.

"Have you noticed the hills?" he asked.

"Yes."

"We come out into the Yukon Flats pretty soon."

She turned and looked at him, said nothing.

"Then Fort Yukon."

Her hand responded, for the first time, and Lloyd's heart began to pound.

"How far is Forty Mile from Fort Yukon?" she asked finally.

"A few hundred miles. I don't really know."

"That's very far."

"Yes. What will you do in Fort Yukon?"

"Find my parents."

"I know. But after that."

"I don't know."

"Do you suppose I'll ever see you again?"

"Oh yes. You must. I'll always be there. Maybe in the spring you can come down river."

The spring! Months and months—nearly a year—away! "We'll be going back to Seattle in the spring," said Lloyd. "Or at least that is the plan."

"Seattle! I've heard of it. A big city. How far away is it?"

"Thousands of miles," said Lloyd. "Across the Bering Sea and the North Pacific. I don't know how far."

She turned and looked at him. He put his arms around her, his pulses hammering violently.

"Oh, we'll see each other again," said Adorée. "I know we will. We must."

"Yes," said Lloyd. "We must."

And then, somehow, they were in the bunk, lying together, and all that happened afterward seemed so right and natural to Lloyd that it was impossible for him to comprehend—even to remember—all his qualms and fears and difficulties of the past.

He felt a sort of worshipful awe of Adorée. As if by magic, she'd changed him from a nerve-wracked adolescent into something resembling a man. He could hold his head high now, even with Jim and

Hoxie.

They clung to each other in silence, as the steamboat battled its way toward the Arctic Circle through the treacherous currents of the Ramparts, while the Old Man snored in his cabin, and Jim and Hoxie chinned with Kobo in the saloon and shouted and cursed over their penny game of seven-up.

Hoxie ran yelling down the gangway, pounded on the Old Man's cabin door, then banged it back, while Jim stood at the rail, gaping.

"Nollys! Lloyd!" Hoxie shouted. "Come look at this, for the love of God! Come look!"

He joined Jim at the rail. They had reached the Flats and there was no land in sight whatsoever. It was just as if they had returned to the sea and were on their way back to St. Michael. The sun burned in the heavens and the water danced with thousands of diamond points of light. There was nothing in the sprawling immensity of the Flats but river and sky. The steamboat was dwarfed to the size of a toy and its heaving and puffing struggles seemed to be fruitless. How could a small conglomeration of wood and iron conquer this vastness?

"Yep," said the Old Man, scratching his beard. "Gets pretty wide here—maybe up to ten miles."

"Ten miles!" cried Hoxie. "Why, hell, boys, you can put this here stream right up against old Father Mississippi."

"Yep," said the Old Man. "That's right." Then he turned and looked up at the wheelhouse. "Carl's got his hands full right now, with the crosscurrents and all. Good man, Carl."

"Sure is," said Hoxie. "Says nothing, but gets you there. Say, where the hell's Lloyd?"

"Oh, he's about," said the Old Man, quickly dismissing it.

They stood in silence now, staring off across the water. In a moment Hoxie noticed something down to his left and turned: Lloyd and his little Injun girl at the rail in the curve of the stern! Without a word, Hoxie hurried away forward, climbed the stairway to the top deck, then moved back toward the stern.

"Now where'd he go?" asked Jim, irritated.

"Up to get a better look, I guess," said the Old Man; then he clapped Jim on the back. "We're really getting there, boy. Next stop Fort Yukon, then the last leg. We been lucky. No trouble at all."

It was true. No real trouble, except for Gabe. But, after all, there had been days of grinding boredom, fear, and lassitude. Didn't the Old Man count *that*? Apparently not.

Hoxie stood at the stern rail of the upper deck staring down at Lloyd and Adorée. He'd never got a good look at her before and he was startled now at what he saw. "Jesus, what a pretty little girl!" he thought. "A real dolly girl!" She'd left her blanket in the cabin and looked slim and straight in her jacket and her felt pants as she stood at the rail beside Lloyd, looking off at the river in silence.

"It ain't fair," Hoxie mumbled. "It just ain't right him having her to himself all that way up the river—and now she's leaving. Goddamn that hayshaker, Jim Hardy!"

There was no regular way down from the deck except the front stairway, but Hoxie did not want to be seen by Jim and the Old Man so he went to the port side and climbed down hand over hand to the second deck.

He chuckled to himself at the sight of Lloyd's startled face as he joined them. The little Injun glanced up at him, then looked away.

"Hoxie!" said Lloyd. "Where'd you come from?"

"Why don't you introduce me?" asked Hoxie, grinning. "All this time on the boat and I ain't once had the pleasure."

Lloyd's face looked grim and tight. "This is Hoxie Thicke, Adorée."

"Mr. Thicke," murmured Adorée, not looking at him.

"Your servant, ma'am," said Hoxie, grinning. "You'll soon be leaving us, eh?"

"My parents are in Fort Yukon."

"Lloyd ain't going to like leaving you, Adorée, and I can't say I blame him."

Neither Lloyd nor Adorée made any reply. They glanced at each other, then lowered their eyes.

"Hoxie! Hoxie!" It was Jim calling and he sounded as fractious as a bear with a sore head, Hoxie thought.

"Coming, Jim, coming," he called back; then: "Pleased to make your acquaintance, Adorée. Sorry it wasn't sooner."

Jim took Hoxie by the arm and hustled him back down the deck. "Didn't I tell you to let that girl alone?"

"What did I do?" cried Hoxie. "I was polite as all hell even if she is an Injun. I was a real gentleman, Jim. You'd've been proud of me."

"You're not fooling me any."

"I'm not trying to. I was curious, that's all. Just wanted to see what she looked like. Did you see her up close? Boy, is she a pretty dolly girl, hardly a Injun at all, looks kind of Frenchy even—maybe a little dark; not Frenchy like Alberte, though: Berte's a natural blonde...."

He talked on. Jim ignored him. When they got back to the rail, forward, the Old Man asked no questions and made no comment.

Later, Hoxie had a private conversation with Kobo in the saloon.

"You sure about that Mr. Brant business with the girl?" he was asking. "Positive?"

Kobo shrugged and giggled. "Pretty sure. I hear all about from sister, Elka. Lady fire Adorée. Say, get out!"

"How about other men—any you know about?"

Kobo giggled nervously, then shrugged and shook his round, close-cropped head. "No. She pretty young, you know."

"Yeah," said Hoxie. "Well, okay, Kobo. Thanks."

"You like that little Indian girl, eh? You like marry?" asked Kobo, not quite understanding the reason for Hoxie's inquiries. What difference if girl have fun with other men? *All* girl have fun men, like the sun rises and the wind blows!

"You might put it that way, Kobo," said Hoxie, grinning. "Yep, you might."

It was afternoon again, but unless you kept close tab on the passing hours you could not have told it from morning, or from night, for that matter. The steamboat was nearing the Arctic Circle, still fighting the contrary currents of the Flats, which had narrowed considerably during the last few hours.

Lloyd was in the galley, talking with Kobo, who was fixing a special tray for Lloyd to take to Adorée. "She leave boat pretty soon now," Kobo was saying. "I fix—nice. Tea. Biscuit. Sardine. Captain won't miss one can sardine." He glanced hopefully at Lloyd, wondering when the promised largesse was going to put in its appearance; but, after all, there was plenty of time, as Lloyd was bound to Forty Mile—the end of the voyage. Plenty damn time!

He grinned at Lloyd, who had to struggle to make himself meet Kobo's eye. Lloyd was embarrassed and ashamed at the way he'd been tricking the Indian steward, but then... he had no other recourse: Adorée must have her tea!

Jim and the Old Man were sitting at the gangway rail, looking out over the wide, flat waste of waters. Land was visible on both sides of them now, land as flat and featureless and dreary as the rolling tundra they'd passed through on their way from St. Michael to the Ramparts. The sun beat down with a sort of unnatural frenzy and the gangway rail was hot to the touch.

"Mighty near the Arctic Circle now," said the Old Man. "When we get to Fort Yukon we'll be spang on it. Something to tell your grandchildren, Jim."

"Yep," said Jim. "Back on the farm I always wanted to see the Pacific Ocean, and I've seen it, plenty of it. But I never thought I'd be riding a steamboat clear up on the top of the world. Makes a fellow kinda dizzy, thinking about it."

The Old Man nodded and smiled; then he asked: "Where's Hoxie?"

"Down talking with Rudy Kelpak, maybe helping out with the stoking. Hoxie's a strong fellow and he likes to show it off at times. He was the strongest boy in our whole community; and his father was the strongest man, a blacksmith. My father couldn't stand Hoxie. Said his muscles had gone to his head."

Jim bent forward to laugh and at that moment they heard the first scream; it was followed immediately by another and then by such a hullabaloo of yelling, trampling, and crashing that Jim sat frozen for a moment.

"What the tarnation...!" the Old Man began; but before he could finish, Jim had recovered from the shock, had leaped out of his chair, and was down the gangway and around the curve of the stern, out of sight.

The first thing Jim saw was a round tin steward's tray, bent, dented, and empty, rolling about the deck. Beyond it was a mess of smashed crockery and spilled food. Still farther along, Adorée stood in her cabin door with a long knife in her hand, crouched forward slightly, as watchful and wary as a tundra wolf. Lloyd was just getting up from the deck, and Hoxie, with a smear of blood on his left shirt sleeve, was standing over him. Lloyd got to his feet and, with his head down, ran toward Hoxie blindly, trying to butt him in the stomach. Hoxie stepped aside nimbly, tripped Lloyd, then, with a contemptuous shove, sent him sprawling face down twenty feet along the deck.

Adorée saw Jim now and recoiled from the look on his face, which was livid in color and hard as flint. Now Hoxie saw Jim and tried to back away from him along the gangway rail, yelling: "She cut me, Jim. Look at all the blood. *Jim!*"

Then he staggered back from a hard punishing blow on the jaw and pitched forward to his knees as Jim hit him a second time, in the stomach, a blow so hard and resounding that Lloyd, who was just getting up from the deck, winced and looked away.

Hoxie crouched down against the rail, his head lowered, his arms crossed over his stomach.

"I told you to let that girl alone," yelled Jim.

"She invited me in," whined Hoxie. "Swear to God she did."

Jim glanced at the girl. "Did you?"

"Yes," said Adorée. "I thought Mr. Gracey had told him to come because he said he wanted to see Mr. Gracey. I knew he would be back soon. He was just getting our tray."

"Look at that coon-skinning knife, Jim. She cut me with that. If I hadn't throwed my arm up she'd have got me real bad."

"Yes," said Adorée. "I tried to kill you."

"You see, Jim? Real nice little girl."

Jim's face looked pale and implacable. Jensen was above them on the top deck, watching now; and Kobo had appeared from the galley and Rudy Kelpak from the boiler room, but Jim ignored them. "What did he do?"

"He threw me in the bunk and tried to pull my trousers off."

"It's a lie," cried Hoxie. "A damned lie. She's only putting this all on, Jim, because Lloyd come and caught us."

Lloyd darted forward, pale as chalk, and tried to get at Hoxie, but Jim held him back. Then there was a long silence and Jim stood looking from Hoxie to Adorée, his face puckered with thought; and at last he said in a calm voice: "Hoxie, better go let the Old Man look at that arm. It's bleeding quite a lot."

"All right, Jim," said Hoxie, suddenly all docility. "I'll do that. Yes sir, Jim."

He got up and quickly disappeared around the curve of the stern.

"That dirty animal!" cried Lloyd, his face still deathly pale.

Jim looked at Lloyd for a moment in silence, then said: "I don't blame Hoxie entirely. Not entirely. Get her inside and keep her there till we get to Fort Yukon."

Now he turned on his heel and started back for his cabin. Jensen, on the deck above, followed along with him.

"All under control, Jim?"

"Looks like it, Cap."

Jensen threw back his big head and laughed. "Oh, these boys and girls will play. Glad you handled it for me. Though I'm captain, I hate to step in when it's a private matter. Thanks."

Jim found Hoxie sitting in his bunk, with the Old Man beside him, bandaging his arm.

"How bad is it, Nollys?"

"A long, mean cut in the flesh of his forearm. It'll be all right."

Hoxie kept staring at the floor, wouldn't look up at Jim; finally he said: "You shouldn't have hit me like that, Jim. Me, with my arm cut to hell by that little Injun vixen—and I didn't even really see you coming. You took me by surprise, Jim. You sneak-punched me. Now did I ever do anything like that to you?"

"Yes," said Jim.

Hoxie's shoulders began to shake. He was laughing. "Well, Jim," he said, "I've swung and missed before, but I'll be goddamned if I was ever butcher-knifed. That little girl must hold her possum high. Remember what Sadie said about rape? 'Wrong man.'"

"Hoxie! Hold still," said the Old Man, with some impatience. He'd deliberately stayed out of the trouble, feeling that Jim could handle it, but he was worried and knotted inside with anger. In spite of Hoxie's easy laughter and Jim's apparent acceptance of the knifing as an episode that was now concluded and could be forgotten, the Old Man felt certain that they had not heard the last of this business.

"You know what scared me most?" Hoxie said. "Lloyd! Why, he was green in the face and snarling like a mean, cowardly little dog—the kind that gets in behind you and bites you in the calf of the leg. What in hell has that Injun done to Lloyd? What would Lena think? Remember Lena, Jim?"

Kobo and Rudy Kelpak stood side by side in the galley, swaying with the motion of the boat and sipping black coffee from big thick white mugs.

"They crazy?" asked Kobo. "Big fight over little Indian girl. Why not one at time? Where the bother?"

"Oh, them Americans are funny. Some of 'em. I'll be glad to get her off this boat. Women bad luck on boats. Remember her mother, Maria? She was purty, too."

"I remember Maria. Remember Maria's father? Big white-head Swede. Hudson Bay Company. Maria still young yet. Maybe thirty year."

"All the same," said Rudy, "I'll be glad when we get to Fort Yukon."

"There she is, off there," said the Old Man, pointing. "See? That's Fort Yukon. See that side river? It's the Porcupine. Town's right between 'em. Used to be quite a place, headquarters for the Hudson Bay Company in Alaska. Now I hear it ain't so much."

"Hell, Nollys," Hoxie grumbled, "your eyes are better than mine. I can't see nothing. We're too far away."

Jim and Hoxie stood beside the Old Man at the rail, shading their eyes against the sun's glare.

"Look up ahead there—further," said the Old Man, who seemed excited for the first time since the start of the trip. "See all that water? That's the Great Bend of the Yukon, where it turns south. Once we leave Fort Yukon we're on the last lap, boys; the last lap!"

"Damn, I don't see nothing but some old shacks along the shore," said Hoxie. "Just kind of strung out haphazard."

"That's Fort Yukon," cried the Old Man. "That's her!"

"That's Fort Yukon?" cried Hoxie in disgust. "Oh, for God's sake! Don't they have no sure-enough towns in this goddamned country? Looks like Lousetown, back home."

Fiery specks were dancing before Jim's eyes now so he looked away, then turned his back. "That glare on the water's got me," he said. "Not much to see, anyway."

Now the boat changed course and headed in for the shore, and Jensen pulled the whistle cord and there came three long shattering blasts that vibrated along the deck and set the metalwork to buzzing.

Something far down the deck caught Jim's eye: Lloyd and Adorée, holding hands, standing at the rail, looking off toward Fort Yukon. In spite of his irritation with Lloyd, in spite of the Indian girl's savage readiness with the butcher knife, in spite of the fact that Lloyd had selfishly and thoughtlessly put the whole expedition in jeopardy (and with his own help!), Jim felt sorry for them. It was love, no doubt about it. Hoxie could jeer all he pleased. With those two, it was love; and Jim felt a momentary stab of envy. When would he find it? Would he ever? He was tired of loudmouthed, chiseling whores and all they stood for. But what was a man to do?

"I didn't make myself this way," thought Jim. "I'm not responsible for what I need. All I can do is keep it in reasonable check and not run wild like that bull of the pasture, ole Hoxie!"

There were three more blasts on the whistle; then Jensen leaned out the wheelhouse window and yelled down to them: "Don't understand it. Nobody around. There's always a flock of people to meet the boat at Fort Yukon. I don't see anybody, except a few Injuns."

Jim turned and the three of them looked at one another in silence. Another Village of the Dead?

V

TO CIRCLE CITY

But Fort Yukon was not quite a Village of the Dead. It had merely been deserted and was now a ghost town, its sagging frame buildings covered with dust that had blown in from the northern tundra, its streets full of rank weeds, its few windowpanes shattered, its doors swinging loose in the Arctic wind, and an air of almost terrifying desolation hanging over it. Myriad hordes of mosquitoes had taken it over and their humming was like the sound of a distant sawmill.

On the bridge Jensen stared openmouthed as the boat was warped in by Rudy, who'd hurried up from below at the skipper's frantic shout.

"Good Christ!" cried Jensen. "Everybody's gone!"

Half a dozen Indians squatted by a beached canoe and stared at the big white steamboat in an awe mixed with fear. They'd seen it passing for years, back and forth, but they still did not trust it nor comprehend what made it walk so easily on the water.

"Well I'll be damned," said the Old Man, as he noticed Jim and Hoxie looking at him, waiting for him to say something. "Likely they've all lit out for Circle City and the gold strike."

"You figure we're too late?" gasped Hoxie.

"Boys," said the Old Man. "I've told you time and again this ain't the big one. I know Circle. I've prospected it. There's gold, all right; but it's the coarse kind. Poor quality. Cinch up your belts and have a little more patience—just a little bit more—and I'll take you where the *real* gold is."

"Old Man," said Hoxie, "you sure we ain't just chasing the sun like a fox terrier after his tail?"

"I'm sure. Dead sure. You think so, don't you, Jim?"

"Yes," said Jim, and Hoxie groaned, then subsided.

Far down the rail, near the curve of the stern, Lloyd, looking off at the desolation that had once been Fort Yukon, did not know what to say to Adorée. He was so elated that he could hardly contain himself, and yet what a terrible disappointment, what a terrible shock, for her.

"Where could everybody have gone?" he said finally.

"What will I do, Mr. Gracey?" asked Adorée, her face rigidly composed, almost masklike. "What *can* I do?"

"I'll think of something," said Lloyd. "Please don't worry, Adorée."

She turned to him, her anxious eyes becoming soft, docile. "Will you really think of something, Mr. Gracey?"

"Yes," said Lloyd.

Little by little her face lost its masklike quality and then her fingers grasped his and held tight. She said nothing more, but stood looking off at the town as it drew closer and closer to them and the margin of the river narrowed to a mere strip and then to nothing.

Lloyd's heart was pounding. Earlier that morning he'd been resigned to leaving her; it had seemed like the only sensible thing to do. But suddenly the decision had been taken out of his hands by a power over which he had no control. He *couldn't* leave her now, no matter what that entailed. He just could not leave her.

Hoxie was the first one ashore, followed by Jensen, Purdy, the two old sourdoughs, and finally by Kobo and one of the stokers, Alf.

Jim glanced down the rail to where Lloyd and Adorée stood silent; then he said to the Old Man: "Nollys, we've really got a problem now."

"I know, I know," said the Old Man. "Goddamn, I wish he'd never seen that Injun girl."

"We can't just leave her out here, you know."

"Why?" barked the Old Man. "She's Injun. This is her country."

Jim stared at the Old Man in unbelief. He'd noted something different in his manner ever since they'd sighted Fort Yukon across the broad river. "Goddamn, Nollys," said Jim, "for once you're just not thinking straight. She's been to school. She's worked in town. She's a quarter-bred at most. Think she's got much in common with those dirty-looking creatures over there on the beach by that canoe?"

"Jim, Jim," said the Old Man. "It's you ain't thinking straight. We come for gold, remember? We got a hard row to hoe but we can hoe it if we all keep sensible. You going to let a little Injun girl...?"

"We don't leave her," said Jim, interrupting.

The Old Man looked straight into Jim's pale, narrowed eyes and knew at once there was no use to argue with him.

"All right, Jim," he said, sounding just a little like Hoxie. "All right."

Jim leaned on the rail, lost in thought for a moment; then he said: "Circle City ought to be pretty big with all this rush, eh, Nollys?"

"Yep. Ought to be."

"Maybe we can leave her there, find maybe a decent family she can stay with. Goddamn it, Nollys, she's only fifteen."

"Maybe, maybe," said the Old Man dubiously. "But let me tell you something, Jim; you got some pretty silly ideas regarding fifteen-year-old Injun girls. They ain't like fifteen-year-old white girls back home. 'T ain't the same thing at all."

"Maybe not," said Jim. "But I wouldn't leave a dog in this God-forsaken place, Nollys. Not even a dog."

The Old Man said nothing. He needed Jim; he needed him bad. The others were mere supers; he'd always known it. But without Jim he'd never make it. Never for a minute.

They were all ashore now except Lloyd and Adorée, who still stood silently at the rail. A wood party was making the chips fly to the south of the town in a grove of new-growth spruce, while Alf and Kobo were demolishing one of the most ruinous of the shacks and carting the boards off to the steamer in a wheelbarrow.

Shouts arose down one of the streets, and the two old sourdoughs turned the corner, half dragging a big old Anglo with a long white beard.

"Look who we found!" shouted Blaik. "It's ole Bill Messerschmidt."

Bill had made one of the first gold finds in Alaska; had sailed away for Juneau where he had stayed drunk for nearly eight years, then had sailed back, broke but hopeful.

He was immediately surrounded; and Jensen, Purdy, and the sourdoughs all tried to talk to him at once.

"You been living here, Bill?"

"Damn right—and I'm staying. They'll all be back. Me and them dirty Injuns down on the beach are holding the fort."

"Why ain't you in Circle?"

Bill laughed derisively. "That's all bosh," he cried. "False strike. Oh, there's gold all right, but you'll end up working your ass off for wages. Not Bill. When I hit, it'll be for millions. I ain't aiming to swing a pick no more for beans. Circle is a mirage. They'll all be back."

"How long you been here, Bill?"

"In and out, for two years. Was a right nice place. Had everything. Fresh meat. Women. Booze. What more could a man want? Now look at it! Nothing left but mosquitoes and Injuns—and ole Bill."

Hoxie groaned and said to Jim: "Here's where Hansen told me I'd find white whores. I don't even see a Injun woman. Maybe Circle City's deserted, too, by now. Maybe the whole damned place is deserted. Maybe there ain't no gold. Maybe there ain't no nothing. Maybe that damned old Nollys Harp is as loony as that white-whiskered old coot over there."

Hoxie's words sent a frightening suspicion across Jim's mind, but he dismissed it at once after a glance at the Old Man, who was listening to Bill Messerschmidt on the edge of the group. No! Whatever Nollys was—and Jim had begun to wonder—he was not loony!

Finally he took the Old Man aside. "Nollys, that Messerschmidt fellow says he's been here for two years off and on. Maybe he might know something about the girl's parents."

"He might at that," said the Old Man, looking sideways at Jim and scratching his whiskers. "Soon as these other fellows here talk him out, we'll see. You better go get her. She ought to ask the questions."

Old Bill kept chewing tobacco and spitting, as Adorée talked to him, with Lloyd, the Old Man, and Jim looking on. Cursing, in a fearful humor, Hoxie had joined the wood party at the south of town and was now taking out his spite on innocent spruce saplings, the chips flying, and the sound of his ax ringing all along the river's edge.

"Yep, yep," old Bill was saying. "Frenchy Belleau and his breed wife—very pretty woman. They were here, left, though, quite a while ago. Long before all these idiots galloped out of here. Let me think. Goddamn, I'm getting old; getting so can't remember anything except where I keep my liquor and tobacco." Bill slapped his thigh and roared; then: "Yep. Yep. Oh hell; I got it. Sure. They went to Circle. Frenchy got a job there, working for the A. C. Company. Don't know what. Sure. They're in Circle. Got there well before the rush, too. That's it. I remember talking to Frenchy now. Went upstream in a big Injun canoe. Frenchy's pretty handy with a paddle if you remember. Been over many a portage, Frenchy!"

Now he looked at Adorée as if seeing her for the first time. "So you're Frenchy's kid. Maria's, too. I can see both of 'em in you, honey. Yes, I can. You're a real pretty girl, but not so pretty as your mama. No, not so pretty as her. She's got them Swedish looks, strong—a real woman. You're kinda on the puny side, honey, like your pap, Frenchy. Sure, sure, I knew 'em, sure, sure... so you're Frenchy's kid. Sure, I knew 'em...."

Once he got started, they couldn't turn him off. Finally Jensen came and dragged him away to the boat for some sardines and crackers.

"Sardines and crackers!" shouted Bill. "Why, by God, you fellows live like rajahs in St. Michael. Just like rajahs!"

Adorée and Lloyd neither looked at each other nor spoke, but they were both thinking the same thing and both were happy. Circle City was a hundred miles upstream; they might make it in twenty-four hours, but this was very unlikely because of the current. Yet even a mere twenty-four hours was better than nothing, far better!

A little later they were back at the railing, holding hands in silence and looking down at the formerly prosperous Alaskan town of Fort Yukon, now abandoned to mosquitoes, a handful of Indians, and old Bill Messerschmidt.

"What are you looking at, Nollys?" asked Jim.

"Them two," said the Old Man, jerking his head toward the silent pair at the rail.

"It's going to work out all right," said Jim. "She'll find her parents in Circle City and that will be that."

"I hope so, Jim," said the Old Man. "I hope so."

Old Bill Messerschmidt, stuffed with crackers, sardines, ship's biscuits, and black coffee, stood on the little shelving beach, towering over the short, squat Indians surrounding him, and waved his hat in a series of wild, frantic good-bys as the *Nils K. Jensen* angled out into the middle of the glittering big river and headed south, upstream, for Circle City.

At the rail Jim and Hoxie looked out at the Great Bend with awe, while the Old Man smoked his pipe tranquilly beside them, smiling to himself from time to time.

"Jesus, some river," said Hoxie. "Look how she sweeps around. Say, ain't this boat pitching a little?"

"Yep," said the Old Man. "She'll bump a bit till we get clear round the bend. Currents're all mixed up here. How'd you like to try it in a canoe?"

Overhead there was a tinkling of bells and hollering; then Jensen came out of the wheelhouse, fuming and cursing, and stamped up and down.

"Matter, Cap?" Hoxie called up to him.

"It's that goddamn new boiler!" yelled Jensen, almost purple in the face. "Slow to get the pressure up; can't hold it; fast to let it go. I wish to God I had my old boiler." He shaded his eyes and studied the currents swirling around the steep shelving banks of the Great Bend. "Once we get past Circle the current comes down powerful on us. Ain't going to be no picnic getting to Forty Mile with this damned boiler. Got to get her looked at in Circle."

He went back into the wheelhouse where Purdy, the A.G. official, had been spelling him at the wheel.

Lloyd and Adorée were standing at the stern rail on the gangway. Beyond them a huge wake was fanning out from the laboring steamboat, and from time to time the jarring slap of the huge paddle wheel shook the deck under their feet. They noticed this vaguely, also the tinkling of bells and the hollering of Jensen on the bridge. Vaguely they saw what had once been Fort Yukon, headquarters for the Hudson Bay Trading Company in Alaska, disappearing astern, across an immense gap of uneasy swirling water; vaguely they noted that Bill Messerschmidt and the Indians were now mere dots in the vastness of tundra and river.

Everything outside themselves had a vagueness, a sort of unreality. They stood, holding hands, silent, happy, but worried about the future. Only too soon Circle City would loom up on the bank. The steamboat, slow but inexorable, and in spite of Jensen's pessimism and the new boiler's deficiencies, would get them there at last.

Finally Lloyd spoke. "Circle City must be pretty big now, with all the people rushing in."

"Yes," said Adorée.

"Maybe your father has a good job."

"He's had many good jobs. He never stays. All he talks about is going back to White Horse. That's where he came from."

"Where is White Horse?"

"I don't know. Somewhere in Canada. He came to Alaska from Canada many years ago."

There was a long pause; then Lloyd asked: "Do you think you will be happy in Circle City with your parents?"

Adorée glanced at him, but said nothing. Suddenly her fingers grasped his, hard. They avoided looking at each other, and, without speaking, side by side, hand in hand, they disappeared into Adorée's cabin.

Later Lloyd went to the galley to get Adorée's tea. Kobo was asleep, with his head on one side and his mouth wide open, dead to the world. Not wanting to disturb him, Lloyd started to get the tea for himself, but Kobo woke with a start.

"Tea?" he said. "No tea. All gone—except for little I save for captain. Yesterday captain say, 'Kobo, you red bastard, where all my tea?' Sorry. No more tea."

But this was impossible! Adorée just had to have her tea. She looked forward to it like a child. And like a child anticipating a treat, she would be dreadfully disappointed.

"No tea," said Kobo. He had finally decided that the soft-spoken, polite, gentlemanly Anglo with his kind eyes and his silky red beard had been "taking" him. This irritated Kobo considerably and embarrassed him, too. He, Kobo, was the exploiter, not these careless, easy-to-fool Anglos. It wasn't right, him being "taken." In fact, Kobo's feelings were a little hurt.

Suddenly Lloyd remembered the lucky piece he'd been carrying for years—a silver French franc that had been given to him by an old retired seaman the first day Lloyd had gone to work at the lumber company on the docks. But should he let it go? Since he'd carried it his luck had been reasonably good. He'd had no serious illness; he'd met Jim and Hoxie—though in the case of Hoxie that had turned out to be a dubious benefit; but above all, he'd found Adorée. Would it break his luck if he let go of this lucky piece in order to give Adorée a little pleasure? What better use could he put it to? It might even increase his luck to pass the coin along to Kobo for a reason so unselfish.

He took it from his pocket and held it in the palm of his hand. "See this? A French franc—silver; my lucky piece. It came to America all the way across the Atlantic Ocean from Marseilles, France. Give us tea till the boat gets to Circle City and it's yours."

Lloyd always kept the coin shining like new. At the moment it glittered in his palm in the sunbeams coming in through the porthole. Kobo's little slanted black eyes showed greed—silver cash money!—and all the way from some country of the Anglos far across the eastern sea! But Kobo veiled his eyes and looked away. Another trick. He'd give the tea but then would never get the coin.

But at that moment Lloyd reached out and put the coin into his little thick fat hand. Kobo's eyes lit up at the pleasant feel of the smooth, hard metal.

"Captain maybe kick my butt," said Kobo, grinning, "but, okay—I find little tea for you."

So Adorée had her daily tea as usual and she was so childishly happy about it that Lloyd felt very proud of himself and of his new-found ingenuity. He was learning to depend on his own resources. He was learning to stand on his own feet. And it was all the work of Adorée; she alone was responsible.

The Old Man was sitting in the wheelhouse with Captain Jensen, looking out over the vast reaches of the powerful, roily, treacherous

Yukon, Father of Northern Waters.

"Little better here," said Jensen, his huge knotted hands grasping the wheel, his blue eyes narrowed and staring vigilantly straight ahead, "since we made the bend. I don't think we'll have any trouble before Circle, but after that the water really piles up and smashes at you. I've seen it when you had to have the engines quarter speed ahead to stay tied up to the bank. There'd be nothing to it, really, though, if it wasn't for that goddamned boiler Purdy made me put in. He ain't saying nothing now, you can bet. He's been spelling me lately and he knows. Why is it, Old Man, you can never tell anybody anything? They always have to learn the hard way."

The Old Man laughed. "Been wondering that for years, Captain. Yep. Never found the answer."

There was a brief silence as the boat jolted slightly and tried to twist its bow toward the shore. Jensen threw the wheel over with a curse, then said: "Feel that? It's rough. But I got all new steering equipment put in this old bottom. It's the only worry I had, till along comes that blasted company official...." He broke off with a derisive grunt, then after a moment said: "That red-bearded partner of yours—he's got all the makings of a squaw man, if you don't mind me saying so."

"Oh, I don't mind. But I wish he'd never seen that pretty little Injun girl."

"You know about her?"

"Well, I've heard a few things," said the Old Man warily.

"Too goddamned pretty for up here," said Jensen. "Mother was, too. Lots of trouble over Maria till she married Frenchy Belleau; then they let her alone. Frenchy'd cut your heart out and show it to you. Made me laugh when the girl took a whack at your partner, Blackbeard. Just like Frenchy."

"There was some trouble, I believe, in St. Michael," said the Old Man, offering Jensen the lead.

"Trouble! The way I heard it the old lady caught Niles Brant cold with the little Injun. And Niles is fifty years old—ought to be ashamed of himself. Can't say I blame the girl much. Only a kid, you might say. Niles is a big man around St. Michael. What he says goes—except for the old lady." Jensen threw his big head back and laughed. "One day I saw her hit him with an umbrella. It was damned embarrassing but funny." Suddenly he turned: "Look over there. Moose! Two of 'em."

The Old Man whirled, then got to his feet.

"Gone already! Look at 'em go." Jensen jerked the whistle cord and a shattering blast shook the boat, and the sound bounded and rebounded across the river, confusing the moose for a moment. They stopped stock-still, threw up their heads to sniff the wind; then they were off again like shots from a cannon, one behind the other.

"Damn," said the Old Man. "I was figuring I might get myself a moose. But the gun's in the cabin."

"Sorry, Old Man," said Jensen, "but I ain't stopping for no moose in this current. They're pretty thick beyond Circle to Forty Mile. Game's scarce around Circle with all them people hollering and carrying on. What do you think about the strike, all them people leaving Fort Yukon?"

"There's gold around Circle, but it's not for us. We're pushing on as planned."

Jensen turned and glanced at the Old Man. "Don't you figure to have a little trouble with them young partners of yours?"

"How do you mean?"

"Once they get to Circle—all that excitement and liquor and whores and such. The two big ones, anyway. The little one's a mooncalf and he's already got his heifer."

"With Hoxie, maybe," said the Old Man, tight-lipped. "But Jim can handle him. Now the little one I ain't so sure about."

"That so? I'd think he'd be the easiest."

"No," said the Old Man. "Him, I'm not sure about."

Jim and Hoxie sat with their chairs tipped back and their feet on the gangway rail, looking off across the river. They were in their shirt sleeves, and sweating. The Arctic sun burned down with its unexpected frenzy, and heat rose from the deck because of the laboring boilers. Mosquitoes dived at them occasionally with a high, thin humming, and they slapped and cursed and kicked.

"If anybody had told me," Hoxie began, then broke off. "Aw, the hell with it."

"Know what you mean," said Jim. "Summer sun, mosquitoes, heat— on the Arctic Circle. Don't make sense."

"Nothing makes sense up here. And Nollys—he's getting so he don't make sense either. What's eating that old man?"

"How do you mean?"

"He's changed. He's got a different look in his eyes. At times it's almost like he was a stranger. Bothers me."

"He's anxious to get to that gold, Hoxie. That's why we made this damned long trek, and we're getting close."

"Yeah," said Hoxie. "Circle City's round the corner with a gold strike and we're going on into the goddamned woods, for what? On that old bastard's say-so. You like that?"

"He's been right so far," said Jim.

"I don't know," said Hoxie dubiously. "These old coots, they all seem a little crazy to me up here. Look at Blaik and Dogett. Won't pass the time of day with a man even. And how about Bill Messerschmidt! He's a historic character, like, up here. And, hell, he's nothing but a damned old drunken bum! He took gold out, too, Jim. Now look at him,"

"Hoxie, we can't call the turn up here. We just don't know. Look. We made an agreement. We stick to it. Very simple."

Hoxie groaned and sighed, then cursed wildly as a mosquito got him in the back of the neck. "Look at the blood, for Christ's sake!" he yelled, showing his hand where he'd killed the mosquito with a slap. "Must be the granddaddy of all of 'em. Full of blood as a Buckwheat Creek leech." Then he sighed, shifted uneasily, and wiped the sweat from his face. "Buckwheat Creek! I see it in my dreams sometimes, Jim. Nightmares, I mean. I never drowned that girl like some people said, Jim. I was just sore and careless. You believe me, don't you, Jim?"

"Yes," said Jim. "I believe you, Hoxie."

Lloyd had climbed to the bridge and stood looking off across the river. He wanted to talk to Jensen, but the captain stared straight ahead in the wheelhouse, ignoring him. Lloyd had hardly exchanged half a dozen words with Jensen during the trip. He had the feeling that Jensen did not like him, did not approve of him at all.

Ordinarily Lloyd would have stalled around for a little while, then gone away. But this had to do with Adorée and he wasn't going to be put off. Steeling himself to a rebuff, he moved over to the wheelhouse and spoke to Jensen through the open window.

"Captain?"

Jensen stared straight ahead, his lips set. "Yep?"

"May I ask you an important question?"

"Can't stop you, can I?"

Jensen's tone was unfriendly. Lloyd swallowed hard, then asked: "Will you tell me where White Horse is?"

"*White Horse!*" Jensen was so surprised that he took his eyes off the river momentarily to glance at Lloyd. "Why, hell, it's more than five hundred miles south of Circle, maybe further; in Canada, north of

Chilkat Pass, in the Lakes country."

"Is it hard to get there?"

"For you—son—impossible."

"But for an experienced Alaskan?"

"Let me say this," said Jensen. "I'd hate to try it myself."

"Is it on the Yukon?"

"No. It's about fifty miles west of the headwaters of the Yukon, near a big lake; in the portage country."

"Thank you, Captain," said Lloyd politely.

Jensen turned again to look at him. "And if you're thinking about trying to go there—forget it, unless you want to leave your bones up here."

"Oh, I was just curious. Thank you."

He got away as quickly as he could, sweating and nervous; but all was calmness and peace and rightness once he got back to Adorée's cabin. She was sitting cross-legged on the floor, mending one of her moccasins with a big bone needle and a piece of thong.

He sat down beside her and as she worked he explained all about White Horse and where it was.

"Yes," said Adorée. "I remember him talking about the Lakes. Make portage, he said. Only he called it 'por*tahje*'—like in French. They carry the little canoes on their backs from lake to lake; and they have rollers for the big ones. Oh yes, I remember now."

She looked up at Lloyd and smiled happily. And he felt proud of himself and very pleased that he'd been able to find out for her about her father's birthplace. But there was something else at the back of his mind that he would hardly acknowledge to himself. Supposing her parents had gone to White Horse, Frenchy's former home. It was five hundred miles away across an almost impenetrable wilderness, according to Jensen. There would be no way for Adorée to reach them. She'd be alone—and his sole responsibility.

Such thoughts made him feel guilty and he tried to dismiss them. Adorée must find her parents. She needed them badly.

"This is more like it," said Hoxie as they left their cabins and walked aft toward the saloon.

There was a high, thick mist over the river, blotting out the sun, a touch of pleasant coolness in the air, and no mosquitoes.

"Oh, the interior ain't so bad," said the Old Man, "once you get used to it."

As they turned in at the saloon door, Lloyd left them and went on down the deck.

"Has to see his Injun," grumbled Hoxie. "Well, we'll soon be shut of her. Say, Nollys, tell me this—how much time does he spend in his cabin at night—or whatever they call it up here?"

"Don't know," said the Old Man. "Been sleeping like the dead on this voyage—ten–twelve hours at a clip."

Hoxie put his arm across Jim's shoulders, patted him. "Country boy, did you ever think we'd be in a place where it's all topsy-turvy like this and you can't tell night from day?"

"No," said Jim.

The saloon was empty. Purdy, Blaik, and Dogett had eaten earlier and Kobo was in the galley. They sat down at the table and lit their pipes.

"Doggone, that there mist looks good," said Hoxie, stretching luxuriously. "Feel almost like a new man. That goddamn Midnight Sun, or whatever you call it, blistered my neck yesterday. How about a guy getting a sunstroke at eleven in the evening? Jensen says it's happened."

"Stock Alaska joke," said the Old Man. "First one I heard when I got here in the eighties."

"You make this same trip then, Nollys?"

"Yep."

"About the same?"

"Tougher then. Fort Yukon was a big place. Lot of changes. More spruce along the river then; more game; more Injuns. Hell, I must've seen fifty moose on that trip, maybe a hundred. Ain't seen but three this time."

"Have they been killing 'em off?"

"No. It's all this noise and ruckus and steamboats and hoosiers coming in. The game's just backed off to the empty country. Plenty of it, God knows; plenty water, plenty grass in the summer. Fifty more years you won't know this country. You boys may live to see it. I won't."

Kobo came in, yawning and stretching.

"Oh. You here. You like breakfast?"

"How about some Java right away?" said Hoxie.

"Sure, sure," said Kobo, but first he proudly displayed his French franc lucky piece. "From way across eastern sea in faraway Anglo country Maysay."

"That's from France," said the Old Man. "I've had pocketfuls of 'em."

"You been to France, Nollys?" asked Jim, surprised.

"Once. Another fellow and I jumped ship in Marseilles...."

Kobo interrupted quickly. "That's right. Coin come from Maysay...."

"That's in France, Kobo," said the Old Man. "This was over forty years ago, you understand, in the days of sail. Chris and me saw the rats leaving the ship in the harbor, so we jumped, too. Later we was thrown in jail by the gendarmes. The ship sailed without us. Hit a storm. Sank off the Canaries, sixty miles from the west coast of Africa. *Elias Marcus*, it was called, out of Corpus Christi. Only time I ever sailed the Atlantic; that, and when I went back on a French boat to New Orleans."

"You've been around, haven't you, Nollys?" said Jim, looking at the Old Man curiously, as if he'd just met him.

"Yep, Jim. I've been around."

Hoxie examined the coin, then made as if to put it into his pocket. Kobo reacted in horror, stiffening, his eyes bulging, but saying nothing. Blackbeard was so big an Anglo, with forearms like the stoker's—Alf! "Oh," said Hoxie, "excuse me. This is yours, isn't it, Kobo?"

Hoxie roared at the look on Kobo's face, then gave him back the coin.

"Where'd you get that French coin?"

Kobo giggled and winked. "From Redbeard."

All three men looked at him. He did not understand the look and began to wilt. But Jim laughed, reassuring him.

"Never know about Lloyd," Jim said to the Old Man. "Didn't even know he had a coin like that."

"It was for tea," said Kobo. "Every day tea for pretty breed girl, Adorée."

"Well, I hope he's getting what he's paying for," said Hoxie. "But, knowing Lloyd, I doubt it."

"You never know," said the Old Man; then he sat shaking his head for a moment as Kobo, carefully pocketing his magic lucky piece from Maysay—a great treasure!—hurried off to get the coffee.

"Don't look at me," said Hoxie to the Old Man. "All Jim's fault. He give him some of his own personal money so he could bring the girl along. More than he'd do for me."

"You're a liar," said Jim, with sudden heat. "If it hadn't been for me you wouldn't be here either."

Hoxie had forgotten; it seemed so long ago now. He ducked his head in embarrassment and avoided the Old Man's probing gray eyes. "It's true," said Hoxie sadly. "It's true, Nollys; Jim loaned me nearly three hundred dollars so's I could pay my share."

"Yes," said Jim, "and I've been paying whores since we left Seattle."

"Only a few times, Jim," said Hoxie. "Just two or three times."

"Then shut up your mouth about me helping Lloyd."

"I was only kidding, Jim," said Hoxie contritely, "just kidding."

The Old Man looked from one to the other, but made no comment.

The sun was breaking through the mist now, and Jensen noticed a shadow lying across the bridge and turned to see who was making it; then he grunted irritatedly to himself. Little Redbeard again: Barbarossa!

"Can I ask you another question, Captain?"

Jensen nodded curtly.

"How soon do you think we'll be in Circle City?"

"If the current don't get any worse—and I'm sure surprised it's not stronger—in about two–three hours."

Lloyd was staggered, but tried not to show it. Where had the time gone?

"Thank you, Captain."

Jensen merely nodded, kept his eye on the river.

Depressed, apprehensive, Lloyd stood at the upper railing for a while, looking off at the shore, which was sliding slowly past: empty, featureless, dreary—mud, tundra, king grass, spruce, just as before. Nearly eighteen hundred miles of identical landscape—except for the Ramparts, hills as featureless and dreary as all the rest of this God-forsaken lost world of the Alaskan interior.

"Oh God! Why did I come?" he asked himself, aloud.

Adorée's parents would be at Circle City, and he would have to leave her there and go on up the dreary big river with Hoxie, Jim, and the Old Man to look for gold and spend the long dark dismal winter, like a benighted Eskimo, in snow and ice, all of them jammed into one log hut they'd have to build.

"I couldn't stand it," he told himself. "I just couldn't stand it. Not without Adorée."

And taking her was of course utterly impossible, the idea alone preposterous, nearly insane.

Adorée was sitting at her end of the bunk—at first, at least, it had been her end of the bunk—waiting for him. She looked up, read his face immediately, then lowered her eyes.

"Should I get my things together?"

"In a little while."

"How long have we got?"

"Maybe three hours."

"So soon? Seems like we just left Fort Yukon—but that was early yesterday morning."

"Yes," said Lloyd.

"I don't know where the time has gone to."

Lloyd sat down on the bunk and put his arm around her. She reached up and held his hand on her shoulder, patting it.

"I'll never forget you, Mr. Gracey. I never met anybody like you. Those friends of yours—they are just like all the other white men I've seen. But not you."

There was a long pause; then Lloyd said: "Sometimes I wish we'd stayed in St. Michael. I could have got a job there with the company."

Adorée looked at him quickly, then lowered her eyes. "The company is also at Circle City, and the town is larger than St. Michael now, I'm sure."

"But you'll find your parents, Adorée, and everything will be all right—and I'll go on and look for gold, and then maybe in the spring...."

"Yes," said Adorée. "In the spring. I'll wait. I'll be there."

Sometime later Adorée began to gather up her meager possessions and pack them into the canvas bag. Lloyd did not even have the energy left to help her. He felt terribly tired and depressed and as if he'd like to lie down and sleep forever.

Why did this have to happen? It couldn't happen. It just couldn't. Lloyd raised his head to say something, then lowered it again, with a long internal groan. Things were too complicated. The opposition would be too powerful for him—first the Old Man, then Jim. He'd never be able to stand up to them, and there wasn't the slightest chance in the world that they'd return his money to him. Why, the Old Man wouldn't even advance him eighty dollars back in St. Michael! Now they were getting close to the gold country the Old Man had told them about; Forty Mile was only a few days upstream... no, it was all over. He was going to lose Adorée, and in this vast unpredictable country it was unlikely that he'd ever see her again....

> *Swing low, sweet chariot,*
> *Coming for to carry me home....*

Hoxie had a deep baritone voice, and after a shot or two of "white whisky" from a bottle Kobo had managed to wangle out of old Bill Messerschmidt he was showing it off in the saloon for the benefit of Kobo and Alf, who were deeply impressed.

"Hey, you sing pretty good," said Alf, when Hoxie had concluded.

"*Pretty* good!" cried Hoxie. "I sing *great*. What do you say we finish that bottle, Kobo?"

Kobo shrank back. "Cost me pretty much in trade. Lots stuff."

"Yeah," said Hoxie, laughing. "But whose stuff? The company's."

"Sure," said Kobo. "But it's all in a little book. Maybe I get fired."

"Kinda late to think about that, ain't it? Tell you what. I'll borrow some money from my pal, Jim—and stake you to a drunk in Circle City."

Always these Anglo promises, almost always forgotten or repudiated.

"Aw, come on," cried Alf. "Don't be a killjoy."

So they finished the bottle of white liquid that was strong enough to take the varnish off a table or jolt a mule. Kobo fell down on the floor and slept—had it been like that in the Village of the Dead, Hoxie wondered? But Alf was of sterner stuff; he managed to stay in his chair, but he kept looking cross-eyed at Hoxie, who roared with laughter at such weaklings and whooped and yelled so vociferously that Jensen came and put his head in the door; then at last Jim arrived and dragged Hoxie away, singing a bawdy song at the top of his lungs.

His loud, robust voice penetrated Adorée's cabin and Lloyd shrank slightly. Adorée raised her head to listen, but made no comment as the obscenities poured out.

Jim shoved Hoxie into the cabin and then tossed him into the bunk like a sack of meal.

"Damn, you're strong, hayshaker," cried Hoxie. "It's pitching all that wheat—takes a man with a back of iron. That's you, Jim, old iron back."

"What a beaut you've got!"

"Aw, this is nothing. Wait till I get to Circle City where there's whores and excitement."

"On whose money?"

"On yours, damn your eyes, Jim Hardy—on yours!"

"Shut up, and go to sleep."

"Call me early, mother," Hoxie shouted after Jim; "I'm to be Queen of the May."

Jim burst out laughing in spite of himself.

It was late in the morning of the twentieth of July, 1896, as the *Nils K. Jensen*, laboring hard against the swirling current, edged its way closer and closer to Circle City on the west bank of the Upper Yukon. Although the town was not yet in sight there were already signs of unusual activity for this empty country.

Jim and the Old Man stood at the gangway rail, forward; Lloyd and Adorée at the stern rail, while Hoxie snored in his bunk in drunken sleep, dead to the world.

Groups of Indians moved southward along the west bank toward Circle City—men, women, and children, with their possessions packed on travois that were being pulled by huge, wolfish-looking dogs. Many canoes were in the river, pulling for Circle City, with here and there a big clumsy rowboat, manned by bearded Anglos. Jensen tooted the whistle from time to time; the Indians screamed and waved a welcome from the bank, and on the river paddles and oars were raised in greeting.

Jim noticed that the Old Man's lined, heavily tanned face was flushed with excitement. He grasped Jim's arm with surprising strength. "Luck's with us, Jim," he said, grinning. "We've struck it just right. Every fool in the country will be headed for Circle now, and we'll have the creeks of Forty Mile to ourselves. They'll get wages, maybe a little dust to take away home; we'll get rich. You hear me, Jim? Rich!"

"You been right so far, Nollys," said Jim, infected little by little by a restless, feverish feeling that was hard to resist.

"You know what it means to be rich, boy, and not beholden to any man, for work or help?" cried the Old Man excitedly. "You got no worries, Jim; no worries. Gold in the bank. Sleep like a baby at night; wake smiling. Best hotels, best liquor, best everything. Your own man, Jim—taking nothing from nobody, neither help nor abuse. By next spring we'll be rich; all of us; rich, Jim. Pretty word, ain't it?"

It was a Nollys that was unknown to Jim, and he turned and studied the Old Man curiously. "You never talked like this before, Nollys," he said. "In fact, you've hardly talked at all about the gold."

"We had a long hard way to go, Jim," cried the Old Man. "It was not the time to talk about it. It would have made you young fellows impatient. But now we're almost there. Nothing to it. In less than a week we'll be prospecting them gold creeks of Forty Mile. You'll see gold in the pan'll shock you, Jim, it'll be so rich. It's in the sand of the creeks, in under the moss of the tundra. You could take it out with a sieve or a tablespoon in some places. You listen to me. I was a fool to leave when I did. I could have had my own railroad by now."

Such talk made Jim a little uneasy and he remembered old Bill Messerschmidt and what Hoxie had said about him. He studied the Old Man narrowly, noting the twitching of the creased, sunken cheeks, the glitter of the pale eyes, the grim, satisfied set of the wide mouth. This wasn't patient, quiet old Nollys at all. This was another man altogether, a kind of visionary fanatic, maybe; far from reassuring.

"You certain you know what you're talking about, Nollys?" asked Jim bluntly.

The Old Man gave him an odd look. "You beginning to doubt me now, Jim? It's a little late for that, ain't it?"

Jim turned away and stared off over the glistening big river. Yes, it was a little late for that. Well over a month late; maybe three thousand miles late.

Jensen was yelling at them from the bridge, waving for them to come up. Purdy was at the wheel spelling him. Jensen was showing unusual excitement himself, and when Jim and the Old Man had joined him he pointed off toward the south and cried: "Look at that."

Circle City was still a long ways off, hardly more than a misty blur on the horizon, but from various points of the western half of the compass groups of people, mere specks on the vast tundra, were converging on it, while to the south canoes and clumsy rowboats dotted the bosom of the big river.

"First one I ever saw like this," cried Jensen. "Where in the hell are they coming from? And what are they going to eat?"

"That's a good point, Jim," cried the Old Man. "You hear that? These fools are going to end up working for wages—if they average out ten, fifteen dollars a day, they'll be lucky—and what are they going to eat? The river freezes over before October. They'll be caught like rats in a trap. But not us, Jim. We'll be snug in our cabin with plenty of food and firewood, and practically alone in Forty Mile, with all the creeks open to us. See? See?"

Jim was beginning to see.

Lloyd and Adorée stood at the rail, looking on unresponsively. Indians waved from canoes, bearded Anglos from rowboats. They merely stared.

"I didn't think there would be this many people," said Adorée, shrinking slightly.

The steamboat was nearing the town, which was spread out unbelievably along the low bank of the river; thrown-up shacks, clapboard stores and saloons, big log houses and huts, and to the south, surrounding the log stockade of the American Commercial Company, was an Anglo tent city, the white canvas giving off a blinding glare in the Arctic sun. Farther to the south, along the river bank, was a sprawling Indian settlement, with rounded, skin and mud wickiups and smoke rising from the cooking fires.

A steady hum of activity went up from the town: men yelled, metal triangles were struck, saws screeched, hammers thudded, and there was a continual trampling through the muddy thoroughfares.

Adorée stared in awe and fear at the largest collection of human beings she'd ever seen in her short life.

"Is Seattle as big as this, Mr. Gracey?" she asked.

"Much, much bigger," said Lloyd. "Forty times as big."

Adorée stared at him in unbelief. "But how could it be? Where do all the people come from? How do they know where to go?"

Lloyd took her hand and they stood staring now in silence at Circle City, metropolis of the North Country, while the *Nils K. Jensen* changed course and headed for the west bank, its whistle shattering the air from time to time. Canoes bobbled precariously in its big, fanned-out wake; bearded Anglos, in plaid or red flannel shirts, stood up and gestured wildly, almost upsetting their boats.

A sort of triumphant frenzy seized Circle City as the first steamboat of the year sheered in for a landing.

Jim couldn't wake Hoxie. He yelled at him, shook him, pounded him on the back; finally, swearing with impatience and irritation, he grabbed him by the ankles and flung him out of his bunk. Hoxie fell hard, then lay groaning and blinking for a moment. At last he sat up with a start.

"What's all that noise?" he cried; then he hit the side of his head just above the ear with the heel of his hand, as a bather does to get the water out. "Jim, boy, that white liquor of Kobo's was bad stuff, bad raw unaged stuff. I'm hearing things. My ears are buzzing so it sounds like a lot of people yelling and talking. Jim, I'm in a bad way. Do something."

Jim stood looking down at him, laughing. "We're in Circle," he said. "And is she roaring!"

Hoxie stared in blank unbelief, then ran to the porthole and looked out. "Oh God," he yelled. "Women! I see women! White ones, whores a-dancing out there. Hey, look. A guy with a cornet. Hear him a-playing." Hoxie began to sing and caper.

> *Waltz me around again, Willie,*
> *Around, around, around.*
> *The music is dreamy*
> *As peaches and creamy—*
> *Oh, don't let my feet touch the ground....*

He ran out on deck, yelling at the top of his voice. Jim followed him, laughing and shaking his head.

Lloyd and Adorée stood frozen at the stern rail, looking off in dismay at the wild hilarity and excitement of the hordes of Circle City.

"Can't we wait to get off?" asked Adorée, clutching her canvas bag.

"Yes," said Lloyd

They went back to her cabin.

"Here I am, girls!" shouted Hoxie, waving his arms from the bridge. "Ole Hoxie Thicke, a country boy from Ohio—but don't let that fool you—there's no hay in my collar, no green in my eyes, and I'm dry behind the ears."

He was answered by loud laughter and shouts of greeting. A man in a red shirt appeared with a bass drum and began to beat it fiercely in time with the strains of "Waltz Me Around Again, Willie," as played by the cornet, the gold of which glinted in the Arctic sun and cast wavering reflections over the deck and across the faces of Jensen, Hoxie, Jim, and the Old Man. Purdy and the two old sourdoughs had already landed and were trying, with poor success, to get away from the greeters and go on about their business.

A group of big bearded Anglos, headed by Shag Galloway, chairman of the Miners' Protective Association, and virtual boss of Circle City, came aboard and dragged Hoxie, Jim, and the Old Man ashore. Jensen begged off. "Got to get the boiler looked at. Have to work on it round the clock. Want to be out of here by tomorrow afternoon at the latest. You fellows go on ahead. Enjoy yourselves."

Shag Galloway was six feet eight, and as wide as two average men. He had a bristling brown beard, salted with gray, a big bulbous nose, and small yellowish close-set eyes. There was no formal law and order in Circle City; no peace officers, no police. They weren't needed. Shag and his committee policed the town and administered a kind of rough justice. They were very lenient in regard to drinking, whoring, gambling, and fighting. But two things they were adamant about. All white women, or breed and Indian women for that matter, deserving of respect, should be shown respect—no exceptions. Stealing, of any kind, was taboo and severely dealt with. A man who stole another's supplies was hanged out of hand; the same applied to the stealing of gold dust. Petty thievery, except by Indians (it was tacitly expected of them and often overlooked), was punished by enforced exile or sometimes by what was called in Circle City "a good lacerating." The man "lacerated" seldom stole again.

"Where to?" cried Hoxie.

"Why, to the Walrus, boys. The Walrus!" yelled Shag. "Women, liquor, everything: we even got a piano and a girl who can play it; Indian girl at that. Learned in the mission way down the river. Hip, hip, and a buzz saw!"

The other miners gave the "buzz saw"—a loud ripping screech that was hard on the ears. This delighted Hoxie. After a few abortive tries he got the idea and shortly was pronounced "one of the greatest and loudest fellows at the 'buzz saw' on the Upper Yukon."

To Jim's surprise the Old Man joined in with a will.

"You going along, Nollys?" cried Hoxie.

"Yep," said the Old Man. "I've conserved my strength long enough. I'm ready. Might even take a roll with a woman, if it comes to that."

"Oh, it'll come to that all right," cried Hoxie. "You can bet your bottom dollar!"

All at once Hoxie grew thoughtful and took Jim aside. "Jim, boy, I ain't got a penny, not a sou. You ain't going to embarrass me in front of our new friends, now are you, Jim? I got to have a little spending money."

Jim, almost as exhilarated as the others, made no protest, unpinned his "personal" money from the inside of his shirt, and handed Hoxie a good-sized bill. Hoxie's eyes popped; then he hugged Jim and danced him about, in spite of his laughing struggles. "That's my boy," cried Hoxie. "My Clark County boy!"

The miners surrounded them once more and hustled and half dragged them off toward the rambling, clapboard building known as the Walrus: dance hall, saloon, gambling hall, brothel—the center of Circle City's social activity.

Hoxie stopped suddenly. "Where the hell is Lloyd and his little Injun?" he cried. "Ain't seen hide nor hair of 'em."

Jim shoved him forward. "Mind your own business. Plenty of ready women here by the looks of things."

"Oh, I wasn't thinking about *that*," said Hoxie. "I was just curious, Jim. Just curious."

As they went through the door into the Walrus, Jim, to his surprise, noticed that the Old Man was capering as agilely as if he were twenty-three instead of sixty-three, and it struck him, all at once, that he did not know Nollys Harp at all, not at all. He kept eying him.

In the cabin aboard the *Nils K. Jensen* Lloyd and Adorée stood in silence with their arms around each other. Hot sunlight flooded in through the porthole, one long thick golden beam in which motes danced in fantastic patterns.

Little by little Lloyd noticed that the hubbub outside had died to nothing. It had to be done. It just had to be done.

"Adorée," he said, bending back to look into her veiled, dark eyes, "I think we'd better...."

She looked at him, then slowly turned away, said nothing, and reached down to pick up her bag. Lloyd tried to take it from her, but she said: "No, Mr. Gracey. It's not right for you to carry it. It embarrasses me."

But Lloyd took it anyway. "I want you to stop feeling like that," he said. "It's wrong."

"For you, maybe," said Adorée. "But with others, no; and you'll soon be gone."

Lloyd struggled hard to keep from bursting into tears. Adorée's face showed nothing, but it had assumed that noncommittal, Indian-like quality—with its suggestion of a mask—that Lloyd had come to understand meant that she was deeply stirred in one way or another. He remembered her slashing at Hoxie; he remembered her on deck as they neared Fort Yukon and at other times when she'd been under a strain—always the mask, the shield held up before the world.

They left the cabin and walked down the gangway together for the last time. The crowd had deserted the steamboat and had moved back uptown. They heard the cornet playing shrilly some place off among the buildings. Employees of the A. C. Company, most of them breeds, were unloading cargo from the hold, at times using a jerry-built winch made of ropes and wooden tackle that screeched and groaned as if it might give way at any moment. Loud hammering and curses came from the boiler room.

They started up the steep, shelving, muddy road that led to the town, which lay before them, an immense cluster of shacks and log houses, dominated by the American Commercial Company's stockade. Big whitish and bluish-gray dogs loafed through the streets with the slanted eyes and oblique gait of tundra wolves. Indians were everywhere, squatting against the buildings and looking on at all this Anglo activity with awed, bewildered eyes. In the Old Days there had been nothing: just tundra and Father River and a few scattered Indian villages: now *this!*

New shacks and log houses were being put up all along the streets, with huge men, bare to the waist and sweating heavily in the scorching sun, swinging axes and sledge hammers, crouching over saws and augers, and from time to time turning to spit long streams of tobacco juice over their shoulders.

"I think we'd better inquire at the stockade," said Lloyd, looking straight ahead.

"Yes," said Adorée.

They found the streets thronged by whiskered men in plaid, red, or blue shirts and heavy woolen or corduroy trousers held up by violently colored suspenders. They all chewed tobacco, they all spat about them promiscuously, and many of them turned to stare at the pretty little breed girl, with her beaded jacket and her thick, chopped-off black hair, ignoring her red-bearded escort, who seemed at a superficial glance to be one of them.

Some place the cornet was playing "Sweet Rosie O'Grady," and from farther on came the metallic hammering of an out-of-tune piano, banging out "Waltz Me Around Again, Willie," the tunes and the sounds clashing in an ugly musical battle, setting Lloyd's teeth on edge. Far down a wide street they saw men pouring in and out of a big rambling frame building whose weather-stained and battered sign read:

THE WALRUS
LAFE WEED SOLE PROP.

Occasionally they saw a white woman with high-piled hair, carefully picking her way through the hordes of men. These women were all wearing cotton, summery dresses, pinched in at the waist and with ballooned out leg-of-mutton sleeves. Adorée eyed them surreptitiously, noting their style and their manner. In the past she had tried to model herself on such women, but since the fiasco in the cabin, when Lloyd had shown such marked distaste at seeing her dressed "white lady style," she felt confused about the matter, although she still secretly yearned to be like them, with a corset—such as Mrs. Brant had worn—little pointed-toe shoes, and maybe even a parasol and a hat with a bluebird on it or a bunch of artificial flowers.

The huge gate at the stockade was never used any more. It stood wide open now and was tied back against the palisades with heavy rope. The courtyard was thronged with crowds of both Anglos and Indians coming and going. Now and then the men stood aside to allow a dog-drawn travois to pass as an Indian brought in a load of hides. The general store at the far eastern end of the courtyard was jammed and there was a long queue waiting to buy supplies. Men crossed through the throng carrying big boxes filled with canned goods on their backs, staggering from the weight. Two hunters came bumping through the crowd, lugging a partly flayed moose carcass to sell to the A. C. Company where there was always a good market for fresh meat.

Lloyd and Adorée were pushed about and trod on as they tried to make their way toward the general offices. Finally they managed to get to the far edge of the crowd along a little walk or trail just inside the towering palisade wall. At the far end they ran upon Kobo, who stopped and grinned.

"How do," he said, ducking his head in a bow. "Pretty big crowd. Biggest ever see. Pretty exciting."

"Yes," said Lloyd. "Is that the general office there?"

"Yes," said Kobo. "Pretty busy there. No time to talk. I try to talk, they make me go." Kobo threw back his head and giggled.

"Who is the man in charge?"

"Boss? Mr. Baker. But he busy with Mr. Purdy. Very lot business. What you want?"

"To find Adorée's father. He works for A.C. here."

"Come. I take," said Kobo; then he gestured for them to follow him, guiding them skillfully past a crowd of men who seemed to think they had business in the general offices, but could not get into the front door because of the press, then around the edge of the log building, down a little passageway hemmed in by the wall and the tall palisades, and at last to a huge porch at the back where half a dozen breeds, stripped to the waist, were sorting a big pile of hides of all sizes and descriptions.

"Pete," called Kobo.

A small, dark-faced older man glanced at Kobo, then showed marked irritation. "Go 'way, Kobo, I'm busy."

But Kobo was not so easily discouraged. "Pete, gentleman here from steamboat. Passenger. You talk with him one minute?"

Pete wiped his filthy hands on his makeshift apron of sacking, then turned. He ran his eyes over Adorée, peered at her carefully, frowning slightly, then asked: "Don't I know you? Wasn't you a kid in St. Michael?"

"Yes," said Adorée.

"My God," cried Pete, "that's been only five years ago—and look at you!" He seemed overwhelmed and kept surveying Adorée from head to foot.

Kobo grinned at Lloyd and Adorée. "I go now; very busy."

Lloyd thanked him profusely, still feeling guilty about the tricks he'd played on him in order to get Adorée's tea.

"See you tomorrow," called Kobo, as he moved away, "when boat sail."

Adorée's hand reached out suddenly and took Lloyd's. Her fingers clung. But she kept her eyes lowered, said nothing; yet Lloyd understood only too well. Anguish stabbed him. It couldn't be. It just couldn't be.

"This is Adorée Belleau," said Lloyd, his lips feeling stiff and tight. "She's looking for her parents. Her father works here for A.C., we understand."

"You Frenchy's daughter?" asked Pete, his expression changing in a marked but unreadable manner.

"Yes. That's right," said Adorée, still clinging to Lloyd's hand, her eyes still lowered.

Pete looked about him momentarily, as if for help; then he said: "Frenchy's not here any more. Gone."

Adorée looked up quickly, her expression as unreadable as Pete's. "Gone? Where?"

"Don't know for sure," said Pete. "But I heard he was heading back for White Horse."

Lloyd's heart began to beat unevenly. Was his dream coming true then? But what about Adorée's mother? Had she remained in Circle City? He could not bring himself to ask.

"And has my mother gone, too?" Adorée inquired, squeezing Lloyd's fingers hard.

Pete shifted uncomfortably. "No," he said, "she...." He broke off and looked at Lloyd. "Could I... uh...." He gestured to indicate that he wanted to speak to Lloyd alone.

They moved a few feet away from Adorée and Pete said: "This is rough. Just couldn't tell her. Maria's dead, buried over there beyond the stockade in the Old Burying Ground."

Lloyd suddenly felt cold as ice. It had all come true; not as he hoped, of course, as it would be impossible for him to wish anyone dead; but in fate's own way. Now fear stabbed at him. He saw the struggle ahead all too clearly. Was he equal to it? Could they force him to leave Adorée at Circle City and go on into the wilderness with them? How? And did he have guts enough to remain behind, thrown on his own resources in this wild, remote, unpredictable country? He was positive that the Old Man would not return his money to him. He'd made a bargain. He'd be held to it.

"What happened to Adorée's mother?" asked Lloyd.

Pete squirmed. "Nobody's sure. She got stabbed, died. Some men think Frenchy did it. But Mr. Shag—the boss—did not. So Frenchy left for White Horse. Nothing to keep him in Alaska. Never would have stayed at all except for Maria. We all liked Frenchy. I don't think he done it."

"I can't tell her this," said Lloyd. "I'll think up something."

"Yes. Sure," said Pete. "That's why I talked to you personal. Now I got to get back. They loaf if I don't keep my eye on 'em."

Lloyd thanked Pete at length and shook hands with him; then Pete returned to his work. Lloyd, so mixed in his thinking and in his emotions for the moment that he felt incapable of facing Adorée, hesitated for a long time and stood lost in thought. All at once he felt a hand on his arm and started.

"My mother," said Adorée. "She's dead, isn't she?"

Lloyd turned and looked at her, noting that her face showed nothing; neither was it masklike; this he could not comprehend at all. "Yes," he said. "She... passed on."

Adorée's eyes now showed some vague, mysterious emotion, but it did not look like grief to Lloyd. "Passed on," said Adorée; she'd never heard the phrase before and liked it. "Yes. Passed on. It's like what the Indians say. Gone away—to where the game is plentiful and there are no enemies. My mother has passed on."

Lloyd was pleased that he had used the genteel American phrase. To him it had always sounded silly. If a man was dead, he was dead; it was the phrase of undertakers and preachers. He'd used it merely out of awkward nervousness, but it seemed to give some comfort to Adorée, and that was the important thing.

He explained where her mother had been buried and asked Adorée if she wanted to go there now. Adorée said that she did.

They circled the rear, or eastern, palisades of the stockade and finally found the little cemetery on a hillock above the river. It was poorly tended and rank with weeds, but some effort had been made to keep it from returning completely to the nothingness of tundra. A low wall of small stones gathered from the margin of the river had been built around the roughly rectangular burying ground; and inside were a few irregular rows of wooden grave markers, all leaning out of plumb, all battered and weathered, a few completely illegible. It was a country of transients; here it was easy to die, be buried, and forgotten in a very short space of time.

They found Adorée's mother's grave marker at once. It was the newest, the least battered, the straightest. It read:

Maria Svendtsen Balo
1863-1896
R.I.P.

It seemed odd to Lloyd that the difficult Swedish name had been correctly spelled while the comparatively easy French one had not.

Adorée stood looking down at her mother's grave, her face showing nothing. Finally she spoke as if to herself: "She never loved me. He loved me more than she, but not very much."

Lloyd, who had extremely conventional ideas regarding the family, was deeply shocked. "Adorée! Why do you say that?"

His tone puzzled her. It seemed to her to have more than a hint of disapproval. She turned and looked at him. "They left me," she said. "They went away and left me. I was only ten years old. They never cared for anything except each other. I was an accident."

"Adorée!"

"That's what my aunt told me. She said my mother told her I was an accident."

"I don't believe it." He tried to keep the outrage from his voice.

"Why do you speak like that? Are you angry with me?" She couldn't understand it.

"You shouldn't believe things like that."

"But I do. It's true. They never wanted me. I was a burden. My father liked to keep moving about; and my mother wanted to be with *him*, not *me*."

"We can't always do what we want."

"*They* did."

Lloyd sighed, took Adorée by the arm, and they walked slowly back along the eastern side of the palisades, toward town.

"What will we do?" asked Adorée.

"I don't know yet," said Lloyd.

Adorée showed a quick flash of dismay, then veiled it. "But you're not going to...."

"No," said Lloyd. "I'm staying. But I... I've got to work it out."

But how? How?

Adorée grabbed his hand and held on tightly. They said nothing more as they walked slowly back toward the outlandish uproar of the new metropolis of the Yukon.

Lloyd took her back to the steamboat. As they were getting aboard, Jensen looked out at them from the hold, then climbed up to the gangway. His face was dirty, and his shirt was soaked with sweat and covered with big grease spots. He looked ready to bite nails.

"What's she doing back aboard?" he asked, his blue eyes cold and unsympathetic.

"I just want her to wait here for a short time while I make some inquiries in town," Lloyd explained.

"No," said Jensen. "This ain't no hotel. I carried her from Fort Yukon to Circle City for free and that's enough."

Adorée turned away, her face showing nothing, and started to get off the boat, but Lloyd reached out and stopped her. Jensen did not like him, did not approve of him, and he was well aware of it, and inwardly he felt himself shrinking away from a clash, but Jensen's contemptuous attitude in regard to Adorée angered him, and, steeling himself, he said: "She can stay in my cabin. I'm a passenger and I've paid my way to Forty Mile."

Jensen's big face turned red under the grime and he took a step toward Lloyd, but checked himself. Hell, Jim, Hoxie, and the Old Man were friends of his. Why take a chance on alienating them merely for the satisfaction of kicking this squaw man, this *klutchmon* lover, off his boat? Besides, Jensen was fair-minded enough to realize that he was not really mad at Lloyd and the breed girl at all, but at the new boiler which at the moment was stubbornly resisting all efforts to readjust it.

"All right," he said angrily; then he disappeared back into the hold.

"Should I?" asked Adorée.

"Of course," said Lloyd. "We've got every right to use my cabin."

"But if Mr. Harp should come back while you're away...."

"He won't."

They climbed to the gangway and went round the deck forward, Lloyd carrying the canvas sack.

"When I was about nine," said Adorée, "Captain Jensen gave me a little rubber ball and a handful of jacks. I guess he's forgotten."

"Yes," said Lloyd. "I guess he has."

As at St. Michael, Lloyd wandered disconsolately through the town. But here it was different, very different. He was bumped, pushed, trod on; not in malice, but merely out of wild, heedless excitement. Men kept arriving from north, south, and east, some with heavy packs of supplies on their backs, some empty-handed, but all with a kind of feverish hope showing in their eyes.

Earlier Lloyd had located Jim, Hoxie, and the Old Man. They were at a table in the Walrus with a bottle before them, watching the girls cavort on a little low stage at the far end of the bar. The uproar was tremendous, with big whiskered men jammed every place, and the hammering of the out-of-tune piano just barely audible. But the squealing of the girls in tights on the stage could be heard plainly as they flung themselves about in a clumsy dance, the sole object of which was to display various parts of their anatomy.

Lloyd had even made a move to join his partners, then had changed his mind. He'd be questioned regarding Adorée, that was sure. And how could he talk about this very serious matter in the midst of the wild uproar of the Walrus? No, he'd have to bide his time. The boat did not sail till the next afternoon.

So Lloyd wandered about through the thronged, muddy streets of Circle City, lost in thought, seeing little, hardly feeling the bumps and pushes. Regrets for the past, fears for the future plagued him. What would he say to Jim and the Old Man? How would he begin? From a rational standpoint he had no case at all. They'd laugh at him, hold him up to ridicule. If the Old Man was right about the gold, he was proposing heedlessly to throw away a fortune—for what? Why, for a little breed girl and the unsavory role of squaw man.

At least that is the way it would look to Jim and the Old Man. And how could he make it look otherwise? How could he explain to them, so they would understand, that he owed a great debt of gratitude to Adorée? That she'd changed him from a feebly fumbling boy to a man?

Hopeless! They'd laugh at him all the harder, remembering the old joke: "Ma, now I am a man." They'd explain to him, no doubt, that it happened to every young male eventually. That it was not a unique experience in any sense, and that he was making too much of it.

Reason definitely would be on their side. But actually, as Lloyd was well aware, reason had nothing to do with it whatsoever. Could reason explain the flash of beauty that was his first glimpse of Adorée? Could reason explain why it was that other women were mere shadows to him, that he was hardly aware of their existence? (The plump, shapely, half-naked girls cavorting on the stage at the Walrus had meant no more to him than the jam of whiskered men watching them.) Could reason explain why it was that he knew deep in his heart he'd rather die than never see Adorée again?

They waited hour after hour in the cabin for Jim, Hoxie, and the Old Man to return and finally it got so late that Lloyd took Adorée to her own cabin and made her go to bed. She was nervous about it.

"But Captain Jensen said...."

"Never mind about him," said Lloyd. "Lock your door and sleep."

"What are you going to do?"

"I'm going to talk to them."

"No matter what they say..." she began, then broke off.

"That's right," said Lloyd. "No matter what they say, I'm staying."

He returned to his own cabin and sat on the lower bunk, with the door open, waiting. The boat was silent now, accentuating the loudness of the vague, confused medley of sounds rising from the town. Against his will he finally dozed, his head falling forward on his chest....

"Well... Lloyd! What are you doing sitting there like that?"

Lloyd woke with a start. The overhead lamp had been lighted. The porthole showed grayish, as a sort of brief twilight fell outside. It was nearly three in the morning.

The Old Man kept looking at him curiously.

"What is it, Lloyd?"

"I want to talk to you. Where's Jim and Hoxie?"

"Jim's still at the Walrus, pretty drunk, for the first time since I've known him. He's got hold of a redheaded girl from Cincinnati, Ohio, he likes. Them Ohioans are sure clannish. What difference if a whore's from Ohio or Timbuktu? A whore's a whore."

The Old Man seemed to be a little bit drunk, too, and Lloyd noticed how he put out a hand to steady himself as he sat down at the other end of the bunk.

"Hoxie has disappeared," said the Old Man. "Went off with that Shag fellow and some of the miners. Don't know where. You talk to me, Lloyd. I'm the soberest one of the three."

The Old Man's gray eyes, steady and cold in spite of the liquor he'd drunk, probed at Lloyd's face, and Lloyd swallowed hard, then explained haltingly what had happened to Adorée's parents.

"Too bad," said the Old Man, but offered no further comment, deliberately making it as tough for him as possible, Lloyd was sure—a wily, shrewd, conniving old man, not at all what Lloyd had thought him in those first exciting days of planning.

Lloyd hesitated, stopped for the moment. But this cat-and-mouse business went against his grain, and finally, with his heart pounding and sweat starting from his forehead, he burst out: "I'm staying here with her. I want my money."

The Old Man's face showed no reaction. He cleared his throat and crossed his legs. Then: "Well, Lloyd, you know as well as I do that this is a partnership. Why talk to me? You've got to talk to all of us at once. It's no good this way. I ain't got the say."

"You know damned well you have," cried Lloyd heatedly.

"No! No, I haven't," said the Old Man mildly. "Tell you what. We'll sleep on it, take ourselves a little siesta, as they say down in Mexico. You ever been to Mexico, Lloyd? Enseñada—that's the place. Bluest water I ever see; whitest sands...."

Lloyd leaped to his feet, hot with anger, and yelled: "Nollys, you can shut up about Mexico. You're not going to get me off the subject that way. I want all my money."

The Old Man turned sideways now and lay down in the bunk, his feet in the spot Lloyd had just vacated. "Getting old," he sighed. "Should've stayed aboard. No more carousing for me. That was the last. Lloyd, get up in your bunk. Make yourself comfortable. When the boys get back, we'll talk this over."

Lloyd had a sudden, almost uncontrollable impulse to jump on the Old Man and start pounding him; this was followed by another impulse to rush out on deck and over the side into the water—and so make an end. He felt so frustrated that he almost burst into tears and stood, hardly knowing what he was doing, wringing his hands.

"Come on now, Lloyd," said the Old Man. "It ain't that bad. They should be back in an hour or two. Get in your bunk."

With a cry, Lloyd rushed out the door, banged it behind him, then took up his place at the gangway rail, to wait for Jim and Hoxie to come back aboard.

"I'll stand right here if it takes hours," he told himself, struggling with his desire to break down and cry. "I'm going to stay in Circle. They can't stop me."

Hoxie came back to the Walrus alone and found Jim still sitting at the table, with his arm around the redheaded girl from Cincinnati. Her name was Nina and she had the best shape in Circle City, a fat, cute face and an impudent turned-up nose. Hoxie pulled up a chair.

"Hi," he said. "Hi, Red. Jim, I got to talk to you pretty soon."

"Go 'way," said Nina. "Let my boy alone."

"For God's sake," cried Hoxie, "ain't you got him wrung yet? Jim, boy, they ought to put you out to stud."

"Shut up. It ain't that," said Nina. "We're friends."

"Oh sure," said Hoxie. "Friends—for how much a roll in the hay?"

"Shut up, Hoxie," said Jim wearily.

Hoxie subsided and sat nervously drumming on the table.

"We're just the same age," said Nina. "I was born in Hamilton and he was born in Roxabelle—not so far apart."

"Do tell," said Hoxie.

"Yes," said Nina.

"Well, I was born in Roxabelle, too," said Hoxie, "or near by. So what's so wonderful about that?"

"You're the first Ohio boys I've met up here," said Nina. "Christ, we're a long ways from home, ain't we?"

"Yep," said Hoxie. "But I ain't figuring to go any further. This here town suits me."

Jim gave Hoxie a surprised look, but was distracted by Nina, who flung her arms around his neck and began to nibble at his ear lobe.

"You hear that, honey?" she cried. "Blackbeard stays; you stay. Find lots of gold and we'll ship out for Juneau. That's a civilized place, for the love of God, and close to the States, with plenty boats coming in. I been there—I know. What do you say, honey?"

"Yeah, yeah," cried Hoxie. "That's the talk. We stay here in a real sure-enough town where we can have some fun." Then: "Jim—look— I got to talk to you. It's serious."

Jim patted Nina on the back, kissed her on the cheek, then disentangled himself. "Got to go, Nina. Back aboard. See you tomorrow."

"Boat leaves in the afternoon, I hear," said Nina. "Don't desert me, pet. Ohioans ought to stick together in this Godforsaken place. Talk to him, Blackbeard. Talk to him."

They went outside into a sort of grayish-blue twilight. It wasn't really night at all, but like a bright day that had unaccountably clouded over and would soon be clear again.

"You got a real girl there," said Hoxie, as they walked along the street.

Jim snorted a laugh. "*I* got. Listen, they tell me on Saturday night there's a line a block long waiting to get in the Walrus at the girls."

"Well, you could take her out of there, set her up; let her keep house for us. She's my idea of a real girly-girl. Course the two I had ain't to be sneezed at either."

Jim pushed him hard and Hoxie, surprised, staggered and almost fell. "Are you crazy?" cried Jim. "What are you talking about? Keep house? In the woods?"

"Woods? No, goddamn it. Right here in Circle. Hell, this is some place! Got everything. Two more boats coming in, maybe three before the season's over. A tug from St. Lawrence and a small A.T.T. steamer from St. Michael, I think—touches here, anyway. If we don't like it, we get out. And it's just a breeze going downstream. Engine quarter speed just to steady the boat. Boy, you really ramble."

"Shut up," said Jim, pushing him again. Jim felt drunk and was fighting it, as he always did: no staggering and silliness, no asinine antics for him. A man ought to be able to hold his liquor!

"Jim, let's stop—let's sit down some place. I got to talk to you."

"What about?" Jim asked wearily.

"About Nollys. About where we're headed for. About a lot of things, very important."

Shrugging, Jim allowed Hoxie to lead him down a side street to a pile of logs that were stacked in front of a half-built cabin. They sat down.

"Boy, you've had a busy day. Don't go to sleep on me."

"I'm wide awake," said Jim, yawning.

Hoxie put his arm across Jim's shoulder and shook him gently from time to time as he talked. "Listen, Jim. I spent hours with Shag. He's the big man here. He wants us to stay, says he'll show us where we can stake some good claims. Says Forty Mile is played out. It's been left, Jim. And that's where we're headed for. Shag says old Nollys is living in the past. Just because he took out thirty-five thousand in the eighties don't mean he can do it again, Shag says. And if he does, we don't get rich splitting it four ways. You listening? I want to stay here, Jim. Women, liquor, everything. Shag says our claims wouldn't be more than a mile or two away. We'd have some place to go in the winter, Jim. You'd have Nina—fun. We wouldn't be living like Eskimos—for God's sake—at the tail end of no place. You listening?"

"I'm listening."

"Shag ought to know what he's talking about. He's boss here and he's been in from the first. Right?"

"The Old Man knows, too," said Jim. "He's been right about everything every step of the way. No, Hoxie. Think we ought to stick to our bargain."

Hoxie groaned and sat staring down at his feet. What he did not know was that Jim was tempted, strongly tempted to stay in Circle. He was very tired of the wilderness, of the nothingness of mud, tundra, king grass, and spruce. And there was Nina, who suited him right down to the ground. And, as Hoxie had pointed out, more steamers were coming in. A man could change his mind and get out in time before the bitter bleak northern winter closed down, and the river froze solid, and the world lived in a sort of twilight, with hardly any sun at all, and a man was powerless to leave, no matter what his true feelings were—held, against his will, in a vast prison of ice and snow and howling gales, for months.

Jim felt himself falling asleep and got abruptly to his feet. "Let's get aboard. I'm unraveling," he said.

As they moved toward the boat, Hoxie kept talking and explaining and prodding Jim to stay. And Jim kept shaking his head and trying to brush away Hoxie's arguments. And yet… didn't it all make sense? Was it wise now to follow the Old Man blindly into the wilderness?

As they went aboard, Jim staggered and Hoxie looked at him in amazement. Jim—*staggering?!* He'd never seen him do it before. A little disturbed, Hoxie put his arm around Jim and helped him up the gangway stairs.

"Don't talk… any more," Jim mumbled. "I can't hear you. I'm sleeping."

Lloyd stepped out to intercept them, but Hoxie brushed him roughly aside. "What's the idea? Get out of the way. I got to get Jim into his bunk. He's out on his feet."

Lloyd was so surprised that he stopped stock-still and stared. Jim? *That* drunk? Finally he moved over to the cabin door in time to see Hoxie pitch Jim into the lower bunk as if he were a sack of meal. Jim groaned, then began to snore. The overhead light was lit. Hoxie turned and saw Lloyd watching him and grinned.

"Tit for tat," said Hoxie, "though it's the first chance I've ever got. That's the way old Jim boy tosses me in. Say, Lloyd; I'd like to talk to you."

"I want to talk to everybody," said Lloyd.

"I don't care about that. But you can't talk to Jim now, maybe not for hours, so you listen to me. Okay?"

He shut the cabin door quietly behind him and stepped out onto the gangway with Lloyd.

"It's like this," said Hoxie. "I'm for staying in Circle City, and maybe I can talk Jim around. You want to listen to me for a minute, Lloyd?"

Lloyd stared at him in unbelief. After all his worries and fears, was it going to be this easy? "Yes, Hoxie. I'll be glad to listen."

So Hoxie went over all of his arguments and explanations again, at great length, and Lloyd listened in silence, hardly able to believe his ears. Hoxie was giving him the perfect excuse to stay, and an excuse that had nothing whatever to do with Adorée. But aside from that—aside from Adorée and everything else—Hoxie was making very good sense (and shouldn't Shag Galloway know all about these things?)—and if they could win Jim over, then it was three against one—and bargain or no bargain, the Old Man would have to give in.

Now Hoxie slapped Lloyd on the back, knocking him forward. "What do you say, boy? What do you say?"

"I think you're right, Hoxie," said Lloyd, really meaning it. "And I'm with you."

"Good," cried Hoxie. "No damned wilderness for us. We'll stay close to Circle, at our ease, and we'll get our gold anyway, and in the spring we'll be long gone down the river and on the way home."

Lloyd made no comment about the last part of the plan. It was useless for his purposes, but all right for Jim and Hoxie. How could he take Adorée home with him? People in Seattle would not understand. And as for his... *family*...! But otherwise he was delighted with the plan, and delighted with Hoxie, who was not such a bad fellow after all. Lloyd felt as if suddenly a heavy burden had been lifted from his back. Hope, like a healing tonic, seemed to be running through all of his veins. He wanted to hurry off and tell Adorée the good news at once, but after a brief hesitation he decided against it. He'd have to be sure first, absolutely sure, with everything set.

He happened to glance toward his own cabin. The door was open a few inches and the Old Man was looking at them. The door closed.

"What's the matter, Lloyd?" asked Hoxie.

Lloyd explained, then said: "Do you suppose he heard us?"

"Maybe," said Hoxie indifferently. "He'll have to hear sooner or later. But no use to talk to him now. Wait till we get Jim on our side for certain."

"There's a good chance?"

"You bet. First thing, he's just about as tired of that open country as I am. God, what a place! Second thing, he's found him a redheaded girl—a real warm number—in Circle. Pretty nice for the long winter. Third place, he must figure Shag Galloway knows what he's talking about, or why would all the miners of this here community make him head man? You think they're going to make some stupid bum, some windbag, head man?"

Lloyd stood listening and nodding. Sounded good. Sounded great!

It was late in the morning. The cargo consigned to Circle City had all been taken off the boat, and the cargo consigned from Circle City to Forty Mile, the end of the voyage, had all been put aboard; the boiler had been readjusted, and the *Nils K. Jensen* was almost ready to continue its laborious way upstream against the ever-increasing current. The only thing that remained to be done was the stowing away of the immense pile of wood the wood parties had cut and gathered along the bank south of town; it was partly driftwood, partly green spruce. Rudy Kelpak, Alf, Creeb, and a group of breeds from the A. C. Company were at work now, getting it aboard.

Beams of sunlight were pouring in through the portholes of the cabin, as the Old Man, sitting on the lower bunk with his head down, heard them out. Time passed. First Hoxie talked, then Jim. Lloyd made no contribution whatever. He'd already talked to the Old Man about staying, but for another reason, and felt that anything he said would have little weight now.

Finally Hoxie and Jim were talked out. The Old Man had said nothing from start to finish. Now he stirred, got up, and began to pace.

"You for this, Jim?" he asked.

"Yes, Nollys," said Jim. "I think it makes good sense. A bird in hand, you know."

"Hm," said the Old Man. "Boys, I'd like to remind you of something. Remember Gabe Windhorn? I told him not to sleep in them jerry-built

quarters. He wouldn't listen. Later, you, Hoxie, said: 'Nollys, I'm going to listen to you from now on.' Remember?"

Hoxie wagged his big head impatiently. "I remember, Nollys. But
what's that got to do with staying in Circle City? The gold's here. It's
safe. And we don't have to go traipsing out into no wilderness."

The Old Man turned. "Jim?"

"I agree with Hoxie," said Jim, with an effort, wondering, after all,
if he was doing the right thing. Since when had he started following
Hoxie's lead? Maybe Nina had a hell of a lot more to do with it than
he thought.

"Lloyd?"

"You know how I feel, Nollys."

"Yes," said the Old Man. "I know. All right. Three to one. But maybe
I can change your mind. Okay. Let's go uptown. If I can't persuade you
in a few quick minutes, I'll throw in with you."

"Fair enough," said Jim, somehow relieved.

But Lloyd began to feel very apprehensive. All along it had seemed
too easy to him, far too easy; but he'd thrust back his fears, reassured
by Hoxie's arguments and explanations and particularly by Jim's coming over to their side. But the Old Man was a tough customer, with a
will of iron. Would he find a way to change Jim's mind, and maybe even
Hoxie's?

The Old Man did not seem worried at all, but calm and confident.

There was a big wooden sign over the door that read:

MELVIN PERCIVAL
SURVEYING
ASSAYING
EXPERT ADVICE

Percival was a tall, slender, bard-bitten old man with steely gray eyes.
He was the only man in Circle City who wore a white shirt, a boiled
collar, and a tie. His manner was remote and unfriendly, and he looked
with little show of interest at the four bearded men—three young, one
old—lined up before him at the counter.

"My name's Nollys Harp," the Old Man explained. "Do you know
me?"

"Never saw you before in my life. If you fellows are looking for a
loan, a grubstake, get out of here. I'm bothered every day of my life,

especially by fellows who say I know them, or ought to."

The Old Man turned to the others. "You satisfied he don't know me?"

They all nodded, puzzled.

Now the Old Man took what looked like a little bundle of rags from his pants pocket and began to unwrap it. Finally he brought out a large gold nugget and put it on the counter.

"Take a look at that, Mr. Percival. Give me your honest opinion. I'm willing to pay for it."

Percival picked the nugget up, studied it carefully, went into the back room, where he stayed quite a while, returned finally, and then handed the nugget back to the Old Man. Lloyd had the feeling that Mr. Percival was laboring under some degree of excitement, but with him it was hard to tell.

"Well?" said the Old Man.

"You didn't find that around here."

"That's right."

"You want to tell me where you found it?"

"No. I just want your opinion of it."

"Haven't got much of an opinion. Can't believe my eyes. Never saw anything as rich in virgin gold as that. Man, you've got a strike will turn the country upside down."

Lloyd turned and glanced at Jim and Hoxie. Both seemed shaken, bewildered.

"What do I owe you?" asked the Old Man.

"Nothing," said Percival; then: "Look here. I'm a man you can depend on. I won't say a word. Tell me where you got that and I'll sell out here and go. Just vanish, won't bring anybody else."

"Sorry," said the Old Man. "Can't do it. These here fellows, my friends, don't even know. And they've come all the way from Seattle."

The Old Man started out. Percival rushed around the end of the counter and stopped him. "Now look here... Mr. Hart... didn't you say your name was?"

"Harp. "

"I've got money," Percival went on. "I can finance up to... oh, thousands... just for a small percentage. I've got credit with A.C.; big credit. Anything you like."

The Old Man appeared to think this over for a long time; then finally he said: "Mr. Percival, I'm going to give that offer a lot of thought. May drop around later. I only ask one thing: don't say a word about this."

"Do you think I'm a fool?" cried Percival; then he quickly wiped his brow and hurried to the front to open the door for the Old Man and his three flabbergasted partners.

Percival, who seemed more than a little hysterical now, followed them outside and kept talking, but they finally managed to get away from him.

On the way back to the boat the Old Man said: "You see, boys, I don't even need you now. You forced my hand. You made me do this. It'll get around. Percival will never be able to keep his mouth shut. We'll be followed to Forty Mile, likely. Course that won't help 'em much. I know. They don't. They can look forever in the same area and find nothing."

"Why didn't you tell us, Nollys?" cried Jim. "Why did you hold it back?"

"You would have talked. All of you. Now... what do we do? You want your money back, Hoxie? Jim? Since Percival already knows, he can finance me and I'll pick me up some day laborers. Men that'll work for wages. All right?"

"I'm going with Nollys," said Jim.

"Me, too," said Hoxie.

But Lloyd said nothing. Things were happening too fast; he felt confused and bewildered.

"Lloyd?" the Old Man barked.

"I... I... I...." Lloyd kept stammering.

"Boat's going to sail about one, Lloyd," said the Old Man.

Lloyd nodded quickly, then said: "I must talk to Adorée. Make her understand. She...."

He broke off and then ran to the boat, got aboard, climbed the gangway stairs, hesitated, came back down, went ashore, and started for town on the run.

The others paid little attention to him. Jim and Hoxie were sweating with excitement—gold fever!—and kept looking at the Old Man as if they'd never seen him before. What a crafty, cunning, patient, close-mouthed old bugger he was!

"Had to wait two weeks longer than I expected for the boat," the Old Man explained, "when I was leaving in '86. Picked up this nugget a few days before I left. Stuck it in my pocket. Never found out what I had till I got to Vancouver. But I was too busy spending my money to worry much about it. Pretty soon the money was all gone. I've been trying to keep my mouth shut and get back here ever since. Never was going to say nothing about this nugget, but you boys forced my hand.”

"We were fools, Nollys,” said Jim. “Excuse us.”

"Harm's done,” said the Old Man. “But don't worry. We'll get ours.”

VI

CIRCLE CITY AND BEYOND

Adorée was sitting on the edge of the bunk, with her hands in her lap and her head down. At her feet was the canvas bag, containing her few possessions. Her face showed nothing, but her whole attitude—the slackness of her body, her lowered head—spoke of complete resignation, wordless submission to fate.

Lloyd was so upset that his face alternately paled and flushed. His voice sounded both pleading and plaintive as he tried to explain to Adorée what in his heart he knew to be unexplainable. He was leaving her. After all his big talk, his repeated assurances, his many promises, he was leaving her.

"You understand, don't you, Adorée?" he insisted, trying to get her to look up at him. "I've got to go. It's the chance of a lifetime. We'll be rich, all of us—by spring. And then I'll come right back here. You understand?"

She seemed all Indian to him now, mysterious, remote, unreachable.

"Won't you please say you understand?" Lloyd pleaded.

Adorée nodded slowly, not looking up. "I understand."

"And I've got everything arranged for you. Pete knew your father, liked him. You can stay with Pete and his wife, and maybe help her. She's a very nice woman. I've talked to her. She says she'll look after you till I get back in the spring."

Adorée nodded slowly.

"All right?" asked Lloyd, beginning to feel a little better now. What was the big problem, after all? He was going. He'd come back. People left and came back every day of the year. He and Adorée were young. What difference could a few months make?

Adorée nodded again.

"Good. Now you stay right here. I've got to talk with the boys. Make a few arrangements. Understand? Then I'll take you to Mrs. Pete. She said she'd come down to the boat. Maybe she's on the bank now. All right?"

Adorée nodded slowly. Lloyd studied her for a moment; then, overcome by some obscure emotion, he struggled hard to control his face. It was as if they were back in the curio store at St. Michael, and he had just come in and was now seeing Adorée for the first time, sitting patiently with her hands in her lap and her head lowered, waiting for nothing.

He turned and went out hurriedly.

Jim, Hoxie, and the Old Man listened in silence to all Lloyd had to say; then the Old Man turned to Jim: "What do you think?"

"I think we can spare it," said Jim. "I'm in favor of it"

"Hoxie?"

"Whatever Jim says is okay with me," said Hoxie, lounging at his ease. Things had come full circle. Hoxie was following Jim's lead again.

The Old Man nodded, then he rose, took off his vest, his shirt, skinned down to his undershirt, unlocked the money belt, and counted out a hundred dollars in bills.

"There you are, Lloyd," said the Old Man. "And you made a wise decision. She'll be well fixed for the year with a hundred dollars cash money, and them people to look after her. A wise decision."

"You understand," said Lloyd. "I'm paying for this however you fellows think is fair. I'll give the hundred back later, or I'll take a smaller cut. Leave it up to the three of you. Now I got to go."

"Yep," said the Old Man. "Get it all settled. We're shipping out real soon. The old tub's about ready."

Lloyd left. Hoxie shook his head and slapped his thigh. "If you'd've told me back in Seattle..." He broke off; then: "You know, that damned Lloyd's got more gumption than a man'd think. Got himself a pretty girl; had her all the way up the Yukon. Fought me for her, not that it was much of a fight till you got in it, hayshaker—but he tried; and now he pays her off and gets rid of her. He'll do all right, that Lloyd. Always thought he was a plain nothing."

Later when they went out on deck they found, to their blank astonishment, that Lloyd was running all over the boat like a crazy man. Jim chased him down the gangway and caught him by the arm.

"Here, here, Lloyd! What the hell's the matter?"

"She's gone," cried Lloyd, staring, bewildered. "I've been all over the ship from hold to bridge. And nobody saw her go. I talked to Kobo, Kelpak, Alf...."

"Wait a minute," said Jim, shaking him gently. "Maybe she...."

"If anybody harmed her...!" cried Lloyd, his face going pale as chalk.

"Now who'd harm her? Lloyd, listen to me. Maybe she went ashore. Maybe she's waiting in town some place. Maybe...."

Lloyd pulled away from Jim and disappeared around the curve of the gangway. A moment later Jim saw him going ashore. He cupped his hands and shouted: "Lloyd, ship's leaving right away. Don't get left!"

Lloyd ignored him, ran on.

He found her sitting on the steps of a little store, halfway up the muddy road that led to the main street of the town, with her canvas bag beside her and her hands folded in her lap. Mrs. Pete was standing just beyond, with her arms crossed over her plump breasts, waiting. She was a large breed woman, with a fat good-natured face.

"Why did you run away?" asked Lloyd. "Why didn't you wait?"

"I didn't belong there any more," said Adorée.

Lloyd took her hand, put the bills into it, then closed her slender fingers over them. "There you are, Adorée. It'll be plenty till I get back."

"But I don't need it," she said, looking up at him. "I still have my other money."

"What other money?"

"The money you gave me in St. Michael."

Gradually, out of what seemed like a vast, remote past, it came to him. "Five dollars? Oh, but that's not nearly enough. I won't be back till spring."

Adorée nodded slowly and put the bills away in her jacket. "Don't worry," said Mrs. Pete to Lloyd. "We'll look after her good. I knew Maria. Francois, too."

Adorée looked at her quickly. "Francois. Yes, that was his name. But everybody called him Frenchy."

Now the steamboat whistle sounded, a shattering blast that bounded and rebounded over the river and through the town. Lloyd stiffened. The whistle blew again. Adorée half rose, then sank back. She was looking at him in silence, and in her dark eyes was a sort of animal anguish that he couldn't bear.

Turning quickly, he ran for the steamboat.

His partners saw him clattering up the gangway stairs and yelled to him; but he paid no attention to them, rushed past and into his cabin.

"What's ailing him?" cried Hoxie. "He's green in the face like that time he butted me. He acts crazy."

Jim hurried down the gangway and looked into Lloyd's open cabin door. Lloyd was on his knees feverishly stuffing clothes and other articles into his sea bag.

"What the hell are you doing?" asked Jim.

Lloyd ignored him, pulled up the string of the bag, then rushed out of the cabin, bumping the astonished Jim on the way, tore past Hoxie and the Old Man, who stared after him openmouthed, then clattered down the gangway stairs.

"Stop him," shouted Jim. "He's lost his mind. He's staying!"

Hoxie started after Lloyd, but the Old Man grabbed him, pulled him back. Jim joined them, too confused, too much taken by surprise to act.

"No!" said the Old Man. "Maybe it's best this way. Where we're going... well... it might get a little rough for Lloyd."

"But, good God, Nollys," said Jim. "Think about his family. Think about...."

"Jim," said the Old Man, "the way you talk, you'd think it was forever. We'll be back in the spring."

Hoxie laughed and slapped Jim on the back. "Sure, sure, Jim. Stop worrying. The months'll roll around. They always do." Now he began to count on his fingers. "By God; if we don't get back till April maybe they'll have a little papoose to show us. Yes sir, a little papoose."

Jim looked at Hoxie angrily, but said nothing. The Old Man sighed, went back to his cabin, and got into his bunk. "Better start conserving again," he said aloud. "Whole cabin to myself now. It'll make it easier."

The steamboat was pulling out, heading for midstream. The Old Man was already asleep. But Jim and Hoxie stood at the gangway rail, on the shore side, waving good-by to the people lining the bank.

"Look at him standing there with his little squaw," said Hoxie. "And who's that other fat one? What's ole Lloyd doing, taking 'em on wholesale?"

But Jim did not feel inclined to humor. It was crazy, crazy, but somehow he just couldn't help admiring Lloyd. Damned few men in this world who'd kick away a fortune for the sake of one little Injun girl. Damned few!

"Well," said Hoxie, "at least he knows he'll sleep warm this winter. Maybe he ain't so dumb after all."

They were well on their way now, with the *Nils K. Jensen* moving laboriously upstream, southeastward, against the mounting pressure of the current.

For reasons best known to themselves the two old sourdoughs, Blaik and Dogett, had decided not to stay at Circle City after all but to continue on to the end of the voyage, at Forty Mile. They remained in their cabin, never sat out on the gangway, and ate their meals at odd hours in the saloon.

"Couple of fine old birds, I must say," grumbled Hoxie. "Won't pass the time of day with a fellow."

The Old Man seemed very much amused by Blaik and Dogett, and finally he said to Jim and Hoxie: "Percival's spies."

"What!" cried Hoxie, outraged. "Why, some night I'll throw them old bastards overboard."

The Old Man laughed. "It's kind of a good idea, Hoxie. But not necessary. You see I've talked so much about Forty Mile and I've harped on it so that it's in everybody's craw that Forty Mile is the place. But it ain't."

Jim and Hoxie exchanged a glance; then Hoxie said: "Why, Nollys—you ole buzzard!"

"You see," said the Old Man, "Shag Galloway was right. Forty Mile is played out. Oh, of course you could make some money there—lot better than wages. But where we're going... why, hell, Midas was a piker! Found it by accident, too, you might say. Just scrounging around waiting for the boat. It ain't on Forty Mile Creek, boys. It's close, but on a different watershed, and I could take you there blindfolded. Oh, we'll make monkeys out of Blaik and Dogett, wise as they are."

"You're a caution, Nollys," said Hoxie. "Sometimes I don't know how to take you, you're such a crafty old bastard."

"Stick with me and I'll get you there," said the Old Man. "Do like I say and we'll all be rich."

Jim and Hoxie sat in the lower bunk, sideways, playing seven-up, but with little interest in the game. Beyond the porthole the same dreary monotonous shore line slipped past: mud, tundra, king grass, spruce.

"Going to take two days or better to get to Forty Mile, the Old Man says," grumbled Hoxie. "It's the goddamned current pouring down. Cap says he never seen it any worse. Jesus, I'm getting fed up with this old tub. Seems like I been on it all my life. The *Schoonover* was just a breeze compared to this."

Hoxie had already forgotten the ice floes and the fog and the uncertainty. In retrospect the voyage on the *George B. Schoonover* now seemed fast, easy, and full of fun.

Hoxie was beginning to regret Circle City. "I don't know, Jim," he said, grumbling.

"That's *my* trick," cried Jim. "Goddamn it, watch what you're doing."

"Let's quit," said Hoxie. "Can't keep my mind on the cards. Keep thinking about the Walrus, and them pretty girls in tights—and Bessie...."

Jim grimaced. "Who the hell's Bessie?" he demanded; then he began to gather up the cards.

"Why, the big plump brunette with the white streak in her hair. What a woman! Me and Bessie shook the building. I ain't kidding."

"Do you want that gold or don't you?" cried Jim, violently irritated.

"Sure I want the gold. Sure. But I want to have some fun, too."

"You want everything in this world. You can't have it. Shut up!"

Jim put the cards away, stripped to his underwear, pushed Hoxie aside, and got into the lower bunk.

"I don't know," said Hoxie. "Jim, every once in a while, even now, I get the feeling that that Old Man is just a little you-know-what. It ain't natural him being so cunning, so close-mouthed. Crazy people are cunning as hell. Craziest fellow I ever saw was a hired hand on Tom Byrd's farm. Name of Whitey. Talked like a schoolmaster. Smart? Smart as a whip. All of a sudden one day he put railroad ties on the Pennsy tracks, tries to wreck a train. He was cunning as all hell."

"Oh shut up," said Jim.

Hoxie rose, yawning and stretching, took off his clothes, and climbed into the upper bunk.

"Hope I have a dream about the Walrus," he said. "Wish I was back there, damn it, with Bessie on my knee and that there Injun girl a-playing the piano. Maybe we should have stayed, Jim; like Shag said. Maybe we ain't going to find nothing but trouble. A man that can lie like that for months to his best friends... well, he ain't to be trusted. Would you lie to me like that, just to keep me going along with what you want to do? All the time I thought it was Forty Mile. Now it ain't. But where is it? We don't know."

Jim ignored him.

It was the next morning. The three partners had had their breakfast and were just rising to leave the saloon when Hoxie glanced out of the porthole. "Hey," he cried, "we're heading in for shore. Damn near there."

Kobo had just come in with a tray and had caught the tail end of Hoxie's words. "We go shore. Tie up. Fix boiler," he explained.

"What—again?"

"Plenty trouble—boiler. No hold steam load good," said Kobo; then he shrugged and grinned reassuringly. "Cap'n fix. No worry."

They went up on the gangway. Jensen was on the bridge above them, shading his eyes as he looked off toward the shore. Purdy was at the wheel.

"More trouble, Cap?" Hoxie called up.

Jensen nodded grimly, then said: "But this time she's going to be fixed if it's the last thing I ever do. Tough enough bucking this current, without fighting that goddamned boiler." Now he cupped his hands about his mouth and called: "Okay, Purdy. Turn her. Little more to port. That's it."

There was a jangling of bells and a creaking groan from the hull as the steamboat was warped in at the bank.

Jensen leaned on the rail and looked down at the partners. "Me and Rudy can fix the boiler," he said. "Going to send Alf and Creeb ashore to cut wood. Might as well take advantage of this stop. How about you fellows? Lend a hand?"

"Sure," cried Hoxie. "I'm your man. Been living soft at Circle. Get the kinks out. Come on, Jim."

They started down the gangway stairs. To their surprise the Old Man followed them. "Better start getting my hand in," he explained. "Even my calluses are starting to soften up; and God knows I don't want to get so soft I blister. I'll show you boys how to cut spruce."

And he did. With a sort of awed respect, Jim and Hoxie stood watching him swinging the ax, as if it were a willow wand, and making the chips fly. He seemed almost like a different person to them and they were less aware of his white beard now and more conscious of his immense strength. Knots of muscle rolled across his back under his shirt, and his forearms looked thick as an average man's leg and very powerful.

"Nollys," called Hoxie, "you must have been quite a man when you was my age."

"Yep," said the Old Man, swinging as he talked. "I was, Hoxie. I was."

"Seems to me he's doing pretty good right now," said Jim.

"Yep," said the Old Man, "I can still hold up my end with most. But I creak a little, boys; I creak."

They laughed, then picked up their axes and joined him.

Alf and Creeb had moved southward toward another big clump of spruce and were working their way slowly back from the bank, toward a low hillock, swinging away tirelessly and occasionally whistling or singing.

The partners had quite a pile of wood cut now and took a breather, wiping the sweat from their faces and grinning at each other. It was good to work and sweat, and then relax, slackening the muscles and giving them a brief respite before another attack on the tough green spruce. Set you up. Made you feel good.

"Some country," said Hoxie, looking off westward across the immense, almost perfectly level northern plain; the horizons were so impossibly distant that it seemed likely that mud, tundra, king grass, and spruce stretched to the ends of the earth. "Any place else in the world like this, Nollys?"

"I ain't seen any," said the Old Man. "But I hear tell that Siberia looks pretty much this way, some of it at least."

"No wonder them Russians send their bad guys there," said Hoxie. "That'll teach 'em!"

A faint grayish mist veiled the sun. Beyond them the mighty river moved northwestward, giving off a powerful rushing sound that Jensen said could be heard for miles. Violent pounding and curses came from the hold of the steamboat.

Hoxie laughed. "That new boiler is sure giving Cap hell. But he'll lick it, if I know my man. He'll lick it sure."

They were just about to resume their work when Alf and Creeb, who'd been singing, whistling, and talking, suddenly fell silent, then began to shout.

"Hey, fellows," yelled Alf, "come here. We just found a dead Injun."

Hoxie and the Old Man threw down their axes and started off at once, but Jim hesitated. He did not want to see "a dead Injun" and couldn't understand Hoxie's and the Old Man's eagerness. However, it would be impossible for him to remain behind and go on working. If he did, he'd never hear the last of it from Hoxie, who could make himself pretty obnoxious and tiresome once he had something to tease a man with. "Matter?" he'd say. "You skeered of dead people? Why, hell, there ain't no such thing as a ghost. Didn't your mommy ever tell you that…" and so on.

Jim put down his ax and walked over to where the others were standing in a group looking down at something lying in the grass. Jim pretended to join them, but pulled his hat low and kept his eyes averted. He'd only seen but one dead person in his life—Grandpa Bates, lying in his coffin; and that had scared the daylights out of him when he was nine years old.

"Dogs or something has been at him," said Alf. "He's pretty well chewed up."

"Old Injun. Very old," said Creeb.

"Yeah. They must have run him out to die. They don't fool around in them Indian villages. Too many mouths to feed as it is. When the old people get useless, they run 'em out on the tundra to die. Some kind of ceremony they have with drums and such. Pretty cruel. But it makes sense, by God; it makes sense."

"Hadn't we better bury him?" asked Jim.

Alf, Creeb, and the Old Man looked at Jim in amazement.

"Bury him!" cried the Old Man. "Why, the ground's frozen hard only twelve inches down. Takes picks and a hell of a lot of hard work. Ain't worth it. The dogs'll be back. Save everybody the trouble."

"Yep," said Alf. "Up here they just kick 'em around till they disappear."

Jim said nothing. In a moment he turned and walked back to where his ax was leaning, picked it up, and went to work on a spruce sapling. He felt sick.

Hoxie came back laughing. He'd found something to tease the Old Man about.

"Nollys," he said, "ain't you glad you're not a Injun living on the Yukon? In a few years they'd be running you out to get et by them wolfish dogs."

"Oh, I don't know," said the Old Man mildly. "No worse than dying in the poorhouse back home; and the idea's about the same."

Hoxie stared. "By God, never thought of it that way, Nollys, but you're right. Yeah. I used to see them poor old bastards out at the Poor Farm back home, sitting around, waiting to die. Nobody ever paid no attention to 'em at all, only give 'em some lousy food."

"Besides," said the Old Man, grinning, "I'm eligible for a Soldiers' Home, any place in the States. I'm a veteran of two wars. But don't expect to find me there. Look me up at the best hotel in San Francisco."

Hoxie roared and slapped him on the back. "I'm for you, Nollys, old man," he cried. "I'm for you. We'll have champagne for breakfast, and caviar...." Hoxie paused, then asked: "What the hell is caviar, Nollys?

I've only read it's what the millionaires eat."

"I've et it," said the Old Man. "Fish eggs. Sturgeon eggs. Salty as hell. I'll take *hen* eggs."

"Well, I'll be goddamned," said Hoxie, amazed.

Jim worked on in silence, forgotten.

The Old Man had gone up to his cabin, a little stiff and sore in his muscles due to the long layoff, but Hoxie and Jim remained below and were helping Rudy, Alf, and Creeb store the wood aboard.

"We really got a load now," said Rudy, grinning. "Maybe we can make Forty Mile with it."

"How about the boiler?" asked Hoxie,

"Cap'n's got it fixed to suit him finally," said Rudy. "Current's bad. Getting worse."

"Oh, we'll get there," said Alf, laughing. "We always do. Been making this run five–six years now. Upstream's a little rough. But downstream's one long picnic; don't use one tenth the wood."

"What's Forty Mile like?" asked Jim.

"Oh, little place on the river. Trading post. Store. Maybe one–two hundred people."

"Women?" asked Hoxie.

"Now and then. Not permanent. They always seem to get married. Them miners are lonely. Breeds around."

Hoxie sighed. "It won't be like Circle."

"You can count on that," cried Alf, laughing. "Yes, sir; that you can count on."

It was the next day. Purdy was at the wheel and Jensen and the Old Man were standing together on the bridge. There wasn't a cloud in the sky and the northern sun beat down with patient ferocity. The immense roily roaring river seemed to be afire with sun glare, and beyond it, on both sides, the tundra, almost perfectly level, stretched off in unbelievably vast vistas of distance. From time to time the boat shuddered and seemed to be trying to fight the helm.

"Look at that," moaned Jensen. "Full speed ahead and we're just barely moving. I been around a long time and I never seen the river this bad before. Must be a big thaw up in the mountains, the way it's pouring down."

He went into the wheelhouse, jangled the bell, talked down the speaking tube to Rudy in the engine room, then came back shaking his head.

"It's that boiler," said Jensen. "Don't act like it should. Rudy's going to try to pile on a little more pressure, see what happens. If we don't do better after that we got to pull in again, take a look."

They waited. Up ahead the river took a gradual, easy bend toward the east, and on the west bank at that point a long arm, or spit, of land thrust itself out into the water; and just beyond it was an Indian village, consisting of a semi-circle of mud and skin wickiups.

Jensen watched the action of the boat for a while, then walked to the wheelhouse and spoke with Purdy through the open window. When he came back he said: "No good. And the current's real bad—getting worse—in this bend. Tell you what, Nollys. Why don't you and the boys go see if you can't get us a moose? Fresh meat! This is real moose country. I'm going to pull in, just around that tongue of land; let her cool off, try to adjust her again."

"Good. Fine," said the Old Man, grinning, pleased. "Cap, how far you figure we are from Forty Mile now?"

"Twenty-five, thirty miles. Oh, we'll get there, don't worry about that. But I just don't like the way that boiler's acting. Neither does Rudy and he's down there right up against it."

A few minutes later Jim, Hoxie, and the Old Man were at the gangway rail on the shore side, waiting for the boat to put in to the bank. They'd passed the long sand spit and the Indian village and now the boat was laboring hard and wallowing a little in the open current of the bend. Jensen was at the wheel now, his face red and sweating, big muscles standing out in knots on his forearms, as he strained against the boat's floundering attempts to fight its rudder.

The Old Man stood at ease at the rail, with the big moose gun in his hand and the bandoleer of ammunition across his shoulder, looking off toward a large clump of spruce about a quarter mile from the river bank. Just beyond it was a hollow, then a rise, then a heavier growth of spruce. Might be a lurking place for Mr. Moose!

But Jim and Hoxie were not thinking about moose at this moment, but were absorbed in Jensen's singlehanded combat with the mindless, implacable violence of the river.

"Hey, this is bad," said Hoxie. "Can't get her in."

Jim, tensed up and worried, said nothing, as the boat floundered sideways toward the bank, the engines pounding, the deck hot underfoot from the laboring boiler.

"Now we're getting there," said Hoxie. "Almost in."

But at that moment there appeared to be a sudden stillness in the air; then a scorching violent wind fanned their faces, the deck bucked under them, and then, all at once, with a shattering, whistling, terrifying explosion the world seemed to fly into fragments.

Jim, Hoxie, and the Old Man were blown clear, as another violent explosion wracked the listing, staggering craft.

In a daze Jim scrambled ashore, hardly knowing what he was doing or where he was. Hoxie was already lying on the bank, groaning. Jim turned. As in a dream, he saw the Old Man coming toward him through the shallow water, with the bandoleer still over his shoulder, the moose gun carefully held high.

Jim sank down beside Hoxie, gasping for breath. He thought that he was dying and finally lay back and looked up into the fierce whitish glare of the northern sky. He was not exactly sure yet where he was or what had happened.

"Jesus," groaned Hoxie, "we sure run into that bank hard! Dumped me ass over appetite."

"Boilers blew up," said the Old Man. "That's the end of the *Nils K. Jensen*."

Hoxie sat up with a start. "Oh God," he yelled. "Look! It's burning. Rolling over on its side. Where the hell's Jensen?"

He tried to get to his feet, but sank back. Jim was coming round now and slowly sat up. What he saw on the river terrified him and he struggled hard to keep from jumping up and running away from the sight.

"Nollys! Good God! Look!" he screamed. "Can't we do something? Where is everybody? Nollys!"

He tried to scramble to his feet, but the Old Man pulled him back. "No use, Jim," he said. "Rest yourself. We was just lucky standing where we was. The rest of 'em... well... Blaik and Dogett were in a cabin right over the boiler. Jensen and Purdy probably got pitched toward the river side—and in that current... well... And as for them fellows in the hold...! So rest yourself, Jim."

"Goddamn!" screamed Hoxie. "We should've stayed in Circle. I knew it! I knew it! God blast you, Nollys Harp!"

"Rest yourself, Hoxie," said the Old Man. "It ain't as bad as you fellows think. We're only twenty-five miles from Forty Mile, and it's an easy walk along the bank, flat country."

Jim and Hoxie, still dazed, still not sure of anything, both turned and stared at the Old Man as if at a monster.

"Forty Mile!" gasped Hoxie. "But... all our supplies. All our.... Nollys Harp, you're as crazy as a loon. Told Jim you were; and by God, you are."

"Now, now," said the Old Man. "She's burning out already. Look. Maybe we can get some of them supplies out. Anyway, we got our gun and we've got our money, boys, our money; right here around my waist, and that's mighty important in this here country."

Jim lay back with a groan and stared up at the sky. It was all just too much for him at the moment. Hoxie looked at the grim Old Man for a long time, bewildered, confused, not just sure what he thought; then something attracted his attention and he glanced over his shoulder.

"Hey, Nollys. Look!"

On a hillock fifty feet beyond them was a semi-circle of Indians, men, women, and children, staring, immobile. "Oh, don't mind them," said the Old Man. "They're harmless. May put 'em to work later. Don't know yet."

One of the Indians—a middle-aged man—now moved down from the hillock, approached within fifteen or twenty feet of the group on the bank, then began to grunt out something and point toward the north with his left arm.

The Old Man got to his feet and, carrying the moose gun in his right hand, went over to the Indian.

"What?"

The Indian gobbled at him, pointing; then he went through a sort of pantomime that seemed to indicate that somebody was lying asleep some place. The Old Man gestured for the Indian to lead the way, show him what he meant, but at that moment a figure in tatters rose slowly from the grass, like an apparition symbolizing disaster, and staggered up the bank toward them.

It was Kobo. His clothes had been shredded by the blast and one shoe blown off. He seemed to be all right otherwise, aside from being dazed and scared half to death.

He staggered forward and fell into the Old Man's arms, sobbing. "Oh Mr. Harp. Mr. Harp," he moaned.

The Old Man sat him down in the grass, then crouched beside him.

"Anybody else?" he asked.

Kobo shook his head and big tears started to roll down his cheeks. "I see Cap'n. River carry him away. Mr. Purdy, too. All the rest— boom!—gone."

"Where were you, Kobo?"

"On gangway aft, shore side. Good luck." He fumbled in his ragged clothes for a moment, then brought out his French franc. "You see what Redbeard give me? Save my life."

On the hillock the Indians sat staring, immobile. Though their faces showed nothing, they were shocked, terrified, and awed by the power of the Great Spirit. Somehow, some way, the white man's huge white smoking canoe had offended. Now it was shattered and burning at the water's edge.

Later they would sacrifice to the wooden image of the Great Spirit, Gitchi Manitou, so He would understand that, unlike the bearded whites, they were His true children, His Chosen People, and that they humbly submitted to His will in all things and were not arrogant and defiant of His power as were the whites.

To Gitchi Manitou, the Sole God, Father of All Things, Creator of the World, Devourer of the Evil Ones, Master, Teacher, Ruler of the Sun and Moon and Planets— All Hail!

Kobo had gone to the Indian village and returned dressed as one of them; in fact, he was now indistinguishable from the staring group on the hillock, except for his lucky French franc and his giggle.

"All arranged?" asked the Old Man, as Jim and Hoxie, still dazed and bewildered, looked on.

Kobo nodded. "Chief and two sons take me back to Circle. Report boat."

"Good," said the Old Man.

Kobo looked down at himself and giggled sadly. Then suddenly he stiffened his face, folded his arms, straightened his back, and grunted. "Me Kobo. Belly fine tundra man."

The middle-aged Indian, standing near-by, almost smiled. It amused him to see this clownish white man-owned Indian making a fool of himself. That's what came of living in the towns, kowtowing to the Anglos!

"Wait a minute now," said Hoxie. "Kobo's going back to Circle?"

"Yes," said the Old Man. "In a canoe."

"Why don't we all go, Nollys? For God's sake; here we are at the end of no place, and on foot. Are you crazy? Jim, talk to him, for the love of God!"

Jim wagged his head and stared about him vaguely. He had still not quite got his bearings. "I don't know, Hoxie. I just don't know."

Hoxie glanced at Jim in dismay. He'd never heard him talk like this before. "Jim," he begged, "think! You want to stay here with these Injuns, when we can get to Circle in a canoe, downstream? Should have stayed in Circle. Should have listened to me. Plenty gold there. Maybe it ain't the best, but it's gold."

"You want to go back to Circle, go!" said the Old Man. "You'll get nothing from us. You ain't got much in, anyway. Jim loaned you the money to get here."

"Jim!" Hoxie pleaded.

But Jim merely shook his head.

Later Hoxie walked out on the spit of land to watch Kobo's departure. The canoe was long and narrow but roomy and comfortable-looking, Hoxie thought, as it headed for midstream, battling the current. Kobo, a city Indian, sat amidship, supercargo, while the three tundra Indians wielded the paddles.

Hoxie watched till he lost the canoe in the fierce sun glare on the river; then he turned away and started back up the muddy moss-covered spit. At the end of it a young male Indian rose from behind a hillock and stood staring at him. Hoxie started, stopped, then came on. Peaceful Injuns up in this country—that was one good thing, anyway!—all quiet and harmless.

Now the young Indian spoke, laboring over it. "I spik 'Glish."

"Not too good," said Hoxie.

"You go white-man town?" He gestured down river.

Hoxie stared at the young Indian for a moment, then began to understand. "Maybe."

"You want canoe? I get. Money."

"How much?"

"One silver dollar. I take you."

"What's your name?"

"John."

"Okay, John. I'll think it over. Maybe. Okay?"

"John say okay."

"Fine. Fine," said Hoxie; then he started on back to where Jim and the Old Man were still sitting on the bank.

The sun beat down, the river roared, the limitless tundra stretched flatly to infinity, all as before; but now where there had been dismay and bewilderment and disorganization there was purposeful activity, and the Old Man was the driving power in the center of it. Up to his waist in water, dressed only in his long underdrawers, he was swing-ing an ax at the exposed under-hull of what had once been the *Nils K. Jensen*. Just beyond him, a dozen stark naked Indian men were wait-ing for orders, while on the bank Hoxie and Jim sorted the various casks, barrels, and bundles that had already been taken from the hold.

"All right," yelled the Old Man finally. "Go in, you buggers; in. Look for picks, shovels. You compree picks, shovels?"

All of the Indians stared blankly, except John and his friend Ittak. They nodded vigorously. "Compree! Compree!" cried John; then he swung an imaginary pick and dug with an imaginary shovel.

"Good boy," yelled the Old Man. "You're my foreman. You all like chawing tobacco?"

John and Ittak both grinned and nodded.

"All right. First we get out the picks and shovels, compree? Then we look for chawing tobacco. We got a case or so in the hold, enough for the whole village."

"Good, good. Compree," cried Ittak, getting in ahead of his friend John this time.

"Guess I got two foremen," shouted the Old Man, grinning. Then: "In, boys. In."

One by one the Indians crawled through the gaping hole the Old Man had chopped in the boat's hull.

"That old man, I don't know," said Hoxie, slowly shaking his head.

Jim did not reply, but in a moment said: "Boy, we're really getting the food out. Look at this. Whole cases of canned bully beef. Canned toma-toes. Canned pears. By God, we're going to eat. That's one sure thing!"

"Oh *no!* cried Hoxie; then: "Books! A whole box of 'em. Now who the hell wants a box of books up in this God-forsaken place? Or *any* place, for that matter!"

They worked on, stockpiling the useful cases and articles and toss-ing the others aside. "That's for the Injuns," Hoxie would say from time to time. "Boy, are they going to have some funny stuff in them beehives they live in!"

Finally they took a breather and lit their pipes.

"Jim," said Hoxie, "I got to talk to you."

"All right, talk."

"You going through with this? Walk twenty–thirty miles with a pack on your back when you don't know where you're going…?"

The Old Man interrupted him with a wild, triumphant shout and they both looked off toward the boat. Indians were pouring out through the gap in the hold, carrying picks and long-handled shovels.

"Goddamn, Jim," said Hoxie, "that old man, he just ain't all there. What's he going to do with all our picks and shovels? Carry 'em to Forty Mile? Jim, listen to me. Let's make him give us our money back. We can get to Circle; all you have to do is sit still and the current'll take you. Bet Kobo's there already."

"No," said Jim. "You want to desert Nollys? Leave him out here all alone?"

"Hell, I got to the place I don't care. Let him come back with us."

"Hoxie, listen. That Old Man come three–four thousand miles. You think he's going to turn back? You know better than that."

"Then the hell with him," cried Hoxie. "Let him rot out here for all I care. Let me tell you something, Jim Hardy—straight. I'm going back to Circle. We been friends for years. But if you won't go back, the hell with you, too. I'm going, you hear! Ole Hoxie Thicke's going."

"Go then," said Jim coldly.

"Jim, how can I?" whined Hoxie. "I ain't got but five–six dollars."

"Then shut up. You're getting no money from me. You cost me over five hundred dollars as it is. And are you grateful? No, goddamn it. The more you get, the more you yell for. Now hit for Circle with your five–six dollars or keep your big mouth shut."

But Hoxie was beyond reason now. He wanted out. That's all, out! Jumping to his feet, he hurried down to the bank to talk to the Old Man. Jim watched him ironically, knowing very well how it would come out."

"... no, Hoxie," the Old Man was saying. "No. I'm not going back. Jim's not going back. If you want to leave, broke, that's your business. But while you're thinking it over, go back and do some work. What do you think you are, an ornament?"

"Don't talk to me that way, you old bastard."

"I'm running this expedition till I hear different," said the Old Man, with an icy edge to his voice. "And if you don't work, you don't eat."

Swearing to himself, Hoxie stumbled back up the bank, put out his pipe, and began to throw cases and bales promiscuously about. For a little while Jim watched him undoing a half hour's labor in a few minutes; then he spoke, and his voice was as icy as the Old Man's: "Hoxie, you're going to keep on asking for it till you get it. Boy, you're breeding a scab, as my grandfather used to say. Put all that stuff back the way you found it."

With a curse, Hoxie climbed the hillock, lay down on his back, put his hands under his head, stared up at the sky, and called: "Make me!"

Jim started for him, then checked himself. Hoxie had always acted like a small brat, with tantrums over nothing at all; now he was worse than ever. Why get into a fight with him in front of the Indians? "Hoxie," he called, "you just aren't good for anything. We don't even need you to sort boxes. Take a nap. I'll have one of the Indians bring your supper up."

Jim went to work. In a few minutes Hoxie joined him, but said nothing. In fact he never spoke another word the rest of the day. His face looked mean, sulky, sullen. From time to time he'd take his spite out on a box or crate, banging it unmercifully. Jim ignored him.

At supper he took his tin plate of beans and bully beef up to the top of the hillock and ate by himself.

"Sulking like a nine-year-old kid," said the Old Man in disgust; then: "Jim, even found my augers. Over half our food is okay. Found the blankets—they're drying right over there. Found the hip boots—the lace-ups are gone; at least we can't find 'em. Maybe we can buy some at Forty Mile."

"Nollys," said Jim, "tell me something. How do we get all this stuff upstream?"

"Don't know yet. Might hire the Indians to carry it, but they get tired on you and just drop the stuff and leave, and then you'd be in trouble. If I had a rowboat, we'd try drag portage."

"What's that?"

"Like a canal boat, only I'm the horse, or you. We rig up a harness and pull. It's tough, but you get there. By the way, we found plenty of good tarred rope—best sea quality."

"What about the Indians pulling?"

"Them little fellows? Not strong enough. Don't like that kind of work. And to most of 'em money means nothing. Course I got plenty of tobacco. Already give 'em a case for the village. They'll have a whingding and powwow tonight. They'll smoke their bloody heads off on that chawing tobacco. Don't know much about conservation, them fellows. If they kill three moose they eat three. Like wolves. They eat till they can't move. They eat till their bellies are out to here. They got the idea they can eat enough for a week at one sitting, which is silly; but they never seem to learn."

"So you think we'll make it all right?" asked Jim.

The Old Man turned and looked at Jim, then laughed: "Make it! It's a mortal cinch. Why, hell, you can almost see Forty Mile from here. Jim, if it was two hundred miles away we'd make it. Or four hundred. Jim, there's nothing we can't do—you and me. You stick; don't pay no attention to that damned Hoxie. He's a knucklehead. Wants to eat his cake and have it, too."

"Nollys, you're sure right about that."

"I know. And fellows like that just won't do up here. Why, hell, that damned little fool of a Lloyd has made a better showing than Hoxie. Trouble with Hoxie is he just ain't grown up. Won't act like a man. Jim, listen to me. I like you, and I wouldn't lie to you. Stick with me and I'll make you one of the richest men on the Coast. God's truth—hope He strikes me dead if I'm lying!"

It was about three in the morning and dark. They were nearly two hundred miles below the Arctic Circle now and the sun had become a little more regular in its movements, though it was still high in the sky at eleven in the evening.

Some of the blankets had dried and the three partners were wrapped in them, against the chill of the river and the darkness.

The Old Man, who had the moose gun inside the blankets with him, was on his back, snoring quietly. Jim was a few feet away, dozing fitfully, but unable to get fully asleep. Hoxie had taken his blankets to the top of the hillock.

Huge pure white stars shone with a frosty brilliance in the cloudless, dark indigo sky, and the sound of the river was almost deafening in the stillness of the Arctic night. Small fires of driftwood showed in the Indian village and there was a faint sound of drumming accompanied at times by the bonging and jangling of some weird musical instrument. Once in a while there was a shriek of laughter, and Jim lay wondering vaguely what those poor devils, lost on the tundra and always in danger of starvation, had to laugh about. Was it the tobacco? A great windfall. Probably.

The night wore on. All the village fires died but one. The drums and the jangling stopped. The Indians slept. Jim turned and tossed, dozing. Finally he fell into a restless sleep, troubled by extremely mixed-up dreams about his boyhood in Ohio—seeing faces he hadn't given a thought to for years, even the face of his third-grade teacher, old Miss Mock, who used to snap him on the side of the head with a thimble.

A loud, weird, high-pitched howling brought him straight up out of his blankets. It went on and on and seemed to be getting closer.

Now he heard hurrying footsteps and turned, startled. But it was only

Hoxie dragging his blankets down from the top of the hillock and making his bed between Jim and the Old Man.

"You hear that, Jim?" gasped Hoxie. "What the hell is it? Sounds like I don't know what. Werewolves. You ever hear about werewolves, Jim? I did, and wish I hadn't."

The Old Man got up and began to rake some sticks together.

"What you doing, Nollys?" asked Hoxie.

"Oh, building a little fire."

"What for? You cold?"

"No," said the Old Man. "Them may be dogs howling; and again they may not."

"What then?"

"Tundra wolves. Big buggers. But they won't come near a fire. If they do I got the moose gun."

"Hell," said Hoxie, "I'm going to stay awake the rest of the night. I don't want no wolf making a beefsteak out of me."

The howling continued. Now a small orange flame sprang up and they could see the Old Man bending over it.

"Christ, Nollys, it's got to be bigger than that," said Hoxie. "That wouldn't scare a toad."

"Give me time, goddamn it," said the Old Man irritably.

Soon there was a good-sized blaze going and the Old Man began to put big sticks of driftwood on it. The crackling sounded very fine and reassuring to Jim and Hoxie.

The Old Man went back to his blankets. "Boys," he said, "have you got any dry matches?"

"Dry matches!" shouted Hoxie. "We fell in the river, didn't we? Say... How did you light that supper fire and this one, Nollys?"

"It's all in knowing," said the Old Man. "I keep trying to tell you this. I carry a little metal match container in my shirt pocket—watertight, full of big sulphurs."

"Damn, you think of everything, don't you?"

"Yep. That's why I'm sixty-three and still going strong."

They settled back. The howling stopped. There was a long silence; then the howling started again, but farther away now, to the south.

Hoxie groaned. "You like this place, Jim?"

Jim mumbled sleepily. Hoxie flung himself over on his side, with violent irritation, and thought: "Well, I don't like it. Not by a damned sight. And I'm not staying."

The next morning, while Jim and the Old Man worked, Hoxie made a nuisance of himself by arguing and pleading with first one, then the other. He'd made up his mind to go back to Circle City, and yet how could he manage it with only five or six dollars in his pocket? What made Jim and the Old Man so stubborn? In Hoxie's opinion it was simply insane to think of trying to push on to Forty Mile under present conditions, when Circle City was only a fast canoe ride downstream.

Finally, grabbing the Old Man by the arm, he made him listen. "You fellows act like you're deaf or blind," he cried. "Look. We go back to Circle. Two more steamboats are coming in pretty quick. As soon as the first one comes in we ride it to Forty Mile in comfort. Is that sense or not?"

The Old Man pushed him away. Hoxie became so incensed that he pulled the ax from the Old Man's hand and threw it thirty feet up the strand. "Goddamn it, you listen to me, Nollys Harp!"

The Old Man hit him with his fist. Snarling, Hoxie leaped on him, tried to choke him, but Jim jumped in at once, broke Hoxie's hold, and pushed him away. "Hoxie," cried Jim, his face pale, his eyes glinting, "this is your last warning."

Hoxie puffed out his chest, glared defiantly at Jim, his face almost purple; then, swearing and kicking at the tundra moss, he turned and disappeared over the hillock in the direction of the Indian village.

The Old Man looked after him in disgust and grunted: "And I thought it'd be Lloyd who'd panic. Jim, that boy is sure out of hand. What do we do?"

"Oh, he'll settle down, Nollys," said Jim. "He always does."

At noon they cooked dinner and sat down between two little humps of tundra to eat it. Hoxie hadn't come back. Down the strand from them a dozen Indian men, their helpers, squatted over their own meal. The two foremen, John and Ittak, had gone away somewhere.

As Jim sipped his coffee, he absent-mindedly noticed that there was a canoe beached at the end of the long sand spit that extended out into the river and that two Indians—he couldn't make out who they were at the distance—were squatting beside it. He thought nothing of this and turned to pour himself another cup of coffee, and at that moment he noticed the Old Man's odd look and attitude. He seemed to be frozen into immobility. Jim glanced quickly over his shoulder and gave a start. Hoxie was about ten feet away, holding the moose gun on them. Apparently he'd crept up behind them through the thick, sound-deadening bed of tundra moss.

"All right now," said Hoxie, his eyes mean, his face heavily sullen, his lips drawn back from his teeth. "I tried to talk sense to you crazy fools but you wouldn't listen. I'm getting out of here, and I want that money belt, Nollys. You hear me? And I'll shoot you to get it. I tried talk, I tried argument, I tried everything a man could, but you wouldn't listen. Friendship is friendship, but sense is sense, and you fellows are acting like you didn't have all your buttons, and you're not dragging me to God knows where, just 'cause that's where we started for. So... Nollys, you just take off that belt and toss it over here. And, Jim, you sit still...."

Jim kept staring at Hoxie in amazement. "Hoxie! Put that gun down and quit this silliness. What's the matter with you?"

"It's not silliness," said the Old Man. "He means it. Don't you, Hoxie?"

"You're goddamned right I do," said Hoxie. "Nobody's going to stop me this time—and that goes for you, too, Jim. You been my friend but now you've turned on me and won't listen. All right, Nollys—throw out that belt."

The Old Man, watching Jim out of the corner of his eye, began to un-button his shirt as if to get at the belt. Hoxie smiled slightly, pleased by what seemed like an easy victory, and his eyes followed the Old Man's fingers. At this moment Jim scrambled to his feet and, crouching low, rushed at Hoxie. There was what seemed like a tremendous explosion, a hot wind fanned his cheek, and he heard a cry, then wild cursing be-hind him, as he grabbed Hoxie's legs, upset him, pulled the gun from his hand, flung it away, and then hit Hoxie half a dozen vicious, pun-ishing blows about the head.

Hoxie seemed to go completely mad, his strength to redouble. He flung Jim off his chest with as little effort as if Jim had been a ten-year-old boy; then he grabbed him from behind, got a double headlock on him quickly, and, groaning and cursing, seemed to be trying to break Jim's neck. Jim struggled and kicked futilely, and his face slowly turned deathly pale.

"Hoxie!" called the Old Man, his voice calm but cold as the floe ice of the Bering Sea. "I'm going to kill you in one second."

Hoxie turned, glanced at the Old Man, then let Jim go, and froze, with a look of horror on his heavy, congested face. Jim staggered away from Hoxie and fell to his knees, gasping for breath. The Old Man was still in a sitting position with his back to the hump of tundra, but the moose gun was at his right shoulder and Hoxie's face was in its sights.

"What do you say, Jim?" asked the Old Man. "Shall I pull the trigger? He's no use to anybody now."

"No, Nollys! No!" cried Jim, staggering to his feet and moving over to the Old Man, who showed him the long tear in the right thigh leg of his trousers. "See this? Bullet just missed me. Would have shattered my leg and I'd've died on you, out here. I say shoot him, just like you would a mad dog. In Circle they'd hang him for highway robbery."

"No," said Jim, somewhat recovered now, "we can't do that. Let him go—back to Circle."

"But I... I only got five–six dollars," whined Hoxie. "This place was driving me crazy. I didn't know what I was doing. I didn't mean to harm nobody."

"Oh shut up," cried Jim, disgusted. "Nollys, let's give him a hundred like we did Lloyd and let him go."

"This is getting pretty expensive," said the Old Man. "Good thing you're here, Jim. I'd shoot him and leave him for the tundra wolves."

Hoxie shuddered at the look in the Old Man's eyes; then he began to plead: "Do like Jim says, Nollys. Maybe I can get a fresh start back there with a hundred dollars. John and Ittak are waiting for me on the spit, with the canoe. I'll leave right away. Won't cause you fellows no more trouble."

The Old Man handed the gun to Jim; then he unlocked the money belt and counted out a few bills. "Fifty," he said. "Take it or leave it."

Hoxie looked pleadingly at Jim, but Jim turned away. "All right, Nollys," said Hoxie. "Fifty it is." He came forward cautiously, pulled the bills from the Old Man's hand, then stood hesitating as if undecided. "Well, fellows..." he said.

But they ignored him. With something that sounded like a sob, Hoxie turned and hurried across the tundra toward the land spit.

"Damned good riddance," said the Old Man, pouring himself a fresh cup of coffee. "He'd got to the place where you couldn't turn your back on him."

Jim said nothing at all, but sank down onto the tundra beside the dinner fire. He still couldn't quite realize that it had happened. He felt dazed.

Hoxie, depressed, nervous, as dazed as Jim, did not really take a look at the water until the canoe was out in midstream, in the swiftest current, and going at express-train speed, skillfully guided by John and Ittak. Hoxie crouched amidship, with John in front of him. Suddenly he noticed how low he was, how close to the water; then he became aware of the brutal, violent strength of the river, of its deafening, rushing roar. Panic gripped him. One little mistake by John or Ittak, and over they'd go. The greatest swimmer in the world would drown in this torrent— as Jensen and Purdy had drowned, carried off remorselessly. All of a sudden he remembered Letty and thought: "But I didn't really hear her calling for help. I mean, I heard her, but I thought she was only trying to make a fuss. I should have gone back. Oh God, why didn't I go back to her?"

He leaned forward, tapped John on the shoulder. "John, I changed my mind. We turn."

John did not seem to understand. "Turn? Circle City. Okay. One silver dollar."

Hoxie groaned to himself. The bank of mud and tundra was sliding by at an unbelievable rate of speed; they'd left the bend and the land spit miles behind already. Frothlike spray leaped about the canoe, as divergent surface currents struggled against each other for mastery. Hoxie could not fight off his panic.

He tapped John hard this time. "John, we turn back. Understand?"

The canoe wobbled slightly from the shifting of Hoxie's big bulky body.

"Okay," said John. "Circle City. One silver dollar. Sit still. No touch John. Canoe tip—good-by."

Hoxie groaned aloud; then he took his face in his hands and sat motionless, not looking at the water. He'd been a fool, a damned fool. He wanted Jim. Jim always knew what to do and how to do it. "Oh God," he thought. "I'll never make it in this God-forsaken country all alone. I'll just never make it."

Some time later John and Ittak headed in for the big rambling Indian settlement at Circle City. They were still scared and speechless at what had happened.

They beached their canoe on the strand, then wandered up to where smoke was rising from supper fires. They had made up their minds to shun the Anglo part of town. They felt guilty and yet they had done nothing at all.

They were directed to the chief's wickiup where their own chief, who had brought Kobo into Circle City, was staying. The chief was sitting by the fire with other elders, all smoking. John and Ittak stayed in the background, not daring to approach the chief at this moment. They were young nobodies. They'd wait till the chief indicated that he was aware of their presence.

Finally he nodded to them and they followed him outside, where the women were cooking, and big wolfish, slant-eyed, vicious-looking dogs were playing with the children.

First John talked, then Ittak. The chief kept nodding. He did not seem to think it at all strange that Blackbeard, the huge Anglo, had jumped from the canoe to his death. Finally he explained.

"There are many evil Anglos. There are also good ones. It is the same with all people. The Great Spirit makes the Evil Ones mad. Blackbeard was an Evil One."

This made good sense to John and Ittak. They felt relieved and at peace. They had been afraid that it was through some fault of their own—some spell, some unknown guilt—that the Anglo had died.

They left the chief, went back to the strand, built their own fire, then lay down to sleep. They felt very tired from the long struggle with Old Father River.

VII

TO FORTY MILE

Worn out from their labors, Jim and the Old Man decided to take a nap and continue work later on in the afternoon. The Old Man slept peacefully in his blankets in spite of the glare of the Arctic sun, but Jim could not sleep at all. He lay thinking about Hoxie. He still couldn't believe it had all happened. Why, Hoxie must have been completely bughouse to do such a thing. Maybe they'd been wrong to let him go. Maybe they should have forced him to stay. Hoxie could run pretty wild by himself. Always needed help.

Jim felt terribly depressed. God, he'd never imagined that their journey to the gold would turn out anything like this. Gabe drowned, Lloyd left behind, now Hoxie gone. Of the original five, only himself and the Old Man left. Who would be next? Would any of them ever reach the gold? To Jim, at this moment, their quest began to take on the lineaments of a nightmare, and he remembered what Hoxie had said that day on the *Nils K. Jensen*—now lying on its side on a mudbank, partly gutted by fire and with three gaping holes chopped in the underside of the hull—yes, what Hoxie had said about a treadmill. It was so true; they'd been on a treadmill since they'd left Seattle ages ago in a past that seemed so remote to Jim that he wondered if he had not dreamed the boardinghouse and Lena and Pa and Ma, and the choppy waters of Puget Sound, and the lighthouse and the gulls screaming over the rooftops....

Turning in his blankets, he noticed a shadow across the ground, near by. He looked up. Shatka, a middle-aged Indian, who had taken John's place as foreman, was standing a few feet away, waiting respectfully to be noticed. Jim sat up.

"Yes?"

Shatka, who could not speak English except for a few labored words, pointed off toward the river. "Bo-att."

Jim got to his feet. Far out a big Anglo rowboat, going downstream, was wallowing perilously as the three men in it tried to get it out of the main current and into shore. Jim woke the Old Man, who got up at once and stood, shading his eyes from the glare, looking off across the river.

"Having a hell of a time getting that tub in," said the Old Man. "Guess they saw the steamboat and wondered what was going on. Jim—that's just the kind of boat we need for drag portage. Them fellows are getting a bellyful of the river, going downstream in it. You reckon we can talk them out of it? Injuns can run 'em to Circle in canoes. Can't be headed any place else."

"We can try," said Jim, wondering at the Old Man's never-sleeping ingenuity. Trust Nollys!

"Goddamn it," cried the Old Man. "If they ain't careful they'll upset, the boat'll drift away, and we'll never get it."

Jim did not miss the Old Man's lack of concern for the men in the boat.

Time passed. Jim and the Old Man stood at the river's edge, watching the frantic struggles of the boatmen. They'd veer in, get the boat headed right; then, just when it seemed that all was well, there'd be a change in the current, and the boat would yaw and fall away in spite of all they could do. One man finally dropped exhausted and hung head down across the thwart, while another one frantically caught the oar and just barely saved it from going overboard.

The Old Man whistled with concern. "That was a close one. If they'd lost that oar, good-by. They'd been back in the middle in no time, whirling round and round, on their way to the sea."

Struggling hard, the men succeeded in keeping the boat's bow pointed more or less toward the shore, although they fell away from time to time.

"Come on, Jim," cried the Old Man. "Way they're going they might be able to beach her on the land spit. Maybe we can help. If they miss that, God knows where they'll end up. Clear on the far bank of the bend, maybe. And we'd never see that boat again."

The boat came on, yawing and veering, but as time passed getting gradually into shallower and less turbulent water. Jim and the Old Man ran out on the land spit, and the Old Man yelled encouragement to the boatmen and tried to guide them by gesturing which way to pull the oars. The boat came in closer and closer, and finally the Old Man leaped into the water and started to wade toward it. Jim stared in surprise, then followed suit.

Together, in water nearly to their armpits, they grasped the bow, heaved it around, and, with the boatmen now using the oars for poles, little by little they succeeded in beaching the craft halfway along the southern edge of the land spit. One of the men at the oars immediately collapsed and fell to the bottom of the boat. One was already draped across a thwart. But the other one merely grinned and climbed out.

He was about five feet tall, seemed almost five feet wide, and was like nothing Jim had ever seen before. His darkish hair, thick and coarse as mattress stuffing, hung to his shoulders; his beard, nearly covering his face, came halfway down his chest, and wild hairs sprouted from his nose and ears. Little piglike eyes, with a pleasant, twinkling expression, peered out as if from ambush. He was wearing a tattered old sweater, work pants, and thigh boots.

With his help, Jim and the Old Man got the other two out of the boat and laid them on ground. All at once the Old Man gave a start.

"George Carmack!" he shouted.

"Da!" said the hairy gnome. "You know?"

"Know!" cried the Old Man. "I was with him at Forty Mile in the eighties." Now he turned: "Jim, will you go make up a big pot of coffee and open up some cans? When I get these fellows around we'll eat."

The gnome grinned cheerfully and rubbed his hands.

George Carmack, a grizzled Alaskan veteran, with bleak-looking blue eyes and a thin, grim face, wrapped in a blanket and still trembling from exhaustion, sipped his coffee slowly and kept glancing at the Old Man. His two helpers, Slim and the gnome, whose name turned out to be Igor, had stuffed themselves into unconsciousness and lay on the ground, snoring loudly.

"By God, Nollys," said George, "you're sure looking old. Why, I remember you with kinda reddish-blond hair. Your beard's white as snow. Regular Santa Claus beard."

But the Old Man wasn't offended. He just laughed. "George," he said, "you got a kind of grizzly gray look yourself and damned if you haven't picked up a fine crop of face wrinkles."

"Where the hell were you headed for in that damned old steamboat, Nollys?"

"Forty Mile. Gold."

George laughed in derision. "Forty Mile! Hell, that's nothing. Penny ante. Let the breeds have it. Nollys, I've made the strike of the century. I'll be richer than the Morgans and the Vanderbilts. Forty Mile!" George laughed loudly and slapped his thigh. "Why, Nollys, you old bugger, you was damned lucky to take thirty-five, forty thousand dollars out of that claim you had in Forty Mile—and you worked like a dog. Look at this!"

He took a rag-wrapped nugget from his pants pocket and held it under the Old Man's nose. The Old Man studied it for a moment, then took out his own nugget and displayed it.

"You damned liar!" cried George, his face showing shock and amazement. "That ain't out of Forty Mile! It ain't! It ain't! It's as good as mine. Now where in hell did you get that? My God, Nollys; you'll be rich as me. It ain't fair."

The two old men glared at each other for a moment, then burst out into wild laughter. They ended up by shaking hands and slapping each other on the back.

"I'm glad it's you, Nollys," said George. "You're an old-timer. You've suffered. Just couldn't stand it if some outsider'd barge in and make a lucky hit. I been looking for ten years, ever since you left. Never was satisfied with my claims on Forty Mile—leased 'em. Come on, Nollys. Tell me where you found that bit. I can't do you no harm. I'm on my way to Circle. Won't be back toward Forty Mile till the next boat."

"You tell me," said the Old Man, "then I'll tell you. Word of honor."

George nodded abruptly. He knew ole Nollys Harp well, and that was good enough for him. "All right," he said. "You know a river, oh, about thirty miles south of Forty Mile Town—Indians call it the Throndeck, something like that?"

"Yes, I do. Never worked it though."

"Well, I picked this up off one of its creeks. Ain't saying which. Me and two other fellows, we got two thousand feet of that creek and we'll have so much money by spring we wouldn't even speak to Queen Victoria. Now. Where'd you find yours?"

"You know Sixty Mile River?"

"I do."

"Off one of its creeks and that's where I'm heading, Jim here and me. We started out with five and now there's only the two of us left."

But George did not seem to think that this was strange. He nodded. "That's the way it goes up here. Say, you'll be needing some help. You want them two fellows of mine? They were figuring to look for work in Circle."

"I can use the hairy one, I think," said the Old Man. "What in God's name is he, by the way?"

"Oh, some unholy mixture of Eskimo, or Indian, and Russian. I was in Japan once when I was sailing before the mast and I saw a whole heap of fellows that looked like him. Hairy Ainus, they called 'em. But he don't even know where Japan is or if it's any place. He was born up here and has never been away. He's as strong as a moose and as good-natured as a healthy baby. So you don't want Slim?"

"Nope," said the Old Man. "Too scrawny. Won't do."

"You got a point," said George. "Collapsed on me out there in that goddamned boat. Almost lost the oar. That'd done for us, all right."

"Say," said the Old Man, "how you figure to get to Circle now?"

"Have one of the Injuns take me in. It's a cinch in a canoe; you ride in style."

"How about that boat?"

"Now what the hell would anybody want with that thing?" cried George. "Never should have started in it. One oar's shorter than the other and the wood round the oarlocks is all worm-eaten to hell. We almost capsized two–three times. Tried to make an Injun village on the other bank but couldn't cut it. Then luckily we seen the steamboat."

"Okay. I'll take the boat," said the Old Man. "What do you want for it?"

"You can't go upstream in that, you old fool. But give me ten dollars and it's yours."

"Done," said the Old Man, smiling with grim satisfaction; then: "Say, by the way, would you mind telling me, George, what the hell you're going to Circle City for anyway?"

"To be on the safe side."

"What do you mean?"

"I'm registering my claims there."

"What the hell's the matter with Forty Mile? Save you all this trip."

"Ain't you heard? Forty Mile, Sixty Mile, all that territory around there has been declared Canadian territory."

"No!"

"Yes. There's a British police post at Fort Cudahy now. The boundary line is the 141st meridian, drawn from Point Demarcation to Mount St. Elias. Wouldn't be surprised you're in Canadian territory right now."

"Well I'm damned," said the Old Man. "But even so, what's wrong with registering your claims with the British? They're mighty damned honest people. More honest than we are, if you come to that."

"I'm taking no chances," said George. "I'm registering 'em both places. And you'd better do the same. There's millions at stake, Nollys; millions. And I'm going to have my share or bust."

The two old men talked on, and Jim sat listening, feeling younger and more inadequate and more foolish minute by minute. How had they ever had the audacity to question any of the Old Man's suggestions or decisions? Jim realized now how silly they'd all been in regard to Nollys. Here was a man who had not told them one lie. Everything he'd said had turned out to be true. Step by step he'd been leading them to a fortune in spite of themselves. Gabe had been unlucky; he knew the Old Man well and would have followed his lead without question. But Lloyd and Hoxie had fallen by the wayside not only because they had doubted the Old Man but also because they could not subdue their own natures long enough to see the expedition out. And now God knows what would happen to them. As for himself, he'd doubted the Old Man really only once—and that had been in Circle City when, out of largely unacknowledged reasons of his own, he had joined Hoxie's puerile revolt.

Jim felt very strange sitting there as the talk flowed on. It was as if a steady hand—not his own, not even the Old Man's—had guided him firmly past the pitfalls and the snares that had been too much for Lloyd and Hoxie. He felt like giving thanks, but he did not know how to go about it.

Jim, the Old Man, and Igor stood on the land spit, gesturing goodby, as the big canoe pushed off and headed diagonally out toward midstream. Three Indians were paddling; George Carmack and Slim sat amidship. Soon the sun glare on the water swallowed them.

"Well," said the Old Man, "let's get to work. First we got to rig rope harness; then we got to pull the boat up from the spit to our camp. Or what about rollers? What do you think, Igor?"

"Name's Igor Bunak," said the hairy gnome. "I work good. One dollar day. All right?"

"That's fine," said the Old Man.

"Every day. Sunday, too. I work Sunday. One dollar."

"All right, Igor. Sunday means nothing to us. We work just the same. I say, rig up the harness, and we'll test the drag-portage idea, getting the boat to our camp. All right, Jim?"

"Sounds all right to me, Nollys."

The Old Man and Igor started back for the camp. Jim stood for a moment on the land spit, looking off across the river. Now and then a little dark speck danced before his eyes. The canoe—with Carmack on his way to Circle, where Lloyd and Hoxie and even Kobo now were.

Loneliness stabbed at him briefly, but he fought it off. The gold lay ahead, and the thought of the long winter did not disturb him now as it had done in the past. He'd seen many a bad winter in Ohio with below-zero temperatures and snowdrifts piled ten or twelve feet high. Many times he and his father and brothers had shoveled their way out of the house. How much worse than that could it be in Alaska?

The boat had been loaded, the drag harness perfected, but the Old Man was still not satisfied. For hours he worked on, installing new blocks for the oarlocks, shortening one oar and laboriously carving out a new handle. Igor slept tranquilly on the strand, waiting to be called to duty, but Jim, feeling useless, paced about with growing impatience.

The Old Man had set up a temporary workbench and was now busy at it, with saw and auger, working on some big, odd-looking blocks of wood. Jim went over to him and watched for a moment, then asked: "What's that? What are you doing now, Nollys?"

"Oh, that boat was a godsend, Jim," said the Old Man, without interrupting his work. "Give me ideas. I'm rigging up a little platform with block wheels. When we get to Forty Mile we're all through with drag portage. We row up Forty Mile Creek to Moose Creek, up Moose Creek to its source; then we wheel all our stuff across to Glacier Creek and then row down Glacier to where we're going. Save us days, weeks, maybe."

He worked on, tirelessly. Jim watched for a while in silence; then he joined Igor on the strand and finally fell asleep.

They were on their way. Igor was in the harness, straining against the wide leather surcingle the Old Man had rigged up, and with the Old Man guiding and steadying it from the bank, the heavily laden boat moved forward through the quiet inshore water with surprising ease.

The Indians stood watching the departure with mixed emotions. These were good Anglos. They had caused no trouble whatsoever in the village; on the contrary, they had been lavish in their gifts of tobacco and trinkets and many unknown objects that were now piled in the wickiup of the chief. And they had brought a welcome excitement, a relief from the grinding monotony of life on the tundra. And yet... they didn't belong there. They were aliens and unbelievers, who did not acknowledge the supreme power of Gitchi Manitou: unregenerate heathens, arrogant and stubborn in their resistance to the True Religion.

A group of Indian children tagged along at a distance, laughing and skipping and accompanied by half a dozen puppies that yapped, skittered about, and played rough-and-tumble with each other in the thick tundra moss. Igor and the Old Man ignored the Indians, but Jim turned and waved good-by.

The children stopped stock-still and stared, thinking that Jim was waving them back; then they climbed to the top of a hillock and watched till the three funny-looking bearded Anglos were out of sight round a bend.

All three lived through a sort of nightmare of weariness as they took their regular turns in the harness and inched the big loaded rowboat forward toward Forty Mile.

"Now I know what it's like to be a horse," said Jim, as Igor relieved him, and he took up his place beside the Old Man at the side of the boat and helped him guide it through the quiet shallows.

"Never said it would be easy," said the Old Man. "But we're getting there."

Yes, they were getting there, foot by foot, instead of mile by mile.

One night—it was about three in the morning—they made camp on the strand of a little scooped-out bay where spruce grew almost down to the water's edge. Igor, who had been taking a double turn lately, fell down where he stood and began to snore. The Old Man, grim with weariness and very silent, got out the utensils and started to cook sup-per. Jim, who was almost stupefied with exhaustion, felt nervous and restless and wandered away from camp to the top of a hillock, where he lighted his pipe and stood looking about him.

All of a sudden he came tearing back into camp, yelling and waving his arms.

"Nollys! Nollys! I can see lights off to the south there. Regular lights—like in a window, or something."

The Old Man climbed up the hillock with Jim and stood staring off toward the south; then he nodded slowly, put his arm around Jim's shoulder, and patted him.

"That'd be Fort Cudahy where George said the British have now got a police post. Forty Mile's only a few miles beyond. We're damned near there, boy; damned near there."

Three redcoated British policemen were walking up and down the strand at Fort Cudahy when the big rowboat appeared round the bend, pulled by what looked like a gorilla or a small bear.

"Good God," said one of them. "There's that Russian that left the other day. What in the devil is he doing, pulling the boat back?"

And later they could not get any coherent explanation from the three men who finally beached the boat, which, to the amazement of the policemen, was piled high with dunnage of all kinds, and fell down in a heap and began to snore.

Later, in the big common room of the police stockade, the three men, wrapped in blankets and revived by hot toddies made with excellent Scotch whisky, tried to explain everything, from the explosion of the *Nils K. Jensen* to the arrival of Carmack; that is, the Old Man tried, while Jim only put in a word here and there, and the Hairy One kept silent, but chuckled cheerfully now and then over the delicious taste of the whisky.

"You're just in time," said the C.O., a huge man with bristling blond mustaches.

"How so?" asked Nollys.

"Strike! Tremendous strike," the C.O. explained. "On the Throndeck. You know, what the British call the Klondyke. Carmack no sooner registered his claims than the others began to pour in. There's a town already, out there in no place, at the juncture of the Klondyke and the Yukon. Never saw anything like it. Where they all come from I'm damned if I know. It's a panic."

The Old Man's face went a little grim at this and his gray eyes flashed, then were veiled. "Big strike at Circle, too," he said, noncommittally.

"So I hear," said the C.O.

That night Igor slept in the boat, to guard their supplies, while Jim and the Old Man had bunks in the barracks.

The Old Man was so weary that he could hardly hold up his head, but he said: "We'll sleep two–three hours, Jim, then be on our way."

"Good God, Nollys," cried Jim, sagging with weariness, "we're here! Why can't we rest a few days?"

"No," said the Old Man adamantly. "You heard what the C.O. said. Big strike on the Throndeck. That's just down Sixty Mile River from our place, Jim. Suppose we get there too late? Men'll be swarming all over the creeks off the Throndeck now. Some may be smart enough to cross the Yukon River and take a shot at Sixty Mile. If we was real smart we'd be on our way right now. But the hell of it is we really need a little rest."

Jim groaned, fell into his bunk, and was asleep in an instant, too exhausted to care whether they ever got any gold or not. Left to himself, he would have stayed at Fort Cudahy for a week, or maybe even a month...!

... the Old Man was shaking him. It seemed to Jim that he'd just closed his eyes.

"All right, Jim," said the Old Man. "Let's go. Igor's in the harness already. Time's a-wasting, boy, time's a-wasting!"

The Old Man drove them hard, and both Jim and Igor worked and strained as if in a nightmare, but at last, gray-faced, almost dropping with fatigue, they reached Forty Mile Town, the goal of all their dreams. Jim couldn't believe his eyes when they got there. It was smaller and more squalid than Unalaska. But the Old Man's grin seemed a yard wide.

"Well, here we are," he cried. "Now we get in the damned boat and row up Forty Mile Creek. The worst's over, Jim; the worst's over."

Igor fell clown in a heap beside the boat and began to snore. In a moment Jim joined him. But the Old Man sat on, wakeful, and grudgingly allowed Igor and Jim a precious hour of rest.

Time passed. The Old Man drove forward relentlessly, and two days later they made the portage from the head of Moose Creek on the Forty Mile watershed to the head of Glacier Creek on the Sixty Mile watershed, through hilly country.

Jim fought with himself hour after hour to keep going. He lived in a gray haze of fatigue, and even the rugged Igor was getting close to the end of his rope. But the Old Man, tireless as a machine, drove on.

As they neared what the Old Man was now calling the Promised Land, a huge moose started up from a clump of spruce and tore off across the tundra, nimbly showing them his heels.

The Old Man cheered, waved his battered hat, and even wept a little, to Jim's astonishment.

"Oh, that moose, that wonderful moose!" cried the Old Man. "I'll remember him to my dying day."

"But why, Nollys? Why?" asked Jim, shaken by the Old Man's emotional display.

"Why, it means the creek's deserted," said the Old Man. "It means the hoosiers ain't started tramping up Glacier Creek. It means we're in time, Jim; *in time!* We've made it, boy; we've made it. Just like I told you we would way back in Seattle, when you were all maybe thinking I was just a half-cracked old waterfront rat. Eh, Jim, eh?" The Old Man roared with laughter, then capered about like a boy, waving his long arms. "We'll be rich as Midas, I'm telling you, Jim; rich as Midas!"

Igor collapsed and began to snore. Jim sat down with his back to the hull of the big rowboat. Little by little the Old Man subsided and finally fell asleep. Slowly his big knotted hands unclasped, his whole taut body relaxed, and at last his hat fell off as his head dropped helplessly forward.

For the moment he looked very old to Jim, very old and spent.

Jim's eyes closed of themselves. The three men slept on. Finally a huge blue jay flew low over them, then perched in a spruce sapling above their heads and scolded them fiercely, staring hard with its beady eyes at these crumpled interlopers from another world.

It was late August now and at night there was a chill in the air. Working like ants, they had built a big, sturdy log house on a good site near the headwaters of Glacier Creek, and by dint of back-breaking labor—with the Old Man driving relentlessly—all the preparatory work for the winter mining season had been done; and four claims had been registered with the British at Fort Cudahy; and the Old Man and Jim now owned two thousand feet of Glacier Creek, with Igor Bunak for dummy on one claim. Igor did not want any claim, he said. All he wanted was one dollar a day, even on Sundays.

This bothered Jim and he said to the Old Man: "I thought you told me hired miners got ten dollars a day up here."

"So they do, or more," said the Old Man. "But why give a fellow more than he asks? Is that sense? Anyway, it don't matter with Igor. He eats, sleeps, works. That's all he knows. And he's happy that way. Let him get his pocket full of money once and he might go wrong. I've seen it happen, time after time, especially with Injuns, and, after all, Igor's a breed, though he don't look it."

Jim still protested and the Old Man finally said to him: "Trouble with you is, Jim, you just don't have enough greed in your nature. You're lacking that way. Listen to me. It's greed makes a man successful. Just pure greed, never mind the copybook maxims!"

But Jim remained unconvinced.

Time passed. The weather stayed good, with a hot sun in the daytime and not too much chill at night. The big Klondyke gold strike roared on all around them. One day men appeared near the headwaters of Glacier Creek. The Old Man got the moose gun and went out to talk to them, but they turned out to be harmless strangers who did not know that they were trespassing.

"Don't have much trouble with jumpers up here," said the Old Man. "As for me, I take no chances. The man that tries to jump me gets killed."

Men continued to pour into the Klondyke area from all directions, some of them dying of the privations of the long trek soon after arrival.

The town at the juncture of the Throndeck and the Yukon had been named Dawson, or Dawson City, and was now nearly two thousand in population and roaring as loudly as Circle City.

But neither Jim nor the Old Man ever went near it, though it was only a little over thirty miles away, across the big river. They worked and planned, with Jim absorbing knowledge, lore, and techniques like a sponge, while Igor slept and ate mostly, saving his energy for the rugged winter mining season ahead.

"He's a good man," said the Old Man. "We were lucky to find him. He knows his business. Can't talk or explain but in his head he knows. And we don't have to cut him in as partner."

"I've been thinking about that," said Jim. "I say cut him in. He deserves it."

"I say no, goddamn it," cried the Old Man. "You want to cut our take a third? That third might amount to thousands and thousands of dollars. Are you crazy, Jim? Plumb daft? Remember what I told you. Greed. That's the answer. Be greedy. Everybody else is."

"What about Lloyd?" asked Jim.

And the Old Man groaned to himself. "Don't bring him up, for the love of God! He's beyond me. Don't understand him at all. Or maybe I do. Yes, maybe I do. She was his first girl. He ain't found out yet a girl is just a girl. A man can't think straight till he's found that out. But he's got greed in him, don't doubt that, Jim. He's human, ain't he?"

Jim was no match for the Old Man in argument so he fell silent. All the same he made up his mind that he'd take care of Igor, one way or another, Old Man or no Old Man.

One afternoon, with a bright sun and a decided chill in the air, Jim and the Old Man were reconnoitering the creek, looking for likely clumps of new-growth spruce for their newly installed iron stove that they'd bought at Forty Mile and brought laboriously to the log house. They were walking through heavy gravel at the margin of the water.

Suddenly the Old Man stumbled and fell to his knees. Jim helped him up and looked at him curiously.

"What happened, Nollys?"

"Turned my ankle on a goddamned stone," said the Old Man quickly, but all the way back he seemed preoccupied.

Jim began to worry about him. After all, Nollys was nearly sixty-four years old. Actually Jim had never paid very much attention to Nollys before; he'd accepted him as a leader, of course, and he'd always listened carefully when he spoke, but he had never really spent any time just observing him, as a man. Now it came as a shock to him to note that Nollys seemed to be failing. His face looked drawn and haggard, his lips pale, his eyes a little dim, nothing so bright and hawklike as they'd been in Seattle and later on the Yukon. He slept more now, ate less. Did not talk nearly as much as in the past and often seemed abstracted, lost to the world about him.

"Nollys, you sure you're all right?" Jim asked him one day, then was astonished by the Old Man's reaction.

He was furious. "Course I'm all right, goddamn it," he yelled. "Didn't I get us here? Didn't I figure it all out? I made it, goddamn it; just like I told you I would. A man stumbles and people think he ain't all right."

Jim had forgotten about the stumbling. The Old Man's reference to it bothered him, but he never again asked the Old Man if he was all right.

The summer had been excessively long and hot for this Yukon country, and the first days of September were warm and fine, a little like Indian summer in the Midwest.

Jim, in his shirt sleeves, was chopping wood in front of the log house when he saw Igor and the Old Man coming up along the edge of the creek toward him. The Old Man had the moose gun strapped to his back and a mattock in his right hand, and Igor was carrying a sack over his shoulder, the weight of it bending him forward.

Jim waved and the Old Man waved back, seeming more like himself. There was even a certain jauntiness in his manner that surprised Jim.

While Igor cooked supper on the all-purpose stove, the Old Man sat at the table with Jim, displaying the contents of the sack, nuggets of various sizes and coloration, and Jim sat staring blankly at the dirty, jagged little bits of rock, thinking, for a moment, that it was very odd that men would leave their homes and all familiar things to come traipsing three or four thousand miles across the globe just to gather stones along a barren creek. Gold! What did it mean? Did gold move the world as the Old Man said, or was it a curse?

"Jim," the Old Man was explaining, "it's even bigger than I thought. I can't believe my eyes. Was talking to a fellow down at the junction of Glacier and Sixty Mile the other day and he told me in a test on El Dorado Creek, across the Yukon, the gold was running seventy dollars to the pan. I thought he was plumb crazy, or just stretching it for fun. Listen, Jim, Igor and I—we been doing some real digging on Claim 2. I did a little testing myself. What do you reckon my best pan run to?"

"I don't know, Nollys," said Jim. "Couldn't be as rich as El Dorado I don't suppose."

The Old Man roared with laughter. "Not as rich, eh? And you think, like me, that maybe the fellow was lying, eh? Two hundred dollars! That's what it run to, Jim."

The Old Man grinned gleefully and slapped the top of the table. Jim was staggered and a cold chill ran down his spine. So it was true after all? He was going to be rich.

But he still couldn't quite grasp it. It seemed so unlikely, so damned unlikely, that he, Jim Hardy, farm boy from Roxabelle, Ohio, was going to be rich!

"By God, you're turning pale, Jim," said the Old Man. "Good, good. Your natural greed's showing, Jim. Good! Listen to me, in Forty Mile in the eighties a ten-dollar pan was a fine one. And I run a quick test here and get twenty times that. It scares me kinda, Jim—damned if it don't. It just ain't natural. As for nuggets, you can pick 'em up like mushrooms along the margin of the creek. We'll be so damned rich, Jim—so damned rich when we pull out of here next spring that... well, you'd think I was lying, Jim. Yes, sir, you'd think old Nollys Harp had finally blown his wig."

"How rich, Nollys?" Jim demanded. "Tell me. How rich?"

"Well, for one thing," said the Old Man, "when we land on the waterfront in Seattle, say, around the fifteenth of August, we'll be the two richest men in the whole city. Does that answer your question, Jim, eh?"

"Come on now, Nollys!" cried Jim, appalled. "Richer than the man who owns the lumber yards? Richer than the Kinsmans, who own the Alaska and Northern Steamship Lines? Richer than the bankers?"

"Yes," said the Old Man. "Much richer. Maybe we'll buy out the Kinsmans, you and me, and run our own steamship line. Eh, Jim?" The Old Man laughed loudly and slapped the table.

"But, Nollys," Jim protested, "when you was trying to get us to come you said we might get out with fifty thousand dollars apiece. You don't buy any steamship lines with that."

"Didn't want to raise your hopes too high. Besides, Jim—don't you see?—I'm kinda flabbergasted myself. It's much richer than I thought. A hundredfold richer! It means millions, Jim, millions!"

While Jim sat in stunned silence, Igor, chuckling and grinning and ignoring all the talk about riches, put the food on the table, then sat down and poured out the thick black coffee.

"I cook good, no?" he said, looking from one to the other, grinning.

The Old Man patted him on the shoulder. "Igor, you do everything good. You're all right."

Jim ate in silence, confused images racing through his mind; images of home—the old Hardy farm, worked by three generations of Hardys; the spring house with its delicious summer cool; the creek at the foot of the south wheat field; his mother's grave in the little shaded burying ground at Roxabelle; his father, hard-bitten, silent, unapproachable; his hard-working, home-staying brothers. He saw himself arriving in a hired surrey from Chillicothe, where the railroad ended. He saw all the astonished faces. What would they say?

It was a rather warm evening and the door was wide open, giving a glimpse of a spruce thicket and an outcropping of boulders, with the slow-flowing creek just beyond. Suddenly the atmosphere changed, a chill wind began to blow along the floor, and in a little while large feathery snowflakes started to fall slowly down past the open doorway.

"Here she comes," said the Old Man, grinning. "I knew that summery weather couldn't last. Look at them flakes. Some of 'em as big as your hand."

They sat watching the snow, but it was a mere harbinger of winter and melted as soon as it landed.

"Won't be long now till the big freeze," said the Old Man. "Then we'll get the gold out, like it was coal. Yes, sir, Jim—just like it was coal, it's that plentiful."

When they got up the next morning the log house was like the inside of an icebox. Jim opened the door and looked out. The king grass was all covered with hoarfrost that sparkled brightly in the early morning light.

"Yep," said the Old Man, grinning and rubbing his hands together, "won't be long now."

After breakfast he grabbed up his tools. "Not going far," he explained. "Not beyond Claim 1. Just want to look over our property, you might say."

Jim made no comment. Every day the Old Man set out to "look over our property"; for hours he'd work at the sluice boxes or plan and re-plan the spillways; but toward evening he always showed up with a sack of gold dust and a pocketful of small nuggets. It was the gold that drew him, Jim knew; not the carpentry work. And after supper, when Igor had cleared the table, the Old Man would test his finds, and then, when at last it was bedtime, he'd stow away the dust in one sack and the nuggets in another, chuckling.

"Damn it," he'd say, "it's just beyond belief. Why, Jim, we got a fortune already in them testing sacks. A man could live a year in comfort on just what I brought in today—and I'm only just pecking around, after work, you might say."

Each day, as fall came slowly on, was like another, with the Old Man hammering and "testing" along the creek while Igor and Jim cut wood in the spruce thickets and did other odd jobs that always seemed to need doing.

But one day turned out to be different. Jim and Igor heard the Old Man yelling for them. He was nearly a quarter of a mile down the creek but his voice came to them clearly. The chunky Igor distanced Jim as they ran toward the Old Man, and Jim could only marvel at his speed afoot; Jim was pretty fast himself, and Igor looked like a slowpoke if he'd ever seen one!

The Old Man had fallen down a bank in among some boulders and twisted his ankle.

"Maybe we'd better get the boat," said Jim, "and row you back."

"No," said Igor. "I carry back. Very easy."

And carry him back to the log house he did, bent almost double with the gangling Old Man prone across his shoulders. They got him into his bunk; then Jim took off the Old Man's lace-ups and pulled down his sock, displaying a badly swollen ankle, blue in color.

"You're going to be in that bunk for a while, Nollys," said Jim. "That's a bad-looking sprain."

"Oh hell," said the Old Man, "it's nothing, Jim; I'll be out working and testing tomorrow morning, same as usual. You watch."

But even the Old Man's iron will failed in the face of this disability. The ankle grew worse, puffed up to such a degree that it frightened Jim to look at it; and it was so sensitive to the touch that the Old Man would grit his teeth and wince as he drew on his sock. But the Old Man would just not stay in his bunk. There was no way to keep him there. He'd rise at breakfast time and hobble painfully to his chair, where he'd spend the day sorting over his gold dust and his nuggets, while Igor kept bringing in tubs of steaming hot water in which to soak his ankle.

The Old Man talked about the gold constantly and weighed and sacked it over and over again. "If only my foot hadn't slipped, Jim," he'd say, "I'd have ten times this gold in the sacks." And then he'd curse and groan at his enforced inactivity.

There was something hysterical about his whole attitude that began to bother Jim very much, and he'd try to calm the Old Man and divert his attention by recalling incidents of their long trek from Seattle to Forty Mile. From time to time this was successful, and the Old Man would smile at the recollections of First Mate Hansen and Joe Portugee and the remote skipper, Lars Petersen, who hardly ever came out of his cabin except to go to the bridge; and Lloyd with his saintlike red beard; and the carousing at Circle City... but he always some way managed to get back to the gold. It had become an obsession.

One night he said: "Jim, do you realize I haven't even so much as run one pan on Claim 3? I know it's farther along from the headwaters of the creek and don't figure to be as rich as I and 2; but I just got a hunch about it—yes, sir—a hunch. Rich as Golconda, Claim 3. You can bet on it, Jim. Rich as Golconda." And then he began to talk about how wealthy they were going to be. He had decided, he said, to buy himself a big house on Nob Hill in San Francisco, in which he'd live for maybe six months of the year; in the summer he intended to tour the islands of the Pacific in his own big sailing yacht, with auxiliary engine; or maybe charter a railroad car and roll off across the continent to New York—and from there he might even ship out for London and Paris on one of those new luxury liners.

Jim was dazzled and bewildered by the Old Man's plans for the future. As for himself, his ideas were not nearly so grandiose; in fact, he seldom thought beyond a house in Columbus, Ohio, and maybe a pretty local girl for a wife. As for his family, well, he knew his father, proud as hell, would never accept a cent from him and would be content to farm the old Hardy place till he dropped in the harness, but maybe he could give his brothers a lift—especially Tommy, who wasn't exactly like the others and at one time had had yearnings to join the Navy and see the world. But as for houses on Nob Hill and yachts and chartered railroad cars and seeing New York, London, and Paris... well, that just seemed fantastic to Jim, like something you'd read in a book or see on the stage. It wasn't for him.

And then the Old Man would get back to the gold. "By God," Jim said to himself one night, as he watched the Old Man re-sacking a drawerful, "he's like a miser. Playing with it, gloating over it."

And the Old Man kept talking about the probable richness of Claim 3, but finally Jim got so that he hardly listened to the Old Man's obsessed, monotonous conversation and had no real conception what a grip the idea of the richness of Claim 3 had on the Old Man's imagination.

It was a cold morning with a gray sky and a north wind that sang and whistled through the spruce clumps. There were little thin sheets of ice all along the margin of the creek, and the sun, trying hard to break through the overcast, shed a wan, palish, silvery light over the countryside.

Jim, chilled in spite of his flannel underwear, flannel shirt, and Mackinaw jacket, was cutting spruce about two hundred yards north of the log house. Later Igor would come with the sledge the Old Man had built and cart the wood back to the stockpile. A big blue jay seemed to take a great interest in what Jim was doing and kept flying from tree to near-by tree, watching him. From time to time the bird scolded Jim in a hoarse, harsh voice.

Jim kept glancing up at the jay, liking the company.

In some of the hollows there were patches of snow, and at one place Jim came across huge animal tracks, of dog or wolf—it didn't seem to matter which in this country. And then he remembered that for the last three nights they'd heard howling far to the north of them—as if a wolf pack was baying at the moon. Winter was coming on. Game was getting scarce. It was the danger time for wolves, as the Old Man had told him. Jim paid less attention to the jay and began to look about him warily at the large low clumps of near-by scrub where a big animal could lurk unseen. There'd been trouble with wolves on Sixty Mile River, or so he'd heard.

The jay left him, then came back. Jim had his ax poised when he heard Igor's voice shouting for him. It sounded urgent, so he turned and ran quickly back toward the log house. Igor had gone to Forty Mile for supplies and Jim hadn't expected him back quite this soon.

"What's the matter?" cried Jim, running up to Igor, who seemed to be in a very unusual state of agitation.

Igor's face worked for a moment; then he pointed to the log house. "He gone."

"Nollys?" cried Jim. Why, hell, the Old Man could just barely walk and had been no farther since his injury than the edge of the creek, a hundred feet from the doorway.

"I look down creek pretty far, no find," said Igor, staring. Now strange, sinister sounds came to them on the wind from far down the creek—was it barking, howling, what?

A hunch suddenly hit Jim. "That Old Man!" he cried. "He couldn't stand it any longer. He's sneaked off to Claim 3 for the gold."

He started down the creek at a run. Igor dashed into the house and came out carrying a Winchester rifle the Old Man had bought in Forty Mile for use against smaller game and silently handed it to Jim, who stopped and took it with a surprised look.

"She loaded," said Igor.

"Old Man got the moose gun?"

Igor nodded. And at that moment a crashing rifle shot echoed up the creek, bounding and rebounding from the big boulders along the way, and the barking or howling or whatever it was rose to a high pitch.

Igor and Jim tore up along the bank, running as if the devil were after them. There was another shot and more howling, and then Jim, topping a low rise, saw the Old Man crouched in a hollow among big boulders, in an awkward position as if he had fallen and couldn't rise, while above him, in among the rocks, were at least a dozen big snarling, gray-blue tundra wolves. Igor, just beyond Jim, gave a gasp of horror that hardly sounded human; then he began to pick up big stones and hurl them at the wolves, advancing on them step by step.

Jim got the biggest of the wolves in his sights and pressed the trigger. The wolf gave a wild leap and a howl, tried to run, couldn't, then fell and rolled, biting at the ground. To Jim's amazed horror the other wolves leaped on him and began to rip and tear at him before he was even close to dead.

"Okay," said Igor. "They eat him now. You kill 'nother one. I see Old Man."

Igor dashed down into the hollow, while Jim, badly shaken by the fiendish savagery of the wolves, shot another one, which also bit at the ground and thrashed about. But this double windfall seemed too much for the other wolves, seemed to unsettle them, and in a moment they slunk off into the timber beyond the margin of the creek. They'd return to feast on their brothers later.

Jim climbed down into the hollow beside Igor and the Old Man, who cried: "Look in that sack, Jim. Look, I was right. It's richer. Claim 3's far richer. Oh God—will we be nabobs!"

It was a long trek to the log house, with Igor lugging the Old Man on his back and Jim carrying the two rifles and the gold sack, and looking over his shoulder to make sure they weren't being followed by the wolves.

As soon as they got the Old Man in his bunk he began to talk feverishly and rave about the gold in Claim 3. They couldn't quiet him, and Jim, his heart sinking, noticed that a greenish-ashen pallor was beginning to spread slowly over the Old Man's worn face.

"Nollys," he cried, "are you all right? Are you all right, Nollys?"

Igor looked at Jim in puzzled wonder, then took the Old Man's hand.

"Sure, I'm all right," said the Old Man. "Ain't I always been? We're going to be rich, Jim; rich beyond the dreams of avarice. Yes, sir, Jim. Told you, didn't I? Back on that damned old Seattle waterfront. Told you!"

Jim felt a little better now—the Old Man would make it; tough as a pine knot, he was!—and Jim turned away to get him a drink of water.

"He dead," said Igor.

And Jim turned back and stared in stark unbelief. The Old Man seemed to be smiling in his sleep.

VIII

THE RETURN:
JULY 1897

It was July 10, 1897, now and the new A.C. tug, *Pribilof*, which had taken the place of the old *Nils K. Jensen*, had docked at Forty Mile, and eager prospectors, jammed on the decks like sardines in a can, were impatiently waiting to get ashore.

Jim Hardy, all packed and ready to leave, was in the office of the A. C. Company—a little clapboard affair—talking with the British C.O. from Fort Cudahy, who had come to take a look at the new arrivals from the States. Alaska was getting a lot of bad ones now and the British authorities did not fool around with them, but relentlessly kicked them out—that is, deported them back to American territory.

Jim had tried hard to make Igor rich, but Igor just did not want to be rich. Money was too great a burden to him. All he wanted was one dollar a day, even on Sundays, and keep.

"What about a thousand dollars?" Jim was asking the C.O.

"Plenty, plenty," said the big British officer, whose face was beet red and whose blond mustaches were larger and bristled even more than they had a year back. "That will be enough money to keep Igor for twenty years, even if he doesn't work."

"All right," said Jim, pleased. "I'll leave it in your trust."

"In the trust of the British Constabulary," corrected the C.O. "I may be sailing for home this year. But it will be looked after."

"I don't doubt that at all," said Jim, smiling.

The *Pribilof* was about ready to sail back down the big river, and Jim was standing beside the gangplank saying good-by to the dirty, bewhiskered Igor, who was grinning at him shyly. Jim's gold, packed in six huge canvas sacks, was stored in the hold of the *Pribilof*, a powerful ocean-going tug and a great improvement over the rickety old *Nils K. Jensen*. Besides the sacked gold, two checks were waiting for Jim in a Seattle bank: one for two hundred and fifty thousand dollars, another for a little over five hundred thousand dollars. He'd sold Claim 3 to a combine of St. Michael businessmen and the other three claims to the Kinsman Steamship Company of Seattle.

But he didn't feel rich or very different from the old Jim who had come upriver almost against his will, propelled by the Old Man's ruthless, determined, unstoppable drive for the gold. In fact, Jim felt bewildered, scared, and lonesome, and wished that Igor was going back with him.

"Well, good-by," said Jim, wringing Igor's dirty, rough hand, hard as wood. "Any time you need a little money, stop in and see the C.O. at Fort Cudahy."

"For why I need money?" asked Igor, puzzled. "I work. People feed me free. All fine."

"You might get sick or hurt."

Igor's eyes lit up at this. "Oh! Good, fine. Sure. I get hurt, sick, I see Redcoat. Yes?"

Jim nodded; they shook hands again; then Jim got aboard, found his cabin, and climbed into his bunk. Little by little his apprehension left him and he began to think about Ohio and Roxabelle and how strange it would seem to return home a rich man, after his father telling him he was a black sheep and a bum and would come to no earthly good!

He suffered a double disappointment in Circle City, as he'd been looking forward to seeing Lloyd and, against his better judgment, Hoxie. But Hoxie had vanished, no man knew where; hadn't been seen in Circle City since the *Nils K. Jensen* pulled out for her ill-fated voyage to Forty Mile in July of '96, while Lloyd and Adorée had gone back to St. Michael on the last boat out in '96, and Pete at the stockade informed Jim he'd heard that the two of them had left St. Michael for Juneau and then later on had gone into Canada, to the White Horse district.

Jim knew nobody. Even Shag Galloway and Nina had moved on: Shag to Dawson City, Nina back to the States, with a German fellow who'd taken a few thousand out of Circle City.

And even Circle City itself was no longer the same. The Klondyke strike had drained it of young able-bodied citizens. It was now inhabited by clerks, hunters, traders, trappers, and a few whores, Indians, and old men. Its muddy streets were no longer thronged, and by nine o'-clock at night the whole town was quiet.

Things had changed at St. Michael, too. It was bigger, more prosperous, and ships were pouring in from all points of the compass, loaded with goldseekers panting with excitement. Six tugs were now making the Yukon run upstream, and the biggest gold strike the world had ever seen roared on.

Jim got a cabin to himself on a fine big ship—the *Kestrel* of Seattle—that was returning to port almost empty of passengers but heavily laden with cargo, part of which was Jim's six sacks of gold.

As the days passed, Jim grew more and more lonely. He even considered going back to Ma Gracey's boardinghouse and saying hello to Ma and Pa and Lena. But two things kept him from it. First, Lena. Why get the poor girl's hopes up? Second, he'd lost track of Lloyd, who had failed in his quest for gold. How could he explain that?

And yet... Jim wasn't satisfied to just pass on as if the Graceys had never existed. They had been very nice to him, as a stranger in Seattle. And he kept recalling poor old Pa, trying to keep his head above water by giving music lessons when all he really wanted to do was loaf; and Ma, the head of the house, working and slaving from morning till night; and Lena, lonely and frustrated, with her embarrassing shyness which at times changed abruptly to a sort of timid boldness. Yes, they'd all been very nice to him, practically making him one of the family, at a time when he'd felt more than a little lost and unsure of the future.

So when he reached Seattle and had sold his gold and picked up his checks, he made arrangements at the bank for fifty thousand dollars to be paid to Ma Gracey at the rate of two hundred and fifty dollars a month. Wise for his years, Jim was afraid that a sum of that size in a lump might completely demoralize the Graceys, who had been living on the edge of poverty for many years. What he had set up, in fact, was a sort of pension that would see the older Graceys through the rest of their lives if they never managed to make another cent out of the music lessons and the boardinghouse.

The banker, a little bewildered by this amazingly rich young man of twenty-five who seemed to know his own mind so well, was instructed to tell the Graceys that the fifty thousand dollars had come from a mining syndicate in Alaska and represented the money from the purchase of one of Lloyd Gracey's claims.

Jim felt much better now as he got aboard his Pullman for Chicago. Would old Nollys have approved of his setting up of the pension? Jim doubted it. "Boy," he could hear him saying, "listen to me. You may need that fifty thousand before you're through. Yes, sir. Hang on to it. Be greedy." Jim laughed rather sadly to himself as the colored porter brought his bags aboard and helped him to get settled for the long trek eastward.

As the big transcontinental train rolled out of the station, Jim sat in his compartment working out his itinerary in his mind: from Seattle straight to Chicago, and from there to Columbus, Ohio, on the Pennsy, and then the short line to Chillicothe, and so home.

And so... home... to the old Hardy place by the big creek—Buckwheat Creek—where his ancestors had toiled for generations—the first Hardy ever to make a mark of any kind in the great world beyond the confines of the rich, rolling, black-soil farmlands of Clark County, Ohio.

The End

W. R. Burnett Bibliography

Novels
Little Caesar (Dial, 1929)
Iron Man (Dial, 1930)
Saint Johnson (Dial, 1930)
The Silver Eagle (Dial, 1931)
The Goodhues of Sinking Creek
　(Raven's Head, 1931)
The Giant Swing (Harper, 1932)
Dark Hazard (Harper, 1933)
Goodbye to the Past
　(Harper, 1934)
King Cole (Harper, 1936)
The Dark Command
　(Knopf, 1938)
High Sierra (Knopf, 1940)
The Quick Brown Fox
　(Knopf, 1942)
Nobody Lives Forever
　(Knopf, 1943)
Tomorrow's Another Day
　(Knopf, 1945)
Romelle (Knopf, 1946)
The Asphalt Jungle
　(Knopf, 1949)
Stretch Dawson
　(Gold Medal, 1950)
Little Men, Big World
　(Knopf, 1951)
Vanity Row (Knopf, 1952)
Adobe Walls (Knopf, 1953)
Big Stan (as by John Monahan;
　Gold Medal, 1953)
Captain Lightfoot
　(Knopf, 1954)
It's Always Four O'Clock
　(as by James Updyke;
　Random, 1956)

Pale Moon (Knopf, 1956)
Underdog (Knopf, 1957)
Bitter Ground (Knopf, 1958)
Mi Amigo (Knopf, 1959)
Conant (Popular Library, 1961)
Round the Clock at Volari's
　(Gold Medal, 1961)
Sergeants 3 (Pocket, 1962)
The Goldseekers
　(Doubleday, 1962)
The Widow Barony
　(UK only; Macdonald, 1962)
The Abilene Samson
　(Pocket, 1963)
The Winning of Mickey Free
　(Bantam, 1965)
The Cool Man
　(Gold Medal, 1968)
Good-bye, Chicago
　(St. Martin's, 1981)

Essays
The Roar of the Crowd
　(Potter, 1964)

Screenplay Contributions
The Finger Points (1931)
Beast of the City (1932)
Scarface: The Shame of a
　Nation (1932)
High Sierra (1941)
The Get-Away (1941)
This Gun for Hire (1942)
Wake Island (1942)
Crash Dive (1943)
Action in the North Atlantic
　(1943)

Background to Danger (1943)
San Antonio (1945)
Nobody Lives Forever (1946)
Belle Starr's Daughter (1949)
Vendetta (1950)
The Racket (1951)
Dangerous Mission (1954)
I Died a Thousand Times (1955)
Captain Lightfoot (1955)
Illegal (1955)
Short Cut to Hell (1957)
September Storm (1960)
Sergeants Three (1962)
The Great Escape (1963)

Uncredited Screen Contributions
Law and Order (1932)
The Whole Town's Talking (1935)
The Westerner (1940)
The Man I Love (1946)
The Walls of Jericho (1948)
The Asphalt Jungle (1950)
Night People (1954)
The Hangman (1959)
Four for Texas (1963)
Ice Station Zebra (1968)
Stiletto (1969)

9 781944 520298